June's Stolen Rose Seasons of Love and War, Book 4

By

Brenda Ashworth Barry

Published by
Melange Books, LLC
White Bear Lake, MN 55110
www.melange-books.com

June's Stolen Rose ~ Copyright © 2015 by Brenda Barry

ISBN: 978-1-68046-142-8

Cover Art by Caroline Andrus

Dedication:

First, I'd like to dedicate this book to my husband who gave me support while staying up late at night to write this story.

To all four of my children who have encouraged and supported my journey of writing.

To Cindy: Who listened to all my crazy ideas and is an amazing reading partner and best friend.

To all my friends and family, who have loved me through the endless hours of writing.

Of course, to Joyce Sterling Scarbrough, who helped me with so many things. Not only is she a wonderful friend, but an awesome editor.

To Barb who is my editor through Melange and she is awesome! Thank you for all your help and ideas.

Special love goes out to my Melange family and Carolyn for her beautiful artwork and Nancy for her continued support.

Chapter One

Even at the age of twenty-three, Beth Ann still hated the turbulence of an airplane.

She glanced down, trying to focus on *Little Women*, the book she was reading, but another round of turbulence caused her to clutch Kaylob's hand, turning her knuckles white. Holy night, she just wanted to get off the darn thing. She closed her eyes and started to imagine how Jo March might handle this, if they would have had planes back then.

Once the plane landed, she exhaled a sigh of relief and didn't miss Kaylob's attempt at hiding his chuckle by bringing her hand up to his lips and kissing her palm. Okay, she would let it go this once. She met his gaze, her stare holding just enough irritation to tell him he was close to being in the doghouse. He smiled innocently, but there was nothing innocent about her childhood sweetheart who was now her husband.

After a thirty-day Hawaiian honeymoon, it was time to get back to the real world and their new life. They needed to check on Kaylob's restaurant to see how close it was to being ready for the opening that was scheduled in a few weeks.

It would be nice to finally have a normal life now that Blake, her former fiancé, had seen her get married. She could move on without the stress of dealing with his efforts to win her back. It wasn't like she didn't feel bad about hurting him. She did, but come on. Showing up at her wedding disguised as a caterer, with a fake mustache and everything? What was wrong with him? That kind of behavior wasn't normal.

There had been no missing Blake's sky blue eyes as she'd walked down the aisle to meet Kaylob. With her head held high, she'd turned away from his gaze and smiled at her soon-to-be husband, who stood near the altar.

Once her gaze had met Kaylob's, she'd melted and Blake Tanner had vanished from her thoughts. The only place she wanted to be was there with the one and only love of her life.

It wasn't her fault that the Army had declared Kaylob killed in action. She had tried to tell everyone he was still alive, but nobody had listened. They'd thought she had lost her mind. Those two horrible, agonizing years Kaylob had spent in that POW camp were the hardest on her. It had taught her a good lesson. She'd never take life for granted again.

Once they exited the airplane, they struggled to move through the crowded Ontario airport. Beth Ann's mind drifted back to Blake, and she couldn't help but wonder if he had stayed in Hawaii. Or would he be back in Riverside?

"Earth to Beth Ann," Kaylob said, leaning over and waving his hand. "Are you with me?"

"Yes, I was just thinking about our honeymoon and how much I'm going to miss the islands." It was only half a lie.

Kaylob arched his eyebrow. "Me too, baby. Me too."

It felt like it took the length of their flight to get through the airport. Once they arrived at the baggage claim area, Kaylob collected all his suitcases, then glanced around for Beth Ann's, but they were nowhere to be seen.

"What the heck happened to your luggage?" he asked. "I hope they didn't lose them."

Beth Ann nodded in disbelief. "All my bags should have been with yours." She watched anxiously as people gathered their belongings.

Kaylob grabbed his suitcases, then took her hand and pulled her toward the service area. Sometimes he just took the lead and forgot to tell her where they were going. That was something she would discuss with him later.

Once they arrived at the desk, Kaylob did all the talking. The baggage people told them to take a seat while they checked to see if her luggage could be located, but they said they couldn't promise anything and couldn't explain what had happened.

Beth Ann sat with Kaylob and tried not to let him see how agitated she was. After what she'd been through with those two thugs who'd almost raped her, she guessed she was still a little paranoid, but after the way some of her things had disappeared before the wedding, she couldn't help wondering if someone had taken her luggage on purpose.

She had searched high and low for the missing things, but because of all their trips up to Gram's and back, she wasn't sure if she might've just left them there. She made a mental note to call Gram as soon as she got home to see if she'd left anything at her house. She wished she could stop being so paranoid.

* * * *

Now you'll sleep.

Slick bent over to make sure the guy was still breathing. He was, but he was out cold from the combination of getting hit with the bat and the Quaaludes he had slipped into his soda, even though he'd hated to waste them on this little piss ant. He'd been planning to use them tonight when he met with the escort. Quaaludes let him turn those sluts into his sweet Beth Ann.

Anyway, this guy should be out for a while. He dropped the bat and thought about turning off the vacuum, but decided to leave it running because the noise helped drown out those damn voices in his head that his dad had stuck there.

You're such a loser. You couldn't hang on to your other girlfriend, and now you're trying to get one that doesn't give a rat's ass about you!

"Shut the hell up!" He yelled, holding his head while glancing in the mirror, Hell, he was a good looking guy. He smoothed out his five hundred dollar suit. "I didn't like that ugly bitch anyway, and Beth Ann loves me. She's going to be my wife someday!" He glanced down at his shoes that he'd spent a fortune on, hoping no blood got on them and dulled the shine.

Face it, you're obsessed with her.

"No, I'm not!"

He was determined, not obsessed, and if he'd gone off the deep end, it was because of Beth Ann. Why did she have to go and marry that soldier boy and pretend to love him anyway? He knew better, and it pissed him off.

3

The guy moaned so he bent down and took a closer look to make sure he was unconscious. And indeed he was, out for the count.

"It's your own fault you got clobbered," Slick scolded. "You should have stayed home or left sooner, but you had to start cleaning like some prissy little moron. Now, you have spoiled my party plans for later. There's no way for me to get more drugs before tonight, so thanks a hell of a lot, pal!" He shoved the guy roughly with his foot.

The smell of the food from the kitchen drifted through the air and he decided he'd better go turn the oven down so nothing caught fire. No sense drawing a full investigation. Once he got back from the kitchen, he noticed the guy still had blood oozing from his head. Wait, did his eyes just flutter?

Great, the idiot might be waking up, he leaned over to get a closer look, no, he's still a sleeping little dork. If Slick had to, he'd hit him again with the bat, but he didn't think he needed to. He didn't want to kill him. That would mean he'd really lost it. Or would it?

Okay, back to business. What would he take this time? He needed more of her things.

"Let me tell you why I need her stuff!" Slick shouted into the air. "She belongs to me, and very soon she'll understand everything. I don't care if she married another man. She's *mine!* And if I can't have her, nobody can!"

He went to Beth Ann's closet and stopped when he opened it, thinking about the first time he'd sneaked in and taken her stuff. She'd come home while he was hiding in the closet, undressing right in front of him. He had wanted to take her then, but the timing had been all wrong. While she took a shower, he'd been able to make his escape without getting caught.

Okay, well back to the task at hand. "Keep your mind where it needs to be, Slick."

Now, lookie here, a couple of new dresses that still had tags on them. Then,when he spotted her sweater, he nodded in approval. He didn't want her to get chilled. He held it up and noticed it even had her initials on it.

"Now ain't that cute?" He laughed and started singing 'Ain't She Sweet.' When he finished, he held the sweater to his nose so he could inhale her intoxicating scent. He pulled the tablet out of his pocket and added the sweater to his list: slips, panties, six pair of shorts, six blouses and two nightgowns.

He moved into the bathroom and started going through the drawers. He took a hairbrush and almost cheered when he saw a bottle of the sexy perfume she always wore. Oh, how he loved that smell! He dabbed some on her sweater and almost lost control. He bent over, his entire body stiff as a nail, and couldn't move, but knew he needed to regain control and do it soon.

When he finally pulled himself back together and looked at his watch, he couldn't believe how late it was getting. "Time to go before they arrive." After he grabbed a few more items, he leaned over the guy and said with a cackle, "You'll sleep it off. And next time, don't stick around where you're not wanted."

He picked up the baseball bat to take it with him and grabbed the can of soda. No fingerprints that way. He glanced around one more time, satisfied for now, then he left the townhouse.

* * * *

Beth Ann and Kaylob had been waiting for over an hour when she spotted a guy carrying her luggage. They both sighed in relief.

"It was almost put on another plane," the guy said. "We were about ready to give up, but one of the guys found it." He smiled as he set her luggage down and gave them papers to sign.

"Thank you." Kaylob signed everything, then shook the guy's hand. He winked at Beth Ann. "Well, I think this means we can finally head on home. Let's sail, baby girl."

The minute they stepped outside into the sunlight, a sudden chill ran down Beth Ann's spine, as if she were being watched. After being attacked just weeks before her wedding, she knew it might take years to feel completely safe again. The therapy she'd had before leaving for her honeymoon had been helping, but it didn't cure her. But Kaylob was beside her now, and her attackers were in prison, so she had to stop worrying so much. She took a deep breath.

"What is it, sweetheart?" Kaylob asked, glancing at her while he placed the luggage in the trunk.

"Oh, it's nothing. I just got nervous when my luggage was missing. I guess it's because I kept misplacing all those things before our wedding."

Kaylob placed the souvenir bag into the trunk. "You have so many clothes, you probably just misplaced them."

"Maybe," she said. "I guess between the paparazzi and everything else that happened, my nerves were just on edge. I hope they'll leave me alone, now that I've been gone for a month."

"I doubt that. You're the foxiest Tony winner I know, especially with those delicious new freckles." He touched the tip of her nose.

"I'm the *only* Tony winner you know." She gave him a saucy grin.

"Are you sure about that?" He playfully patted her behind and laughed.

"I'd better be!" She placed another bag of souvenirs in the trunk. "Why do they want to take pictures of me anyway? They need to get a life. And I hope they won't be following me to work because they could scare the children and distract them. I want them to have fun learning to sing and dance, not be afraid of strangers taking pictures." She sighed. "I miss working with all my kids."

Kaylob turned her to him so their eyes met. "I know you love your job, sweetheart, and I bet all your students have missed you too. But I told you why they like taking your picture. In case you haven't noticed, you *are* one foxy mama." He pulled her close and nibbled her neck. "Now let's go home. I'm hungry. That was a long flight."

Beth Ann wiggled free and chuckled as she walked toward the passenger door. "You're always hungry, Mr. O'Brien. I'm surprised you don't have a cookie belly."

"Would you still love me if I did, Mrs. O'Brien?" He laughed as he opened the passenger door for her.

"Of course," she said as she got in the car. "It would just be more to love."

Once they were both in the car and on their way, Kaylob gave her a sidelong glance. "We can always order pizza, because I have another kind of hunger that needs to be fed right away."

"Why, Mr. O'Brien!" Beth Ann said, her cheeks growing warm. She fanned herself like a Southern Belle. "Whatever am I going to do with you?"

"Well, my little redheaded dancer, I'm sure you can think of something." Kaylob let his blue eyes skim over her small body.

Beth Ann had known her husband from childhood, so she knew most of his charming looks, and she definitely knew *that* sultry, seductive look. It was what Gram had always called *the hoochie coochie eyes.* And Kaylob's were irresistible.

The drive from the Ontario Airport to Riverside seemed to take forever because of the traffic, so when they pulled into their garage, Beth Ann was thrilled to be home. While Kaylob unloaded the suitcases from the trunk, Beth Ann admired the way his Hawaiian tan accentuated his muscular body, making his blond hair stand out. She licked her lips in anticipation and almost dropped one of the souvenir bags.

"Are you okay, sweetheart?" Kaylob raised an eyebrow.

"Yes, I'm fine," she stammered. "I'm just hot."

"Oh yes, indeed you are!" He laughed, giving her another playful wink.

She smiled and tried to focus on something other than her husband's physique, at least until they made it inside their townhouse.

"I told Jack we'd be home over two hours ago," she said. "I hope he hasn't given up his whole day to wait around for us."

"Did you see his car in the garage?" Kaylob asked.

"No, but I didn't really look for it. He parks out on the street most of the time. Jack doesn't like the garage. He said it creeps him out."

With the bags in her hands and all those souvenirs, she sure as heck was glad they had a bigger place than their first little apartment. Now they had room for all the wedding gifts and everything they'd bought on their honeymoon. Some of the wedding gifts were still sitting in one of the spare rooms unopened, and she reminded herself that she needed to send thank you cards to everyone.

"Hell, the door is ajar," Kaylob said and pushed it open with his foot.

"Jack must have forgotten to make sure it was closed," Beth Ann said. "He does that a lot. Unless he's still here."

The moment they stepped inside, Kaylob turned to shower her with kisses, but he stopped abruptly and lifted his nose in the air, sniffing the fantastic aroma coming from the kitchen.

"Now I'm *really* starving," he said as he set down the suitcases.

"That smells incredible!"

Beth Ann called out. "Hello, Jack! Are you here? We're home!"

When they didn't get an answer, they went to the kitchen and found a casserole warming in the oven.

"Boy, that smells great." Kaylob leaned into the oven to take a closer look. "This is done. I'm pulling it out." He grinned, reaching for the potholder.

"While you're tending to that, I'll find Jack," Beth Ann said. "Sounds like he's vacuuming in one of the bedrooms."

"Okay, baby," Kaylob said, setting the casserole on the counter.

Beth Ann followed the sound of the vacuum to the master bedroom. "Jack? Hello!"

She opened the door and froze in horror.

"*Kaylob!*" she shrieked. "Oh my God, come here!"

She dropped the bags and ran over to where Jack was lying face down beside the vacuum, blood trickling from a gash in the back of his head. Seconds later, Kaylob appeared in the doorway and rushed to Jack's side.

"What the hell happened?" He turned off the vacuum and looked around the room.

"I don't know, but we need to call for help!" Beth Ann cried.

Kaylob grabbed the phone on the nightstand and dialed 911.

Beth Ann gently shook Jack's shoulders while Kaylob told the operator to send an ambulance.

"Jack, please wake up!" Tears rolled down her cheeks. "Jack, can you hear me?"

Kaylob rushed over and dropped to his knees beside Jack, gently rolling him onto his back. "Thank God, he's breathing." Kaylob placed two fingers on the side of Jack's neck. "And his pulse seems good."

Beth Ann fought to control her tears, clutching their friend's hand to her heart. "Jack, please open your eyes! Can you hear me? It's Kaylob and Beth Ann."

After what seemed like forever, a loud knock echoed from the front door and Kaylob ran to answer it. A few seconds later, two very large paramedics rushed into the room and pushed past Beth Ann.

"We need you to step aside, ma'am," the guy said. "What's his name?"

"Jack. His name is Jack." She was trying not to cry.

The man's voice was loud and deep. "Jack, wake up." When the paramedic stuck something under Jack's nose, Beth Ann finally saw his eyes start to flutter and heard him moan.

Thank God he was waking up!

She drew in a breath of relief, then she realized she needed to call Lenard and let him know what had happened. Beth Ann went to the living room to call while Kaylob walked through the house, checking the other rooms. Jack and Lenard had been her first friends after she and Kaylob left Novato and moved to Riverside when she had been accepted at the Lakeside School of Performing Arts. Once she finished with her six month Broadway tour, she started teaching children at the school.

Jack had always been her rock, especially when Kaylob was listed as MIA and then pronounced dead. Thank God, Jack had been there during her nervous breakdown, when she'd hacked off all her hair and couldn't eat. He had supported her with love and compassion, plus the bonus that he was also a wonderful hair stylist and had managed to make her look normal again.

Jack was the sweetest man in the world, with his soft smile and caring brown eyes. The thought that someone would hurt him drove a stake through Beth Ann's heart. What would she have done without him during those dark days when Kaylob was gone? Jack had made her smile many times, even though all she'd wanted to do was cry.

She was about to hang up when Lenard answered, sounding out of breath.

"Lenard, it's Beth Ann." She was trying to sound normal but failing badly. "Please try to stay calm, but when we got home, we found Jack unconscious on the floor."

"What happened?" Lenard said, his voice full of alarm.

Before she could say any more, Kaylob walked up and held out his hand. She handed the phone to him, relieved that she wouldn't have to tell Lenard all the details.

"Lenard, Jack was attacked and hit on the head. He's awake and talking now, but pretty much out of it. They're taking him to the hospital. Do you want to meet us there?"

Beth Ann hurried back to the bedroom and found Jack sitting up as the paramedic examined his head injury.

"Jack, thank God you're awake!"

He glanced up at her and held out his hand, his eyes still dazed and half closed.

"I'm so sorry, Jack," she said, as she squeezed his hand. "What happened?"

"I can't remember," He pulled her into a hug as he spoke, his words slurred. "Apparently, someone hit me on the head. And I feel drugged or something."

He reached up to touch the wound, but the paramedic stopped him. "No, don't touch it. You're going to need stitches."

There was still a small amount of blood leaking from the wound, but not nearly as much as before. A few seconds later, another paramedic entered the bedroom pushing a gurney. Beth Ann moved out of the way again while they got Jack onto the bed. It certainly wasn't the homecoming she and Kaylob had planned, but that didn't matter. The most important thing was that Jack was okay.

Just as they started to step out the door, two police officers showed up, so Beth Ann and Kaylob had to fill them in on everything they knew before they could go to the hospital to see about Jack.

Chapter Two

After spending hours at the hospital, sitting by Jack's side, Beth Ann felt exhausted. She was the only one there at the moment. Lenard had been making phone calls off and on and Kaylob was dozing out in the waiting area. The antiseptic smell and the beeping sounds of the monitors flooded her with memories of her hospital stay after she was attacked, and Kaylob's in the VA hospital. Jack looked so weak lying in the hospital bed with the tubes in his nose and IVs poking his arms, it brought back everything.

The door opened and a nurse came waltzing into the room. She stood on the other side of the bed, checking everything. She pulled out a needle and injected something into the IV.

"You should go home and get some rest," the nurse said to Beth Ann as she flicked the IV, frowning at Jack.

Beth Ann rolled her eyes, crossed her legs and bounced her foot. "We want to hear from the doctor first, thank you." She picked up a magazine and thumbed through it.

"Your name is Beth Ann, right?" the nurse asked, and Beth Ann nodded. "Do you know if Jack does recreational drugs?" She arched one eyebrow and held Beth Ann's gaze.

"Never!" Beth Ann couldn't believe she asked that. Offended, she stood up and straightened Jack's blanket.

"Well, the doctor will want to speak to you and his gentleman friend, Lenard before you leave. You're both listed as family members." She threw something in the trash and left.

What the heck was going on? Jack never did drugs, and how dare she even ask that! Was that why she had been frowning at him? Before she could run down the hall and hit that nurse in the head with the bedpan, Lenard came back.

"Has the doc been here yet?" He walked over to Beth Ann and hugged her before turning to squeeze Jack's hand. "He's still so out of it."

"Haven't seen the doctor yet," Beth Ann replied. "But the nurse was here and had the nerve to ask me if Jack did recreational drugs."

"What? Why would they think that?" Lenard's brow furrowed.

Beth Ann shook her head. "I don't know. She said the doctor wants to talk to us." She sighed. "I'm going to go wake up Kaylob. He should be here when the doctor comes in."

Before she could take one step, the doctor walked in holding a clipboard.

"Hello, I'm Dr. Roberts," he said as he walked over to Jack and glanced at the monitors. "Are you Lenard?" he asked then turned to Beth Ann. "And you're Elizabeth, correct?" When they both nodded, he said, "Jack is suffering from a minor concussion, but we also found methaqualone in his blood work." He flipped the pages of his chart. "Do either of you know why he would have that in his system?"

"Jack has *never* done drugs," Lenard said adamantly.

"He hardly ever has a glass of wine," Beth Ann agreed. "And what is methaqualone? I've never heard of it."

"It's the brand name for what is known as Quaaludes," Dr. Roberts said. "He had quite a bit of it in his system. That's why he's so out of it and why we have to keep an eye on him."

"What?" BethAnn's voice was laced with shock.

"There is no way Jack took Quaaludes," Lenard insisted. "Someone must have given them to him without his knowledge."

"Well, the only way we'll find out is when he comes around, which won't be tonight." He nodded as he made a few notes. "Maybe he'll remember more about the attack when he wakes up in the morning, but I'm afraid he's still going to be groggy and may not remember anything for a few days." He put the pages back down on his clipboard. "You two should head on home and come back in the morning. We'll call if anything changes. He needs the rest."

Lenard shook his head. "I'm not leaving."

"Suit yourself, but he won't be waking up." Dr. Roberts shrugged. "I'll tell the nurse you're staying, but we don't have room for two."

"I understand. We'll come back in the morning." Beth Ann reached up and hugged Lenard. "Call if you need us, okay?"

"I will." He hugged her back. "Thank you for being here."

* * * *

Beth Ann and Kaylob called the police from a pay phone before they left the hospital, but the cops said they had little to go on, other than that someone must have sneaked into the house while Jack was vacuuming. The officer they spoke to reminded them that Riverside was full of crime and suggested it might be smart for them to get new locks and a security system.

By the time they arrived home, Beth Ann was starving. One bag of chips and a few cookies at the hospital hadn't done the trick. The aroma from the food Jack had cooked still lingered in the air, so she headed into the kitchen while Kaylob carried the luggage and souvenirs down the hall. When Kaylob joined her in the kitchen, they both helped themselves to a plate of Jack's delicious casserole.

"Yum," Beth Ann said when she finished. "The last bite is always the tastiest."

Kaylob got up and put both plates in the sink. "I'm going to check the dead bolt while you jump in the shower."

Beth Ann went in the bathroom and turned on the water to let it warm up. After the day she'd had, it felt divine when she got in. After just a few minutes, the door opened and Kaylob joined her.

"Hey, gorgeous, let me help you out." He took the shampoo from her and proceeded to tenderly wash her hair.

"Oh, Kaylob, that feels so good." She leaned back and let him work his magic. "I feel so bad about Jack."

"He's going to be fine. His head will just be sore for a few days. Here, let me help you relax." He used his strong hands to massage her scalp.

"Are you nervous about sleeping here after what happened?" Beth Ann questioned.

"No. Jack must've left the door open. And besides, I have my weapon."

"What weapon?" She turned and looked at him.

"My baseball bat." He swung his arms like he was batting. "*Wham!* After what that asshole did to Jack, I'll take his head off if he comes back."

"Okay, Mr. Headbasher, but before you knock off any heads, let's get some sleep tonight." She turned and gazed into his beautiful blue eyes.

"You're right. It's late, and we do need some sleep. I'll live through a night of sleep as long as I get to hold you." He kissed her neck.

Beth Ann sighed in relief when she was out of the shower and in her pajamas.

"Oh, I love our bed," she said as she threw back the covers and climbed in.

Kaylob walked into the bedroom with a blank look on his face. "My bat is gone."

"Gone?" She stared at him.

"It wasn't in the closet where I had it." He gestured toward the closet. "And I remember putting it there before we left, but it's not there. I bet the person who used it on Jack's head took it."

"Oh God, Kaylob. We'd better call the police tomorrow."

"Yeah, but I doubt that they can do anything about a missing bat. The hell with it, I'll buy a new one." He climbed into bed next to her and wrapped his arms around her.

Beth Ann didn't remember falling asleep, but she was fully aware of being held by her husband for the entire night.

* * * *

The next morning, she awoke to the sun shining through her white curtains, and her first thoughts were of Jack. She reached over to touch Kaylob and discovered a piece of paper.

My sleeping beauty,
I went to the restaurant to see how things are coming along. I called Lenard and he said Jack is awake. He still has no memory of what happened, and they say he might not remember anything. They're letting

him come home at noon though. I would love to have you come and join me as soon as you can. The doors are all safe and you're locked in. I also called a security company, and the neighbors are watching out for us. Your breakfast is in the oven, keeping warm, and my arms are here at the restaurant. Mrs. O'Brien, I love you and miss you already. I wouldn't have left you alone if I thought our house wasn't safe. Call me as soon as you get up and hurry down. By the way, I searched the house for my bat and it is gone. I know that I put it in our closet.

Love you,
At last, your husband

She held the note to her heart. "I have the best husband in the entire world."

She turned to pick up the phone and call the hospital, but it rang before she had the chance.

"Hello?" she said, but no one responded. "Hello, is anybody there?"

Nothing but breathing, then she heard a woman's voice off in the distance saying *the meeting is about to start.* There was a click, then nothing but a dial tone.

Was that a bad connection? If it was, they would surely call back. She hoped it wasn't those hang-ups she'd been getting before the wedding. Everyone thought it had been Blake, but she didn't think he would do that. Not now.

She decided to call the police before calling Lenard and was put on hold after she told them the situation.

"Mrs. O'Brien, This is Sergeant Vincent De Luca. The guys who attacked you are still in prison. And, ma'am, we have no way of tracing or tracking down a missing baseball bat." He sounded short with her.

"Well, thanks anyway." She hung up without saying goodbye. It wasn't unreasonable for her to worry about the guys who'd attacked her. How rude of him to dismiss her that way. She sighed and called the hospital next and was surprised to hear that Jack had already been discharged.

The minute she hung up the phone, it rang again. Holy crap, she was going to starve before she got to eat her breakfast!

"Hi, I'm home," Jack said when she answered.

"Oh, Jack, I'm so glad you called! Are you okay?" Her voice trembled.

"Yes, honey. It's my own fault for leaving the door open while I was cleaning. They must have slipped drugs in my mouth, once they knocked me out. Maybe they were drug addicts looking for cash. Oh my god, I just thought of something!"

"What?"

"My soda was out in the living room while I was in the bathroom cleaning, afterwards, I went out and picked it up and took it with me. Is the can still there?"

"Let me go check." Beth Ann ran around looking everywhere, including the garbage, but she couldn't find any trace of his soda. "Nope, no soda can. Do you remember anything else?"

"The assailant must have taken it," Jack said. "Maybe they were afraid of fingerprints. I don't remember much of anything. Everything is still so fuzzy."

"Oh, Jack, you could have been killed." Beth Ann gulped for air. "I guess the guy covered his bases, because he took Kaylob's baseball bat. That's what we think he used on your head."

"Where was his baseball bat?"

"In our master bedroom closet," Beth Ann said.

"They must have been hiding in there, watching me." Jack's voice quivered. "Beth Ann, they may have already been there before I got there. Maybe I forgot to lock your door the last time I was there. I probably didn't notice because I used the key and had so much stuff in my hands."

"I'm just relieved you're okay, and I'm so sorry this happened."

"This is my fault," Jack said. "I have to start locking the door when I leave and enter places. What a wake up call."

"I don't leave anything unlocked anymore after being attacked." She remembered when she would forget to lock her car. "I guess we both learned a lesson. How's your head feeling?"

"Sore, but it's the effects of the drugs that are still bothering me." He sighed. "They said I should be okay by tomorrow, at least not so much pain. I'm staying in bed today. Lenard is here and won't let me get up for anything."

"Do you need me to come and do anything?"

"No, honey. You just relax and I'll keep you updated. The police are stopping by for more information today, but I don't have much to tell them other than, I know I was slammed in the head."

After she hung up, Beth Ann started to worry about living in her townhouse. First, she had been attacked right in the building, and now Jack had been attacked in her home. She felt a shiver go up her spine and went to double check the lock on the front door. Jack was right about the need to start locking doors.

The next call was to Gram, and Beth Ann smiled as soon as she heard her sweet voice.

"Hi, Gram. We're home safe and sound." She didn't want to tell her about Jack and upset her.

"Oh, good! I was expecting to hear from you yesterday when your flight got in."

"It ended up being later than we thought. They misplaced my luggage." It wasn't a lie, she was just leaving some parts out. "They finally found it, but it took hours."

"Well, I have something I need to tell you." Gram paused and Beth Ann could hear her taking a deep breath.

"Okay ..." Beth Ann felt a twinge of worry.

"Nicky and I want to get married on September twenty-sixth, and we really want you and Kaylob to be there. I know it's a lot to ask with you just getting home from your honeymoon and all, but we really don't want to wait. We've waited what feels like our whole life already."

"Oh, Gram, I'm so happy for you! Of course we'll be there. We wouldn't miss it for the world."

Beth Ann and Kaylob had helped Gram and Nicky find each other again, and brought them together at their wedding in Hawaii. It had been beautiful to see the two lost lovers reunite, it had enhanced their wedding day. They had been childhood sweethearts who had been kept apart by Gram's controlling family. Now they were back together and getting married, and Beth Ann couldn't be happier for them.

Gram laughed. "I'm so glad to hear that, sweetness, and I know Nicky will be thrilled too. I couldn't have imagined you not being here."

After hanging up the phone, Beth Ann twirled around in a circle and started singing.

"Going to the chapel and you're gonna get maaaaarrrried. Gee they really love each other and they're gonna get married. Going to the chapel of love." She did a little dance around the living room while she continued her modified lyrics.

By the time she finished making the rest of her calls and ate her breakfast, the entire morning was gone. She got dressed and decided to walk to the restaurant and enjoy the beautiful day. But before she got very far down the street, she got the creepy feeling of someone's eyes on her. Her stomach took a dive and her hands trembled.

She whirled around, trying to see through the faces of strangers and feeling her throat tighten, but nothing stood out. Somewhere out in the shadows of these people, could there be someone watching her?

Chapter Three

Beth Ann bent over and put her hands on her knees as she caught her breath; she was having a panic attack, something her therapist had tried to help her with. She looked around again, but all she could see was the hustle and bustle of the city. Nobody seemed interested in her at all. She was just being paranoid, and she needed to pull it together and stop all this nonsense. Nobody was going to steal her peace of mind again.

She straightened up and started strolling down the sidewalk, seriously considering those self-defense classes Carol had told her about. She was tired of living in fear. Maybe learning to kick the crap out of anyone that touched her or hurt someone she loved would be just what she needed.

Suddenly a car squealed and almost rear-ended another car. The guy in the front stuck his head out the window and yelled, "Hey, watch where you're going, dickweed!"

"Screw you, asshole! I didn't know you were stopping!"

Beth Ann was relieved when the light changed and they both took off. This was definitely not Hawaii, where the calm ocean waves and seagulls lulled them to sleep. There were good things about Riverside too, like the aroma of roasting nuts, hot dogs, or the bittersweet scent of coffee sweeping through the air. There were plenty of things to like about Riverside, but her friend getting hit over the head with a baseball bat was not one of them.

She passed by the corner store where she used to shop just as the *woo-woo* of the train whistle and echoed through town, tugging at her heart strings. The echoing sound reminded her of Novato and the fun days of her childhood. She couldn't wait to see her friends and family again and hoped it would be soon.

Just when she paused, a soft breeze slithered by and lifted the strands of her hair in different directions. But once again a triple layer of chills ran down her back, and she felt as if she were being watched. Why was she feeling that way? It had to be because of what happened to Jack. She needed to stop letting her fear suffocate her, but she decided to tell Kaylob she wanted him to change all their locks just to be safe.

She walked a little faster down the street, and when she passed their old apartment, memories came pouring back of the good times they'd had there before Kaylob got drafted. They had lived downstairs from Jack and Lenard when they first came to Riverside from Novato, but she didn't know anyone who lived there now since Jack and Lenard had moved. They'd had some harassment and didn't like the crime around here, and with what had just happened to Jack, there was no doubt they'd made a wise decision.

She was still angry they had been harassed because of their lifestyle, after that garbage tabloid had published that they were gay. It was bad enough the damn paparazzi followed *her* around, but to do that to Jack and Lenard made her want to use some of Carol's Kung Fu on them. Jack and Lenard were wonderful men, and she'd stand by them no matter what. Nobody better *ever* be mean to them in front of her or Kaylob. At least now they lived in a cute little country house outside of town, and so far the neighbors had all been nice to them.

She wished she and Kaylob could move somewhere like that, but the restaurant was here. Plus, she loved her teaching job and would eventually be performing again. She'd always wanted to perform and work with children. She knew everyone considered them well off after Kaylob's uncle had died and left them a huge inheritance, but she really didn't feel any different. She wanted to keep their lifestyle simple.

The odd thing was that his uncle had been from Ireland, and Kaylob had never met him. He didn't even know the relatives from there, and none of them had shown up for the wedding. What was that all about? She'd asked herself that before and hoped she would get some answers someday.

The restaurant came into view, and she could see the workers preparing to hang Kaylob's sign. SEVEN NIGHTS AND SEVEN ROSES was engraved across the smooth finish, and below it was *A Dining Experience*. Kaylob had named it after those seven glorious nights they'd shared before he left for Vietnam. He'd sent her seven roses and named each one of them. She still had the petals tucked away and saved.

A wave of happiness rushed through her. Kaylob was finally getting to live his dream. Almost a year ago, he was supposed to be dead. Now they were married with all their visions coming true. He had talked about opening a restaurant since they were teenagers.

Beth Ann put her hand over her eyes to block out the sun and get a better look at the sign. Just watching the workers steadying it brought tears to her eyes, and her hand slid down to cover her heart. There were no words to describe the pride she felt for her husband.

When she went inside the restaurant, chaos abounded. It was easy to be overwhelmed by the kinetic energy. Workers were vacuuming, electricians were hanging lights, and delivery men were pushing dollies stacked with supplies toward the kitchen, all of it accompanied by the sounds of mixers and timers.

Holy hunger alert, the divine aroma of cloves and cinnamon wafted through the air, making her feel like a hound dog following a scent. When she stepped inside the kitchen, there was no way to miss all the cooking taking place. It was clear they were testing the equipment. The chefs were busy mixing recipes in bowls, yelling at each other with taunts and boasts about both their cooking and romantic expertise. It was like a culinary combat zone. She had to place her hand over her mouth to hide her laughter as she backed up slowly, relieved that nobody had noticed her.

"Hey, there, Mrs. O'Brien!" Kaylob's baritone voice rang out over all the noise as he made his way to her. "I was missing you!"

"Hello, Mr. O'Brien." She smiled back and gave him a lingering kiss.

His breath caught and he cleared his throat. "Careful, baby. We don't want the world to know what you do to me."

A short man who appeared to be in his early forties looked up from where he was holding a strip of baseboard in place and scratching marks on the wall. Kaylob released Beth Ann and grinned at the man with the salt-and-pepper hair.

"Tom, this is my wife Beth Ann. Tom's wife is the one I was telling you about. She must be at least twenty months pregnant." Kaylob chuckled.

"Seems more like thirty months." Tom laughed too, and wiped his hand on his pants before extending it. "Nice to meet you, Beth Ann."

Beth Ann greeted him and blushed when he placed his lips on her hand, raising his bushy eyebrows as he looked at Kaylob and back at her.

"I hear you two had a wonderful honeymoon." Tom's Italian accent was thick.

"Yes, it was incredible," Beth Ann said. "We had so much fun."

"I also hear you thought your husband was cheating before the wedding." Tom shook his head. "No man in his right mind would cheat on you."

Why did Kaylob have to blab to everyone about what happened before they were married? He had been sneaking around to surprise her with both the plans for the restaurant and also getting his culinary degree, and his long hours had made her think he was up to something. Then, when she'd seen him walking down the street with his arm around a woman who'd turned out to be Tom's wife, she had been sure he was having an affair. She only saw them from the back, so she had no idea that the woman Kaylob was with was pregnant. She had gotten a bit drunk, maybe even thrown up a little, and accused him of everything under the sun. But what else was she supposed to think?

Tom smiled at Kaylob and winked at Beth Ann.

As if on cue, a woman walked in, cradling her ready-to-pop belly. "Tom, leave the poor girl alone," she said, waddling over to shake Beth Ann's hand with a stunning smile. "Don't mind my husband. He gets crazy around beautiful women."

"Ah, my Bella," Tom said, reaching over to pat her stomach sweetly. "You are my most beautiful woman. There are just so many other ladies in second place."

Beth Ann giggled, watching Bella lower herself slowly into a nearby chair while holding her belly. "I'm afraid I did think my husband was having an affair with you, Bella."

Bella waved her hand toward Kaylob in a dismissive manner. "Ah, your man loves you with all his heart. Every day I was here, all he did was talk about his Beth Ann."

Tom arched his eyebrow. "Bella, Beth Ann said they had a very fun honeymoon. Remember how much fun we had?"

"Yes, I remember well." She touched her belly again and chuckled. "But I thought it might be over by now."

"Every day is a honeymoon with my Bella." Tom lifted her hand to his lips.

The look between the two of them told a story of forever love. Beth Ann placed her hand across her heart and sighed.

A worker came over to Tom, showing him some tile. He listened and instructed the worker, then he helped his wife from her seat. "I have to walk my Bella to the car and make sure she doesn't fall over."

Bella stopped and took Beth Ann's hand. "Nice to meet you, Beth Ann. Maybe the next time I see you, I'll be able to move better." She laughed, her eyes sparkling.

Beth Ann watched them go, thinking how touching it was that Tom was so attentive to Bella. There was no doubt she needed someone to help her stay steady on her feet, but she was both radiant and stunning with her jet-black hair and tanned, toned legs. Her big belly only enhanced her beauty, and she seemed happy to be pregnant. Beth Ann found herself wondering how she would feel if she were pregnant.

Wait, where the heck had *that* thought come from?

"Earth to Beth Ann." Kaylob waved his hand in front of her face. "Come on, let me show you around."

He took her on a tour of the place, with workers everywhere. Beth Ann noticed how many stopped and stared at her as they passed by.

"Hey, what're you looking at?" Kaylob said to the guys, trying to act serious even though he was laughing. "This is my wife Beth Ann. Get back to work!"

Beth Ann's cheeks flushed as the guys nodded and waved to her. She wished she hadn't worn shorts with so many men around, but the heat in Riverside was boiling.

They continued their tour, and the restaurant was stylish as well as luxurious. Vines were elegantly painted above the arches that led into alcoves reserved for private parties.

Kaylob explained about the swinging oak soundproof doors. He said they needed them because chefs could sometimes be boisterous. She'd seen that for herself already.

The restaurant was everything that Kaylob had ever dreamed of and more.

After they finished the tour, he took her hand and walked her to the door, stopping to give her a long, lasting kiss. He had always known how to kiss her in a way that melted her insides.

"Baby, did you walk here?" Kaylob said when he didn't see her car.

"Yes, I wanted the exercise."

"I think you've had plenty after a month long honeymoon. Let me get my keys and drive you home."

"No, honey, I really enjoy walking. Don't worry, I'll be fine." She stood on her tiptoes and kissed him again.

A couple of the guys whistled and Kaylob stopped and pointed. Beth Ann couldn't help but giggle.

"Well, okay, just be careful." She could tell he didn't like it, but at least he agreed.

"I promise I will. I just wanted to do a few things on the way home." She grinned and he seemed to relax.

Once she got home and locked the doors, she got Kaylob's rolling pin and searched the house for intruders. All was clear, so she returned it to the kitchen and got a brilliant idea. She would cook tonight for her amazing husband and put a little romance in the atmosphere, even though he would probably feign passing out from the surprise.

The next step was finding something she could cook without burning down the house. Out of all the recipes Gram had given her, the one for spaghetti looked like the simplest. She wrote down the ingredients, changed into pants and set out for the grocery store. After being gone for thirty days, they were out of everything.

An hour later, when she got home with her groceries, the damn paparazzi started snapping pictures as soon as she got out of the car. They were really getting on her nerves, but she did her best to pretend they weren't there. She carried all the groceries inside and locked the doors again. The cabinets were all bare, so it was easy finding room for everything. Before she started cooking, she decided to call Jack again. He answered on the second ring.

"Hey, Jack, how's the head?"

"Still attached to my neck." He laughed. "I'm glad you called, honey. I remembered something. I was just talking about it with Lenard."

"Really, what was it?"

"I wasn't sure if I should tell you or Kaylob." He drew in a deep breath. "But you guys need to know."

"What is it, Jack?" Beth Ann was starting to get nervous.

"Well …" He hesitated, as if wondering how to proceed. "Whoever nailed me in the head said something before I lost consciousness. My short term memory loss is starting to fade like the doctor said it might."

"What did you remember?" Beth Ann felt the hair stand up on the back of her neck.

"He said that you were *his* and someday he'd get you, or something along those lines. It seemed like he was yelling it at somebody."

"Oh God ..." Beth Ann felt the room start to spin. Fear gripped her throat, and she couldn't swallow. She held the phone to her ear in a tight grip, unable to speak.

"Beth Ann?" Jack said. "Listen, he didn't actually say your name. He said '*she* belongs to *me*.' I can't be a hundred percent sure of what he meant. Do you think it could have been Blake?"

"No, he would never hurt another person!" Beth Ann was adamant.

"Okay, Beth Ann. Take a deep breath and calm down. It's all kind of fuzzy, so I suppose I could have just dreamed it all. I'm not positive about anything."

Beth Ann heard a doorbell chime in the background.

"I'll be right there!" Jack yelled to Lenard. "The police are here, honey. I need to go."

"Okay. And I know it's not Blake, but the police need to know what you think you might have heard, so make sure you tell them."

"I already told them on the phone, but I'll tell them again since they're here. I wish I had more information."

After she hung up, she closed her eyes for a moment and tried to slow her heartbeat. She didn't think the police were taking this seriously enough, even after she'd told them there had been a car following her for months before the wedding, and the two guys who'd attacked her had never been traced to a black car. Since the person in the car had been taking pictures of her, the police seemed to think it must be the paparazzi. Maybe they were right. Still, the whole thing was giving her an eerie feeling. All she could do was hope Jack had imagined the voices, or that his head would heal soon and he'd remember everything.

Okay, time to shake all this off and get back to romantic thoughts. She tried to focus on remembering all the times she had watched her mom and Gram make spaghetti. If she recalled correctly, all they did was throw everything in one big pot, then simmer it for a few hours. That seemed simple enough.

She took out all the ingredients and got out Kaylob's biggest pot. In went the hamburger, the sauce, and all the spices. She chopped onions and garlic and threw them in too for good measure, then she added two cans of stewed tomatoes.

"What the heck?" she said, snapping her fingers. "I almost forgot the most important ingredient—the noodles!"

She went to the cabinet and searched until she found an unopened box of spaghetti that had probably been fresh back in the fifties. She tossed the whole box in as well, hoping it would be enough. Kaylob had a hearty appetite.

Now all she had to do was let it simmer.

While she cleaned the house, the aroma floated through the air. It smelled amazing, but when she lifted the lid to check, the red, uncooked meat was floating on the top. Guessing she wasn't cooking it high enough, she turned it from simmer to medium.

While it cooked, she put out their best table settings and wine glasses. She cut the bread, placed the butter on the table, and complemented everything with a single rose. When the table was set, she turned on some soft music and lit the candles. Everything looked beautiful. She knew Kaylob would love it, but not as much as the surprise she had waiting for him in the bedroom after dinner. The final touch was a rose on his pillow with fresh mints.

Pleased with her handiwork, she decided to call him and see how long it would be before he came home.

"Seven Nights, Seven Roses," he said when he answered. "Kaylob speaking."

"Hi, honey, it's me."

"Hey, you. Whatcha doing?"

"Calling you to see when you're coming home."

"In about twenty minutes. Do you miss me?"

"Yes, very much." She smiled.

"I'll be home soon. And I miss you, too."

With a sigh, she said, "It's hard to be apart after spending thirty days together with no one to intrude."

"Oh, you bet it is," he said with a chuckle. "Maybe I can get home a little sooner."

After she hung up, she went to the bedroom to change. She knew exactly which dress she was going to wear. A sexy pink outfit she'd bought just for Kaylob's eyes. She'd purchased it before they left for Hawaii, but never got the chance to wear it. The closet was big, but where the heck was her dress? She fumbled through all her clothes and even went to Kaylob's side, but the dress was gone. The pink hanger wasn't even there. She looked through all her drawers and suitcases, which needed to unpacked. She didn't think she'd taken it to Hawaii, but maybe she did and had left it there.

Oh, well. A missing dress wasn't going to spoil her evening. She had plenty more dresses, so she picked another pink one and put Kaylob's apron over it. But when she went to brush her hair, she couldn't find her big hairbrush. Good Lord, she must have left that in Hawaii, too. She might be getting that old-timer's disease. She walked over to her suitcase and pulled out her makeup bag and an older hairbrush. When she was finished dressing, she went back to the kitchen and lifted the top of the pot.

What the heck? The meat was still raw and floating in the red sauce.

She was beginning to think something must be wrong with the meat, so she turned the stove up to full blast. She never imagined meat taking so long to cook.

It was almost time for Kaylob to be home, so she went back to the bedroom and dimmed the lights, laying her sexy little gown on the bed and moving the chair over beside it. Once everything was set up in the bedroom, she walked down the hall to the kitchen, but stopped in horror before she got there.

"Oh my god!" she screamed.

It looked like a massive tomato bomb had gone off. Sauce decorated the floor, all the walls, and the ceiling. Some of it had even made its way across the counter to the bar. How could food travel so far? She had never seen such a mess. She dashed over to turn down the heat, and the pan made a horrible popping, gurgling sound as if eager to regurgitate more mess.

Slipping and sliding on the tomato-covered floor and reeling from the shock, she managed to make it back to the hall and ran to the laundry room, grabbing the mop and bucket. She rushed back into the kitchen, and the minute her feet hit the slimy red goo again, she fell and crashed down in an unceremonious swoosh, followed by a loud, squishy thud.

Dazed, she lay on the floor looking up at the ceiling, fully aware that she had become part of the explosion. Her pink dress was now a splotchy red. Tears began to pool in her eyes as she lay there, trying to figure out what the heck had happened, then she heard the front door open and Kaylob's voice echoed from the entry.

"Hello, baby! Are you cooking something?"

* * * *

Kaylob's mouth fell open. After the initial shock, he tried to restrain his laughter, but the sight of his wife swimming in some type of red sauce was too much. Never had he seen anything so damn cute. Pressing his face into his arm, he tried to muffle the laugh so she wouldn't hear it. He knew it hadn't worked when she started to cry and talk at the same time.

"I tried to cook spaghetti for you and make a romantic dinner and … and ..." she paused, crying harder now. Her words were as jumbled as the mess he'd walked into. "And it exploded for no good reason!"

Kaylob walked over and pulled her up into his arms. Sauce covered her face, hair and dress. He knew he was going to lose it if he didn't focus on something else, so he sat her down on one of the chairs in the dining area and hugged her.

She pushed him away and covered her face with her hands as she sobbed. It broke his heart, but she was still so damn cute.

"Don't cry, baby." He pulled her hands down and hugged her again. "I love that you tried to do this, and look how nice the table looks!" The dining table set with candles and wine also showed small signs of spaghetti shrapnel, but he hoped she wouldn't notice.

"I destroyed our entire dinner." Her lips trembled, and she drew in several deep breaths.

"It's okay, sweetheart," he said soothingly. "Hey, the French bread is still good, and look, we still have wine!"

He eyed the bottle, noting that it would have to be wiped off first. Beth Ann swiped the tears from her eyes and looked at the bread and wine, chewing her bottom lip. How could he fix this? Maybe he should call the National Guard cleaning crew, because this was a national disaster.

"I tried to cook spaghetti, but it blew up. I did everything Gram's recipe said, but it still exploded. There's something wrong with the meat, it wouldn't brown." She pointed toward the kitchen accusingly.

He tiptoed over to the stove, trying to avoid the mess, and turned everything completely off. When he peeked into the pot, he couldn't believe his eyes. She hadn't browned the meat. My wife is the opposite of what is known as a good cook. He went back and took her in his arms.

"Sweetheart, I think you need a shower. It's in your hair and all over you." He walked her into the bathroom. "I'm so sorry this happened, Beth Ann. You did your best, and that's always good enough for me. I love you." He leaned down and kissed her forehead.

Her lip quivered again at the sight of herself in the bathroom mirror. Kaylob kissed her and helped get out of the sauced clothes. They were actually damp, so he took them to the washer and noticed how everything in the laundry room sparkled. She had cleaned the house from top to bottom. When he went back to the bathroom, she was sitting on the laundry basket looking down at the floor. He knelt in front of her and took her hands.

"Everything's okay, sweetheart. At least you tried. I'll call and order dinner for us, okay? This could happen to anyone. Don't be sad, the house looks beautiful. You did a great job."

She nodded and laid her head against his chest. "Thank you. I love you and just wanted everything to be perfect."

He felt his heart skipping beats. "You make my life perfect just by being in it." He kissed her again and looked into her eyes. "I've always known you couldn't cook, but look what a great job you did on the house. Thank you for doing all of this."

As she stepped into the shower, he was reminded that she was the sweetest, most beautiful woman in the world, and he almost had to slap himself to keep from climbing in there with her so he could make her forget about what happened. Unfortunately, the mess in the kitchen had to be cleaned up. From what he had surveyed, it was from floor to ceiling.

As much as he hated to leave the view, gawking at his naked wife wasn't getting him anywhere. He forced himself to leave, then he noticed her gown on the bed and his heart skipped a few more beats. The chair was sitting at the end of the bed, which meant she was planning a repeat performance, like she did on their honeymoon. Man, she had shown him some moves that had made his head spin and his knees go weak. Ooh la la. She had the kind of motion that makes a man stand up without moving.

Reluctantly, he changed into some old clothes and headed out to the crime scene in the kitchen. Gazing around at the mess, he didn't know where to start. Spaghetti and sauce was everywhere, splatters on the glasses and even on the little table where she had Gram's pictures and Bible. How in the world did it splatter all the way into what she called her reading room?

With a sigh, he filled a bucket with some cleaner and warm water and started on the floor so he wouldn't track it on their carpet. He had just started scrubbing when he heard the doorbell. Great, this was no time for company.

Frankie and Debra smiled when Kaylob opened the door and motioned for them to come on in.

"Beware of the mess though," he warned.

"We were going to a movie and thought maybe you guys might—" Frankie broke off when they reached the kitchen. He and Debra stood there with their eyes wide.

"What in God's name happened?" Debra asked in a small voice.

"And where'd ya hide the body?" Frankie muttered.

30

Kaylob tried not to laugh. "Beth Ann decided to cook spaghetti and didn't brown the meat first. When it wasn't browning, she turned it up full blast. As you can see, it exploded. She told me there was something wrong with the meat."

All three stood surveying the damage until Kaylob finally couldn't contain his laughter any longer, and it infected the other two.

"I know we shouldn't laugh at her," Kaylob said as he picked up the mop. "But she's so darn cute."

"Let us help you clean it up," Debra said. "Where's Beth Ann?"

"In the shower, washing all the red sauce out of her hair." Kaylob chuckled again. "She was swimming in it when I got home."

Frankie shook his head. "I told you a long time ago to ban that girl from the kitchen."

Kaylob nodded. "No shit. I think I'll lock it up."

The clean up wasn't easy, but with Frankie and Debra helping, it went a lot faster. Frankie ended up on a ladder cleaning the walls while Debra scrubbed down the cabinets.

"Look at your curtains," Frankie said, pointing. "They need to be taken down. Bro, don't you ever let her cook again. This place looks like a scene from *Police Woman*." He cracked up.

"Yeah, but at least Angie Dickinson won't need to hunt anyone down since we know who murdered the spaghetti." Kaylob threw back his head in laughter, but stopped when he heard someone clear their throat and turned to see Beth Ann standing in the doorway with her hands on her hips.

"Gee, so much for *anyone can do this, and how wonderful it is that you tried.*"

"Aw, sweetheart, don't get mad." Kaylob put down his red-stained rag and grinned. "You didn't brown the meat for the spaghetti sauce. That's why it was all mushy and floating on top."

"Brown the meat?" She picked up the recipe card. "I did what it said to do."

Kaylob moved next to her and pointed to the instructions. "Look at the card again. This isn't a grocery list. You have to read the directions *below* the ingredients." He placed his finger right on the information and read aloud. "Brown hamburger in pan with garlic and onions."

Beth Ann frowned. "But it doesn't say not to put it in with the sauce too. I thought it browned in the pan with everything."

Frankie tossed her a rag. "Okay, you screwed up. Help us clean it up and we'll forgive you."

After an hour of scrubbing, everything looked back to normal, except the curtains that would need to be washed. To celebrate, Kaylob called out for two large pizzas.

"C'mon, guys," Frankie said. "Let's go to the movies after dinner."

"No, I think I've been too traumatized and need to stay home and relax," Beth Ann said. "First, my brand new pink dress vanishes, then the spaghetti erupted on me."

Kaylob studied her. "Your pink dress is gone?"

"Yes, I looked everywhere."

"Just like my baseball bat. Maybe the intruder is a baseball fan who likes pink dresses."

"You need to tell the police about all that right now," Frankie said, then he chuckled. "I mean, a guy wearing Beth Ann's pink dress and carrying a baseball bat might just stand out in a crowd."

"Frankie Russo, it's not funny," Beth Ann scolded. "And besides, I think I might have accidentally left it in Hawaii anyway."

"Well, at least Jack's head is much better," Kaylob said. "I don't think he'll be leaving the doors open anymore."

"I'm happy about that." Beth Ann nodded. "But he told me today that he thought he heard the guy say something."

"What?" Frankie and Kaylob said in unison.

"That's spooky." Debra shivered.

Beth Ann agreed. "He remembered the guy saying something like *She belongs to me.* But he's not sure if he heard it or dreamed it."

Frankie shot a concerned look at Kaylob then looked back at Beth Ann. "Do you think it could be Blake?"

Kaylob wondered the same thing, but he didn't say anything.

"No, it's not Blake!" Beth Ann said a bit too loud. "I wish everyone would stop saying that."

"All right, I was just wondering." Frankie raised his hands in surrender.

"I have to agree with Beth Ann. You know I don't trust Tanner, but I don't think he'd hit Jack in the head."

"Well, he did show up at your wedding, dressed as one of the caterers." Frankie arched a brow. "Maybe he's gone off the deep end."

"Frankie, it's not Blake!" Beth Ann's face got red. "He wouldn't do that."

Luckily, for Frankie, there was a knock at the door just then.

"I bet that's the pizza," Kaylob said, jumping up to go answer the door.

Chapter Four

The pizza girl came in and set the pizzas on the dining table. She had long blonde hair and wore tight shorts with no bra. Beth Ann didn't miss the way the girl looked at Kaylob when she took the money. She was glad that her husband was polite, but ignored the girl's flirtations, because she didn't feel like having a conniption fit over the floozy.

After the girl left, Kaylob set down the pizza box on the coffee table and turned to wink at Beth Ann. He came close to chuckling, but decided against it. He must've known it would be dangerous to do so.

When they finished most of the pizza, Frankie stood, holding his stomach. "Man, I ate like a pig." He took Debra's hand and pulled her to her feet. "We hate to eat and run, but we want to go see *The Way We Were*. Thanks for the food."

"You're welcome," Kaylob said then laughed. "Thanks for cleaning up the crime scene."

When Frankie and Debra were gone, Beth Ann shot Kaylob her best dirty look. "Crime scene?"

"Teasing you, Mrs. O'Brien." He tried to look innocent but failed, so he pulled her into his arms. They cuddled on the couch awhile, then he put his hands on her shoulders and turned her toward him. "Sweetheart, I need to talk to you about something important."

She saw something in his eyes and gave him her full attention. "What is it?"

"I was thinking that once I get my restaurant running and organized and if you don't have any other plans, maybe we could go to Ireland."

"Well, I have something I need to talk to you about too." Beth Ann smiled. "Could the trip wait until after September twenty-sixth? Gram and Nicky are getting married then, and they want us to be there. Are you okay with that?"

"I'm more than okay. That's great news!" He jumped up and swung her around in his arms. "We did it, baby! We brought them together, and now they're gonna spend the rest of their lives together."

"I know, and I'm happy too." Beth Ann giggled at the way her husband's eyes were lit up. "And Ireland sounds like fun. When did you want to go?"

"I don't have a date yet." He sat down again and put his arm around her. "I wanted to see how you felt about meeting some of my family back there."

"Of course I want to meet your family," she said. "We can go whenever you're ready."

Both of them jumped at the loud shrill of the phone. They really needed to turn that thing down. Kaylob got up to answer it.

"Hello?" He paused. "Hello, who is this? I can hear you breathing." A few seconds later, he hung up the phone and Beth Ann saw his jaw clench when he turned to look at her.

"It's not him, Kaylob."

"How do you know that? He was at our wedding, Beth Ann. Maybe I need to go have a conversation with Mr. Tanner."

"No you don't, and it's not him!"

Kaylob's eyes narrowed. "Why don't you go on to bed? I'll clean up out here and lock everything up."

"Fine," she said testily. "The whole spaghetti ordeal drained me anyway, and I'm in no mood to discuss Blake Tanner with you." She paused on her way to the bedroom. "But I think we need to get the locks changed, and get a deadbolt put in."

Kaylob just nodded and looked away. Beth Ann didn't want to argue about her former fiancé, so she went into the master bathroom and brushed her teeth, washed her face and climbed into bed.

While she lay in bed reading, Kaylob walked in and stood over her. "Do you know how much I love you?"

She didn't look up from her book. "Well, I might, but you made fun of me tonight. And you also let that pizza girl flirt with you."

He took her hand and sat on the bed. "I wasn't letting her, she was just doing it. And I wasn't making fun of you, I was just laughing at the incident." He pulled her into his arms and kissed her neck, then he started to climb under the covers with her.

She sighed and tried to move away. "Don't do that. I'm trying really hard to be mad."

He lifted her hair and softly glided his tongue over her skin. "Come on, Beth Ann. You know you love it when I do that."

"Kaylob Shawn O'Brien, you're cheating. And I'm staying mad for a while."

He moved his lips close to her ear. "One, two, three, four."

"What are you doing?" She shivered from his husky voice.

"Giving you time to cool off." He moved his hand slowly up her leg and kissed her shoulder.

In almost a whisper, she said, "Kaylob, that explosion wasn't funny. It made me so sad."

"Ah, baby, don't be sad. Let me show you another kind of explosion that will make you forget all about that other one." He gave her a look full of promise as he removed the rose and mint from his pillow.

"You think so?" she said then pushed him onto his back. "Okay, you win." She climbed on top and watched his eyes widen. There was no way to resist his offer, so she pulled off her nightgown and lowered her lips to his chest.

"Oh, Beth Ann…"

* * * *

At his office in Palm Springs, Blake Tanner swore and threw the folder against the wall. *Swoosh*. Papers flew everywhere.

"Damn it! This deal's not going to close!" He picked up a piece of paper and looked at the numbers again. There was no way his client would pay that. He'd have to call Mr. Duncan the next morning and let him know.

A knock on the door added to his frustration. Who the hell was there at midnight?

"Come in!" he yelled.

Melissa walked in and took a survey of the papers strewn across the floor. "What are you doing here, Blake?"

"Dancing the night away," he shot back, as he went to pick up the folder. "What the hell are you doing out this late at night?"

"I came by to grab my scarf and my wallet." She bent down and picked up some of the paperwork. "I left them in my drawer."

"You shouldn't be out this late at night," he said. "It's dangerous for a girl your age. I'll drive you home."

Melissa moved closer to him and reached out to touch his face. "You don't have to do that. I'm a big girl. You do remember that, right?"

He caught her wrist. "Let's get you home."

"What about my car?" she asked.

He stuffed the folder in his briefcase and snapped it shut. "I'll pick you up in the morning around ten."

When they got to her house, he couldn't believe it when she tried to kiss him goodnight. What the hell was that girl thinking? First, she'd tried to kiss him on the plane on the way to Beth Ann's wedding, now this. He needed to do something about her advances as it was starting to bother him. He couldn't let anything happen no matter what, she was only nineteen, for God's sake! But damn the roadrunner if she hadn't blossomed into a beautiful young lady. Maybe he could set her up with that new agent, he'd hired, either that or he'd have to talk to her daddy about moving her to another office if this didn't stop.

As he drove down his street, part of him was glad to be home, but the rest of him still felt so goddamn lonely and hated the emptiness of the place. Being engaged and living with Beth Ann for so long had given him something he'd never known he needed. Maybe he should move back to Texas and find a few ladies to have some good old-fashioned fun with. That was the only place he'd almost gotten over Beth Ann. Yes, sir, the women in Texas, were one of a kind.

He could get someone else to handle the Palm Springs office so he could go back to where the grass was green and the sky was wide. That would also get him away from Melissa so he wouldn't have to talk with her daddy about her behavior. Maybe she'd find herself a boyfriend if he left. That sure as beans shouldn't be hard with her looks.

He mulled over the time frame to see when he'd be able to move. It would take a few months to wrap things up here, but he had a plan. He'd already sold his town home in Riverside because he couldn't bring himself to live anywhere near Beth Ann and her Mr. Perfect. He could keep his place in Palm Springs for when he worked here and had to meet clients—that might be good. Yep, Texas was just what the doctor ordered. Luscious hot-blooded women who would take his mind off the little redhead who'd stolen his heart and broken it into pieces.

He parked his car in the driveway and dragged his ass out to gather his mail. Just as he turned to walk up to his front door, he caught sight of a familiar shadow standing there gazing at him. Oh, hell yeah. She was just what he needed.

"Celise, what a pleasant surprise."

"Heyya, Blake. I was just about to leave." The brown-haired beauty sashayed over to him, sweeping her hair over her shoulders. "I just stopped by to see if America's most eligible bachelor was still ... well, eligible."

"Well, darlin," he said, skimming his fingers over her enticing neck. "I sure am, and I'm as happy as a cowboy on a horse that you stopped by." He pulled her into a devouring kiss. "How about we have a night cap?"

"I do have something in mind." She breezed inside when he opened the door, then she leaned over to whisper in his ear. "Tie me up and have your way with me!"

His body instantly responded from head to toe. She slid off her jacket, and her tall, voluptuous body was completely naked underneath.

"Well, darlin, I guess you did have something in mind." He swept his fingers across her breasts and watched as they rose to the occasion, just like he did.

He locked the door behind him, then he took her hand and led her to his bedroom. All thoughts of work and everything else disappeared in the face of the mouthwatering dessert that Celise was offering.

* * * *

The phone jarred Beth Ann awake the next morning, and she wondered for the millionth time why the heck she hadn't turned down that noise maker. She reached out to the end table and picked it up and said hello.

"I'd like to speak with Elizabeth Ann Rose," a man's voice said.

"This is she, but my last name is O'Brien now."

"Oh, right. I was told you just got married."

"May I ask who is calling?"

Kaylob sat up and propped his head on his hand, watching her.

"Oh, of course. My apologies. My name is Alberto Rios. I saw your show when you were on the road with Mitch. I was quite impressed, Mrs. O'Brien."

Beth Ann almost dropped the phone. Alberto Rios was a well-known name around Broadway, synonymous with a half dozen Broadway hits. His English was better than when she'd seen him on TV.

"I've heard of your shows, Mr. Rios," she said, shaking Kaylob's arm with excitement.

Alberto cleared his throat. "Well, I hope you're available to work with me on the next one. I'm doing a new production called *Midnight Love*. I would like very much for you to play the lead. I would have contacted your agent, but you don't seem to have one. I can make it worth your while, Mrs. O'Brien."

He ended up offering her more than double what she had made on her last show. He told her she'd be traveling in a private tour bus, and the tour would be on the road for six months. He also offered to have a private plane pick up Kaylob whenever they wanted to see each other. She was very impressed, but she told him she'd have to talk it over with her husband before she could give him an answer. After she hung up and told Kaylob all the details, she watched his face closely for a reaction.

"Honey, how do you feel about this?"

He smiled, but something in his eyes was missing. "Beth Ann, I want you to be happy. If this is what you want, I say go for it."

"You're really okay with me traveling and being gone so much?"

"Is it what you want?" He pushed a strand of hair out of her face. "Because if it is, then that's what I want too."

"It's a wonderful offer." She reached up and touched the dimple in his chin.

"I'm proud of you, sweetheart. And speaking of proud, don't forget that Mitch wants to bring your Tony over."

"Oh, that's right. I'll call him today. So you're not upset about how long I'll be away?"

He shook his head. "I'll miss you, but I'll be okay with it." He kissed her then went to take a shower.

"Alberto will fly you out to see me whenever you want and I can come home too on a private plane, but our phone bill will still be high," Beth Ann yelled out to him.

"Yep, it sure will, the offer is great, sweetheart. Come take a shower with me. I'll wash your hair." Kaylob peeked around the corner and winked at her.

No way could she refuse an offer like that. His hands always felt so good on her scalp. He was humming and singing when she stepped in and joined him. She really was thrilled about Alberto's offer, but a part of her wished that Kaylob had asked her not to go, because she was going to miss him so much. It made her a little sad that he was so okay with everything.

She made a mental note to call her job and let them know, they needed to get someone to replace her. She'd be rehearsing for the tour soon, and wanted to spend as much time as she could with her husband. She also needed to call Carol, because they usually drove together. Carol had started working at Disneyland, training dancers and said she totally loved it. Who wouldn't love it though, since on her breaks, she could have fun going on rides. Now that's what Beth Ann called a great job.

But if the truth be known, she was sure as heck glad Carol wasn't training *her* anymore because she pushed so hard. Carol had been at the Lakeside School of Art when Beth Ann first arrived. She was hard to miss with her grace and poise and those long, lean legs that made you know she had to be a dancer. Carol had become one of Beth Ann's best friends and had been there for her when Kaylob had been declared dead.

She had been lucky to have all her wonderful friends around her during those times, and that gave her a brilliant idea. They needed to have a dinner party soon. Maybe the restaurant could cater everything.

One thing she knew for sure was that *she* wouldn't be doing the cooking!

Chapter Five

Weeks later, Beth Ann was dizzy from all the craziness. She had wrapped up her final day at her job yesterday and Kaylob had been looking for a general manager for the restaurant. He needed someone who could run things while he was gone. Beth Ann tried to understand the whole thing. He had a manager, but needed a general manager? Why, Beth Ann hadn't a clue. They had just opened and things were getting crazy. Beth Ann couldn't believe how fast everything had been finished and set up.

As Kaylob and Beth Ann drove into the parking lot, they were both surprised by the amount of customers who were there on a Saturday at noon. Kaylob pulled around back to the alley when they saw the delivery truck leaving, and he was upset to find deliveries piled outside the back door against the wall.

"This is the reason why I need a general manager," Kaylob said, pointing at the boxes of food. "Someone needs to get that stuff inside and put it away before it spoils."

He stepped through the back door, grabbed a dolly and started stacking the boxes. Beth Ann picked up the last one and followed her husband into the kitchen. The storage area was peaceful and serene, but the minute they walked through the double doors they found themselves in the crazy kitchen zone.

"Get the damn chicken off the grill! It needed to chill yesterday," one of the chefs yelled.

"Hey, kiss my ass!" another chef shot back. "Who do you think you are, King Farouk?" He walked away from the grill, leaving the chicken where it was.

Kaylob seemed completely oblivious to everything going on, but Beth Ann took it all in while they moved the boxes into the freezer. What a trip. After the supplies had been put away, she watched Kaylob put on his apron, wash his hands and pull the chicken off the grill. He placed it perfectly onto a plate and put some garnishes on it, then handed it off to one of the prep chefs. If Kaylob hadn't explained what they were, she wouldn't have known what to call them.

There was no way to keep from being in awe of her husband. Her heart swelled with so much pride that she was afraid it might explode. She took a seat on a stool by the freezer and wished she had some popcorn to watch act two.

"Fire up the back burners!" one of the cooks yelled.

"Do it yourself! I'm not your slave."

The insults escalated with increasingly creative metaphors, making the kitchen sound like a longshoreman's bar.

Beth Ann was surprised that no one acknowledged Kaylob, but she guessed it was due to the perpetual activity. There seemed to be no spare time, but she did notice an older gentleman looking at her more than once.

Kaylob fired up the back burner, then started to whip something in a large bowl. Two assistant chefs returned to the kitchen, then started to chop and yell about extra virgin olive oil.

"I don't like this kind, it smells like fish guts!" one guy yelled.

"Ralf likes this flavor and he's the chef!"

"He's one of the chefs, not *the* chef."

A few minutes later, a hostess rushed in all flustered. She was trying to get a word in, her hand on her hip while she waited for the right moment, but nobody was paying any attention to her. Beth Ann thought she was adorable with her strawberry hair, big blue eyes and petite build. At the moment, she was obviously frustrated, drifting her head left and right looking for someone who could help her. Finally, she was able to make her voice heard over the squawking chefs.

"A guy is here for the position of general manager!" she shouted. "Sorry for yelling, but I had to because of all the noise." She looked at Kaylob. "I put him in the office and gave him some coffee."

Beth Ann noticed that the chefs had on nametags.

Juan, the short, heavyset guy, winked at the hostess. "So what positions do you like?"

The younger chef, a handsome blond guy named Ralf, spoke next. "She doesn't want you, Juan. She likes me better, right, Julie?" Ralf raised his eyebrows and gave her a flirtatious smile.

The girl's cheeks turned a bright red color and she shrugged with a bashful smile. "How would I know? I haven't been out with you."

"That can be fixed. Let's go out." Ralf smiled at her as he handed the bowl and spoon he was holding to his assistant.

All the guys started whistling and singing *That's Amoré.*

Kaylob pointed at Ralf and encouraged him to finish what he was doing, then he took Beth Ann by the arm and led her toward the office. "Come on, I'm getting you out of this place."

One of the guys called after them. "Hey, boss, why can't you leave your wife here with us? We'll make her happy."

Kaylob shook his head. "Not in a million years."

The yelling and chatter was blocked out when they shut the soundproof doors. Now Beth Ann totally understood why doors leading into the kitchen had to be specially made, and she knew why it also made sense for the kitchen to be so far away from the dining area and closer to the bar where the music was louder.

When they reached the back office and opened the door, they found a man in the chair who was wearing a conservative blue suit and fidgeting nervously with a folder on his lap. Kaylob walked over and the man stood up to shake hands. He was maybe Kaylob's age and of medium height, with brown hair and pale, gray eyes.

Kaylob introduced himself and Beth Ann. When he shook Beth Ann's hand, she noticed he was wearing a wedding ring.

"Thank you for seeing me, Mr. O'Brien." The man handed Kaylob the folder. "My name is Mike Davidson, and I'm here about the general manager's job."

Kaylob moved around behind the desk and took a seat while Beth Ann sat on the small couch. She didn't want to make the poor guy more nervous than he was already, so she picked up something to read and was surprised to see it was one of the new menus. Wow, she was stunned that two of the chefs had their name above the foods they'd created. That was something new, but she liked it. She was getting hungry reading the dessert menu—Chocolate Peanut Butter Mousse. Gosh, that sounded deadly!

"I see here that you haven't managed anywhere in the last two years," Kaylob said, jotting down notes. "Is there a reason for that?"

Mike clasped his hands together and looked at the floor. "I had to take a couple years off, because ..." He paused and seemed to be collecting himself. "My wife had a breakdown, and I had to take care of her." He fidgeted once again in the chair before taking a sip from the coffee cup sitting on the desk in front of him. "We lost our baby to a rare cancer. It was really hard on my wife, but she's doing better now. In fact, she went back to her banking job just a few days ago."

The small room quieted, and it was as though his story had taken the air out of the room. Kaylob nodded and kept his eyes on the resume in his hands. "I'm sorry for your loss and admire your commitment to your wife." He studied the resume again. "Mike, you have some great references."

"Thank you." The man seemed to relax. "I love working in this field."

They talked for another fifteen minutes before Kaylob stood and extended his hand. "As long as your references check out, the job is yours. Can you start tomorrow?"

Mike jumped up and shook Kaylob's hand. "Yes, no problem. I give you my word you won't be disappointed."

"I have a feeling I'm going to be very happy with you as part of the team." Kaylob moved from behind the desk and walked Mike to the door. "Let me go introduce you to everyone." He looked back and winked at Beth Ann as they left.

When she was alone in the office, Beth Ann felt a tear slide down her cheek as she thought about what Mike had said about his wife. Even though she'd never wanted children, she couldn't imagine what a loss like that must feel like. She was proud of Kaylob for helping him out.

She went back to looking at the menus and realized she must've dozed off while she waited for Kaylob to come back, because the next thing she felt was warm kisses on her cheek. And she knew those lips belonged to her husband.

"Wake up, sleeping beauty." He grinned and took her hand to help her up.

She gave him a gentle kiss before they walked out to the dining area hand in hand. They both paused because it was like stepping into another dimension. Soft music blended with light chatter and laughter from the guests. The place was nearly full, and everything was running perfectly.

Kaylob sighed deeply. "When Mike comes on board, things will only get better."

Beth Ann saw tears fill his eyes. "Honey, are you okay?"

"It's been so busy around here with so many things happening, I don't think I've had time to appreciate all this." He waved his hand around. "For the first time since we got home, I realize that my dream has come true. I have the restaurant and wife that I've been dreaming about since I was a kid."

She stood on her toes and gave him another gentle kiss. "And this wife couldn't be any happier for you."

When they got to his truck, he opened the door. "I'm happy for you too, baby. You just landed a big role in another Broadway show."

"Thank you, honey." When they were both in the truck, she remembered to ask him something. "Kaylob, what's the difference between a general manager and a manager?"

"A manager is in charge of hiring new staff and terminating undesirables. They help keep the books balanced and keep everyone doing their job. They make sure the event planner keeps everything straight, takes care of customer service and oversees a lot of things like the ads and menus. Things like that."

She nodded. "And what does the general manager do?"

"He handles the inventory, including front line items like paper napkins, cleaning supplies and restaurant dishware. General managers also review and approve liquor orders and food requests from the head chef and wine manager." He turned and pointed at the back door. "They're also responsible for making sure deliveries are put up so we won't have food wasting away out back by the door, like today."

Beth Ann held up her hand. "Whew, okay. You're talking to someone who can't cook an egg, so let's pretend I never asked." She wasn't surprised that her husband was so knowledgeable about everything to do with the business. He'd been studying and researching everything since he was a kid.

An hour later, after fighting the afternoon traffic, Kaylob took Beth Ann to a specialty store so she could pick out another pink dress.

The first one she tried on was a hit, at least for a minute. The spark in his eyes told her it was sexy and clung in all the right places, but when he glanced around to see if anyone else was watching, she knew what he was thinking. It took her back to another time years ago when she'd shown him a sexy dress and he'd made it clear he didn't want her wearing it out in public.

"What?" he asked.

"Never mind." She shook her head and went back to start over.

The next one was cute and sexy, but not so revealing. The second she stepped into his view, a smile spread across his handsome face. When they finished and went to pay for everything, Kaylob had added a new pair of tennis shoes for work, and Beth Ann bought some new undergarments along with her new dress.

It was a relief when they stepped outside the store and nobody was taking pictures. Maybe the paparazzi had decided to stalk someone else now. She could only hope.

"Want to go get something to eat?" Kaylob looked at his watch when they climbed into the truck. "It's already four o'clock. By the time we get somewhere to eat, it will be dinner time." He put a hand on his stomach. "I'm starved."

"Don't you want to go to our own restaurant?" she asked. "I mean your place."

"No, you're right, Beth Ann." He grinned. "It's *our* place. I built that stage for you, remember? But right now I want to take you somewhere different."

Something about the way he said it, made her wonder if his feelings were hurt because he'd built that platform for her. Holy smokes, and now she'd be singing somewhere else.

"Kaylob, I'm so sorry. You went through all the trouble to have that done, and now I'm leaving." She scooted over closer to him. "I'm being selfish."

"You're not being selfish. It was my dream for you to sing in my restaurant, not yours. You've always wanted Broadway." He lifted her chin and his lips melted across hers, which left her breathless.

"But, Kaylob—"

"No buts. Now shush. I love you, and what makes you happy, makes me happy."

All she could do was nod. There was no way to put in words how much she loved this man.

Once they arrived at the restaurant, she could see Kaylob observing everything. When he started writing things on a napkin after they ordered, she waited for him to finish, first tapping the table with her nails, then humming, then tapping her knife on her spoon. When the food arrived and he said *thank you* without even looking up, she started to wonder if he'd forgotten she was there.

She cleared her throat. "I'm going to eat my meal nude then do some jumping jacks with nothing on."

"Sounds good," he muttered.

"*Ahem.*"

Still not even a glance. After two more *ahems* with no response, she started coughing and he finally looked up at her.

"Are you okay? Do you have something caught in your throat?"

"No, but I guess you must have something very important you're writing on that napkin." She reached across the table and picked it up. "I told you I was going to eat in the nude and you agreed."

"What?" He looked perplexed.

When she glanced down at the napkin, she saw four different ideas for recipes. "What is this?"

"A formula for some new dessert recipes. I'm sorry, I guess I got caught up in my ideas." He arched an eyebrow. "Now what's this about being nude?"

She giggled. "I was trying to get your attention."

He gave her his undivided attention for the rest of the time, and the dinner ended up being wonderful. They lingered for hours, drinking coffee and talking about future plans.

Before it got dark, they strolled over to their favorite park where they had carved their initials on the old oak tree. They had also buried two glass bottles with unread notes that they would open on their twenty-fifth wedding anniversary. As they sat down on the bench near the tree, the last rays of sunlight flickered across the grass, casting shadows from the trees and lampposts. The aroma of the roses permeated the air as small gusts of wind rustled through the treetops.

Beth Ann was enveloped in nostalgia. The children's laughter was like a melody, bringing back memories of her own childhood and how she and her brothers had played outside at the truck stops, playing catch and running across the grass. But more than anything, it reminded her of the summers at Gram's house. Those times were her stable moments in life and the place she felt at home.

"Penny for your thoughts," Kaylob said.

"I was thinking about all the traveling I did as a child. You know, there were some good times even though we lived in that old car and dirty hotel rooms."

Kaylob wrapped his arms around her. "Well, Elizbeth Ann O'Brien, those days of dirty hotel rooms are long gone."

She nodded and snuggled closer, and they both lost track of how much time had gone by.

When they returned to Kaylob's restaurant much later, the place was almost quiet. The staff was cleaning tables and stacking chairs as light chatter came from somewhere near the bar. The kitchen was spotless, and things seemed to have gone well for the night. Off in one of the alcoves, a vacuum was running while some of the staff was restocking supplies and putting new candles on the tables. These were the late night staff, the ones who set up for the next day. Kaylob went over to talk to a couple of the guys cleaning the bar.

Beth Ann sighed deeply as she watched Kaylob. Their day together had been lovely, and seeing how nice things were flowing in his place filled her with a sense of contentment. She walked over to the front window and glanced outside at the hotel across the street. Things were quiet as the day came to a close. She placed her hand across her heart, and it swelled with love and joy.

Then, out of the corner of her eye, she caught a glimpse of a man standing outside the hotel across the street, watching her.

Oh God, that's my pink dress he's holding!

Shivers ran down her spine, and terror had her frozen to the spot. All she could do was stare at the man out there watching her. His face was hidden by a hat, but she could tell from the position of his head that he was looking in her direction. She fumbled backwards, watching the street lights flicker, casting shadows everywhere.

Everything about him screamed danger.

Finally, she managed to get past the lump in her throat. "Kaylob!"

He must have recognized the panic in her voice because he came running. She pointed at the window, but when she looked out, the stranger was gone.

Kaylob looked outside, then back at Beth Ann. "What's wrong, sweetheart? What was out there?"

"There was someone staring at me from across the street. Kaylob, he was holding a pink dress!"

Kaylob hurried outside to look around, but when he came back, he shook his head. "I didn't see anyone out there, Beth Ann."

"He was there, staring in the window right at me." Her voice cracked. "You have to believe me!"

"I do, sweetheart." He wrapped his arms around her. "But it was more than likely just someone from the hotel. Maybe he stepped outside to smoke. I see people doing that all the time." He lifted her chin and kissed her gently.

She told herself he was right. After all, it was a hotel and people went outside to smoke all the time.

"Okay, honey," she said. "I guess I'm still a bit jumpy. But when I saw the pink dress …" She paused to laugh uneasily. "I don't know why I thought it was mine. It looked like my dress, but that's just silly."

"Maybe it belonged to his wife." Kaylob hugged her again. "But it doesn't matter. I'm here, and nobody is going to do anything to you. I think our home being robbed brought back stuff from your attack, and you're feeling nervous. Remember Frankie got the locks changed for us last week, so don't worry." He pulled them out of his pocket. "Do you still have your set of keys?"

"Yes of course." She smiled. "I keep them in my purse all the time."

He took her hand and guided her toward his office. When they got there, they found Hal sitting at the desk, hitting buttons on the calculator and running a tab. He held a finger up, wrote down a few more things, then looked up and smiled.

"Hey, Hal," Kaylob said. "How'd we do today?"

"Sales are up and we have happy customers," Hal replied. "Not one complaint today, except that one about the shrimp." His smile widened. "By the way, since you cooked that Tortelli di Zucca we have to put it on next week's menu now. The customer couldn't shut up about it, and now we have orders for a dinner party of forty. You, my friend, are making a name for this place. And ..." He paused to look down at the numbers in front of him. "You are exceeding all the projections."

Kaylob shook his hand. "Now that's what I like to hear." He turned to Beth Ann. "Wonder what they'd think if they knew an Irishman cooked that Italian special."

All three of them chuckled.

Hal and Kaylob discussed their new general manager, and Hal assured him everything would be okay while Kaylob was away with Beth Ann for Gram's wedding. He promised to make sure the grand opening that was set for one week after they returned would be perfect. They went over the wine list for the following week, confirming or rejecting the selections the wine manager had made, then they discussed the new chef they had snipped from another restaurant, an Italian woman named Andria Marino with a reputation for being the best.

"I hope you know you're getting a woman who's known for eating men alive in the kitchen," Hal said.

"That's fine." Kaylob waved a dismissive hand and laughed. "Those guys need to be put in their place."

"She liked you, boss," Hal said. "For that reason alone, she's taking the job since we're such a new place. Those are words from her mouth to my ear."

"Yeah, and I'd bet she liked that I'm paying her more money and letting her make her own menu too."

Hal nodded. "True, but don't worry about anything while you're away at the wedding. We have everything under control."

It was really late by the time they left. Beth Ann moved over next to Kaylob in the truck on the drive home and put her head on his shoulder. She must've dozed off, because the next thing she knew they were home and Kaylob was whispering in her ear.

"Don't move." He got out, then went around to her side and gathered her in his arms. "My baby girl is tired."

He was the most romantic, loving husband a girl could ever ask for. She wanted to stay up all night, showing him how lucky she felt, but they had to get some sleep so they wouldn't miss their flight for Gram and Nickolas's wedding the next morning. With new locks and a new dead bolt, everything was safe.

Chapter Six

Maggie Rose, future Mrs. Ballas stood in the sewing room at Nicky's farmhouse, looking at her wedding gown hanging on the hub. A sea of joy filled her heart. She was marrying the man she had loved since she was a young girl, and all because her wonderful granddaughter and her fiancé, now her husband, had found Nicky and talked him into showing up at their wedding in Hawaii.

It was a miracle how Beth Ann and Kaylob had pulled off such a surprise. They had found Nicky through some of the old love letters Maggie had saved. It turned out that he lived only fifteen minutes away, but if they hadn't searched for him, Maggie would never have gone to find him herself.

This is a chance for our happiness that was stolen so many years ago.

What a surprise to find out that Nicky was living in the same farmhouse his parents had lived in. Maggie walked around the room and ran her hand over the antique furniture. It was lovely and felt like home already. She'd never lived in a house this big and wondered how in the world she'd keep it clean with six bedrooms, each with a bathroom attached. His parents had turned it into a place for weary travelers, which had changed their life financially.

Standing there, gazing at her dress, Maggie thought of Beth Ann's wedding day. She'd been the most radiant bride, even after everything she'd been through. Just the thought of what those beasts had done to her granddaughter sent a pain through Maggie's heart. What if they had killed her? Tears filled her eyes, and her throat clogged with pain for her beloved Beth Ann. Maggie adored all her grandchildren, but Beth Ann was the light of her world, and they had a bond that wasn't easy to explain.

She parted the curtains, gazing out at the open pasture and the old barn that had been repainted. Out in the field, she could see a flock of birds gathering around something Nicky was growing. She hoped they weren't doing any damage. Some of the birds landed around the barn, picking at the ground. Memories came flooding back of all the things she and Nicky had done inside that old barn.

It had been July of 1945, the day his parents went to Portland and she had waited just outside of the barn doors while Nicky went to get them some lemonade. His parents had moved from Salem to Woodburn, so it was harder for them to see each other, but that day they were alone for the entire afternoon. Her friend Bee had given her a ride and was going to pick her up later that afternoon. Of course, she had told her parents, she and Bee were going shopping, then out to dinner.

She recalled hearing Nicky's footsteps before she saw him.

"Hey, beautiful," he'd said. "Do you want to go up to the house or hang out in the barn?"

"Let's stay in the barn just in case they get back early." She looked at him and touched her lips.

He knew instantly what she wanted, and with the lemonade in hand, he leaned down and devoured her lips. Within minutes, he led her in the barn after he sat the lemonade inside the old wheelbarrow.

The memory made her shiver. As she stood, gazing outside, she could see them running in the fields and laughing until Nicky would catch her then pull her down into the tall grass. Remembering the touch of his hands still gave her goose bumps.

The view was incredible, and she was the happiest woman in the world. Sixty-five wasn't too old to start over with the man she loved, and she believed they would have many wonderful years together.

A knock on the door brought her back from her daydreams, so she walked over and opened it.

Nicky stood there with his eyes shut. "Can I come in, and is there anything I'm not supposed to see?"

"Hold on a second." Maggie went to cover the dress with a throw. "Okay, now you can open your eyes and come in."

"Maggie, my darling." Nicky put his hands on her shoulders and smiled at her. "Are you ready for today?"

"Oh, Nicky, I'm more than ready." She grinned as she gazed at his handsome face.

They looked into each other's eyes a moment, then he leaned down and gently pressed his lips to hers. It still surprised her that she was feeling things she had no idea she could ever feel again. The truth was, she had never felt them with her first husband, Albert James Rose. They'd never had much of anything between them except friendship. After their son was born, they'd only had sex a few times because they just didn't feel right about it. He had shared with Maggie that his family had pushed him into marrying her as well.

It had been a tragic life for them both. He'd had other women, but out of respect for her, he'd been very discreet. She was glad they'd ended up being the best of friends, and that had made everyone think they'd had a great marriage. What they'd really had was great companionship, and she had loved him like a brother.

"Maggie, you seem far away," Nicky said. "You're not having second thoughts, are you?"

"For heaven's sake, no." She laughed. "I was just thinking about how you make me feel. I had forgotten what it feels like to be kissed by someone you're in love with."

He pulled her into his arms and held her close. "Ah, my little Magpie, tonight I'm hoping to show you just how much we've missed."

"Nicky, there's something I need to let you know." She played with the button on his shirt and felt her face getting warm. "It's been a very long time for me."

"I know your husband's been dead since Beth Ann was a baby." He paused and took a deep breath. "Didn't you ever date after he passed away?"

"Oh, a few little dinners here and there, but it never went anywhere."

"So it's been over twenty years for you? Do you want to be with me in that way?"

She still didn't look at him. "Oh, Nicky, more than you know. But it's been a lot longer than twenty years. After James was born, we moved into separate rooms and well … we were best friends."

He pulled her over to the bed and sat down, pulling her onto his lap. "Well, it will be like our first time again, and we both know how wonderful we were together." He lifted her chin and gazed into her eyes.

She managed not to look away even though she felt the fire heating her face.

He laughed softly. "My Magpie was always a shy one. Well, until we—"

"*Nickolas.*" She stood and gave him her best scolding look. He'd always loved to make her blush, but they were too old to be talking about it and making out like a couple of high school kids.

Bee's voice's echoed up the stairs. "Maggie, yoo-hoo! We're here to set up the food and decorations."

Maggie straightened her dress, smoothed her hair and walked out to the landing, which allowed her to see the entire bottom floor. Looking up at her with wide smiles on their faces and holding boxes of food were four of her dearest friends.

"Maggie, we're going to get started." Bee nodded at the box in her hand.

"Do you need me to come down and help?" Maggie took a few steps toward the stairs.

"Don't you dare take a step down here!" Bee said. "You just relax and get yourself ready. We'll handle setting everything up, and we've got more ladies coming over to finish up the decorations. So, don't worry, Maggie. Everything is going to be perfect."

"Let's get this show on the road, Bee!" Another longtime friend named Betty waved up at Maggie.

"You guys are the best friends in the world." Maggie placed her hand over her heart and hoped Nickolas stayed in the room until her friends were too busy to notice him leaving. She didn't want them to think there was any hanky panky going on.

Beth Ann and Kaylob arrived just then, and when Beth Ann looked up at Maggie tears filled her gorgeous brown eyes. Her granddaughter ran up the stairs and flung herself into her grandmother's arms.

"Oh, Gram! I'm so happy for you!"

She noticed Beth Ann saw Nicky, leaving the room. She didn't want her granddaughter to think that any kind of shenanigans had been going on either.

* * * *

Beth Ann stepped back and gave Gram a tender smile, then looked at Nicky. "I hope we didn't interrupt anything."

"Don't be silly, young lady." Gram waved a dismissive hand, then took Beth Ann's arm and led her into the room to show her the pressed wedding dress. Gram had bought it when Nicky first proposed all those years ago.

Beth Ann gasped. "Oh, Gram, it's even more gorgeous than I remember. I loved this dress the minute you showed it to me."

"I'm so happy I saved it." Gram wiped away a tear as she touched the ivory lace. The old-fashioned gown was made from silk, and covered with lace. The high neck was lined with pearl buttons down the back as well as on the cuff where it closed.

"Come on, Gram. Let me do your hair." Beth Ann took her hand and sat her down in front of the walnut veneer dressing table.

"This table is amazing." Beth Ann reached down and ran her hand across it.

Gram nodded. "It belonged to Nicky's mom."

"How special that he's kept it all these years." Beth Ann picked up the hairbrush and started on her grandmother's snow white hair. When Gram's hair was done, Beth Ann applied some light makeup and some eye shadow to match her blue eyes.

"You look stunning." She moved out of the way so Gram could see herself. When her entire face lit up, Beth Ann knew she was pleased. "Now we need to get your dress on. Are you sure it fits?"

Gram nodded. "The one thing that hasn't changed about me over the years is my weight. I've tried to gain but couldn't do it, except when I was pregnant. I still wear a size two."

Beth Ann smiled. "I didn't know what size the dress was, but it almost looks too big."

She turned around to glance at it again, then she went over and took the dress off the hub and helped her grandmother to slip it on. Once Beth Ann had buttoned it up, she turned Gram to face her, and her breath caught in her throat. "Gram, you're the most beautiful bride ever.

Nickolas is going to die when he sees you in this."

"I sure hope not," Gram said. "I want him alive and well."

Beth Ann chuckled, but she hadn't been exaggerating. Gram was radiant and didn't look at day over forty.

"Oh, sweetness." Gram looked in the full-length mirror with tears in her eyes. "I can't believe this is happening. You made me look wonderful."

Beth Ann stood next to her and gave her a gentle hug. "It was easy because you're so pretty. And believe it because it's happening. You're going to spend the rest of your life with the man you should have been with all along." Beth Ann wiped away her own tear. "And now I'll have a grandpa again. I'll always love my real grandpa, but I can't really remember him."

Gram touched Beth Ann's hand and gave her a soft smile. "Nicky loves you already."

There was a knock at the door and Beth Ann was surprised to see her tremendously handsome dad ready to walk his mom down the aisle. He was dressed in a dark suit with a blue shirt that matched the color of his eyes and complemented his strawberry blond hair. His eyes lit up the moment he saw his mother.

"Mother, you look amazing," he said.

"Thank you, James." Gram reached up and cupped his face.

He cleared his throat as if trying to keep from choking up. "They told me to let you ladies know that the pastor is here. They'll be ready in about fifteen minutes."

"Okay," Beth Ann said. "I just have to slip on my dress and we'll be ready too," she told her dad as he left. "Gram, is it hanging in this closet?" She pointed.

"Yes, I had it pressed and ready for you the minute it got here."

Beth Ann walked over and pulled it from the closet. It was a pretty and delicate peach-colored bridesmaid's dress. Beth Ann was the sole bridesmaid, and her dress matched Gram's bouquet that held a special meaning in Latin: *Carnations, the flower of love*. Perfect for Gram and Nickolas.

Fifteen minutes later, her dad returned and held out his arm for his mother. Beth Ann handed Gram the bouquet and noticed how tiny Gram looked standing next to her tall son. As Beth Ann went down the stairs, she heard the music beginning and saw how amazing the living room looked. All the furniture had been moved and replaced with chairs lined in rows and filled with guests. Flowers and decorations filled the area.

Kaylob was standing up front with Nickolas in his baby blue suit that almost made Beth Ann's knees go weak, and he winked at her when she joined them near the pastor. Then the wedding march started and James led Gram slowly down the staircase. Everyone was *oohing* in awe at how incredible she looked. When Beth Ann glanced at Nickolas, his eyes sparkled with adoration as he watched his bride. He looked wonderful in his dark jacket, light blue shirt and ivory tie.

When her dad and Gram reached the front, the music changed again, and Beth Ann recognized *Day By Day* by Frank Sinatra and thought how perfect the lyrics were: "Day by day, I'm falling more in love with you."

As the song ended, the pastor stepped up closer, holding the Bible. James placed his mother's hand into Nickolas's, and the couple faced the preacher.

"Dearly beloved, we have gathered here together ..."

As he spoke, Beth Ann thought about how many years Gram had waited to marry Nickolas, and now they would get their chance. She wished her brothers could have made it here for the wedding, but neither could get away. Beth Ann wouldn't have missed it for the world.

She found herself wondering what life would be like for her and Kaylob when they were as old as Gram and Nicky. Would they still desire each other as much as they did now? She thought they would.

"Do you have rings?" asked the pastor.

Nickolas nodded to Kaylob who pulled out a box and handed it over to the groom.

"Maggie ..." Nickolas paused as his voice cracked. "These are the wedding bands I bought for us over forty years ago." He took the rings from the box and held them up.

"Oh, Nicky ..." Gram's hands covered her mouth and tears spilled down her cheeks.

Beth Ann could see the lovely vintage wedding bands were engraved with a whimsical pattern of leaves and pansy blossoms. The two silver and gold bands were a matching set, Nickolas's was a wider cut. The engagement ring was attached to Gram's band, and it was breathtaking.

Gram held out her hand, and Nickolas slid the band onto her finger. "This ring is a token of my love. I marry you with this ring and become your husband, with all that I have and all that I am. I pledge to be with you until death do us part."

Gram took the other band and slipped it onto his finger. "This ring is a token of my love. I marry you and become your wife today with love in my heart. With all that I have and all that I am, I give myself unto you."

"You may kiss your bride," the pastor said.

Beth Ann's eyes flooded with tears as she watched them kiss, finally man and wife. She wanted to run and hug them both, but figured she'd better wait a little longer.

"Ladies and gentlemen," the pastor announced. "I present to you Mr. and Mrs. Ballas."

Everyone clapped and yelled hooray. Kaylob smiled at Beth Ann, and she could see the emotion in his eyes. He was as happy for them as she was.

The reception was precious. Nickolas and Gram danced and laughed, and the food was out of this world. The ladies from Gram's church really knew how to cook, and Kaylob was in heaven, flirting with the old ladies and getting their recipes. Beth Ann shook her head and watched him work his magic.

Twilight arrived, and it seemed as though the stars danced in the heavens. Gram and Beth Ann strolled arm in arm into the farmhouse as things were winding down. Gram had already said her goodnights to most the ladies. A few stayed behind and were starting to clean up while the guys took apart the tables and carried them inside the storage house.

When Beth Ann and Gram got upstairs to the master bedroom, Gram said, "Some of my friends were surprised that we aren't leaving for a honeymoon, but there's no place in the world I'd rather be than here. Nicky and I want to spend the next week at home savoring our chance at finally being husband and wife."

"I'm so thrilled for both of you, Gram. And I know you're going to be so very happy." Beth Ann lifted her hand to look at the beautiful wedding band. "How amazing that he kept it all these years."

"I know." Gram nodded. "I had no idea."

"What will the two do for the next week?" Beth Ann paused. "I mean, ah …"

"I can see the questions burning in your eyes, sweet girl. You're wondering if we're going to be together as man and wife."

Beth Ann looked down at her shoes. "Well, now that you mention it."

Gram lifted her chin. "Yes, Nicky and I are very much in love."

"Everyone can see that, Gram." Beth Ann felt her cheeks heat and decided to change the subject. "It was the sweetest wedding I've ever been to."

They hugged and Beth Ann saw Kaylob coming in the room. She wondered if he had overheard them talking.

"Gram, what about saving a hug for me?" he asked.

"Always room for you, Kaylob. Always." Gram hugged him close.

"The ladies got everything cleaned up downstairs and left in a hurry, so we need to leave these two newlyweds alone." He took Beth Ann's hand and chuckled. "They said they'd come back for the chairs and stuff in a few days."

Gram walked over to her purse. "Here's the key to my house. Your daddy and Vera are going to move in next week, so go on over and look around to see if there are any items you want."

"Can I have the paintings off the wall that I did for you?" Beth Ann asked.

"Sorry, sweetie. You can have them someday, but not until I'm long gone. Those were packed up and brought over here. I'm hanging them up in the sewing room."

Beth Ann smiled and gave her a big hug, then she and Kaylob took off to Gram's old house. She was happy that it was staying in the family because she couldn't imagine never going to it again.

* * * *

After everyone left, Gram wondered why Nicky hadn't come upstairs yet. She moved over to the bedroom window and glanced down, smiling when she saw him gazing into the sky at the moon and stars. Could she be dreaming? It had all happened so fast. Was she truly ready to give everything to him again? Her eyes focused on the moon and followed the trail of its luminous light on the trees below. Nicky's silhouette made her heart quiver. Even in the darkness, she could see the outline of his broad shoulders.

Just as she started to step away from the window, he turned and their eyes met. The love and affection swept its way up into the bedroom and sang to her heartstrings. And it answered all her questions. She knew without a doubt that she was more than ready to spend forever with her husband.

She smiled down at him and gently glided her fingers across her lips like she had when they were teens. He'd always known what that simple motion meant. She inhaled deeply and looked up at the sky again, thanking God for this most wonderful blessing.

The second he came into the room, she knew, even though he'd made no sound. Slowly, she turned to face him.

"I must be dreaming," he said, tears glittering in his eyes in the dim light. "Because I never thought this day would ever come. You're the most beautiful, radiant woman I've ever seen. I love you beyond the moon and back." He reached out his hand to her.

"Nicky, look at the sky." She walked forward to lace their fingers together, then she led him back to the window. "Doesn't it remind you of all the nights we sat under the stars, talking about our future together? We were so young."

"Yes, it does. And look—all those dreams finally came true."

He kissed her cheek, then he walked back over and shut the door. When he turned to look at her again, the look in his eyes told her their honeymoon was about to begin.

Chapter Seven

The coast is clear. I'm going in again.

He turned the handle on the front door of Beth Ann's townhouse, but the door was locked, just as he'd suspected. He tried the new key and it went right in. Yep, he'd overheard Beth Ann at work saying she had to change the locks. It had been easy to get into her purse, slip out her key and go make a copy, then return it. He had walked right up to Beth Ann that day and spoke to her. Hell, he had the keys in his hand and she was clueless. It was fun to be so close to her while he was plotting out all the things he was going to do.

This time he was going to look for more personal and sentimental items. He knew Beth Ann was in Salem at her grandmother's wedding. As far as he was concerned, the old gal was too damn old to be getting married, but it gave him a chance to get some more of Beth Ann's things and for her to see her grandmother one last time. Very soon now, none of them would ever see Beth Ann again. Where he was taking her, nobody would ever find them.

What a surprise it had been when she'd spotted him outside their restaurant through the window. That hotel was his home for now. He'd been staying there to keep an eye on her while he waited for his house to be finished. The pink dress had been in his hand, and he couldn't help wondering if she had noticed it. She probably had since her big brave Soldier Boy had come running out the door, looking around, acting all tough and shit.

But once again brains had outsmarted bravery, because Soldier Boy hadn't seen him dart behind the soda machine. But damn, that had been close. He'd been bringing her dress inside after picking it up from the dry cleaners, since it had gotten a bit dirty in his trunk. He couldn't have that, being it was new and all.

At least his house was almost done and ready to go, and that was making him a very happy man. He'd been mapping out this plan for a long time.

The minute he stepped inside the reading room, he saw something he knew he had to take. On a special little table were trinkets and a lovely picture of Beth Ann and her grandmother. "Oh, how special." Next to the picture was a Bible. He picked it up and flipped through the pages. "I'm going to hell in a Lambergini." He cackled.

"This is a score!" It was an entire journal of Beth Ann's life, and all the events appeared to have been written by her grandmother. He was taking all these things for sure, because the one thing he knew about Beth Ann was, she loved her grandma.

He stuck the picture and the Bible in one of the oversized bags he'd brought, then he headed to her bedroom and went straight to her closet where her dresser was. Man, she sure had a lot of shoes. He'd better take at least two pair and some flip-flops. She wasn't going to miss these.

When he opened the drawer on the bottom of her dresser, he scored again. Inside was a tiny pink bikini. He held it up. "Ah, I remember how she looked in that other one and this one is even skimpier."

He felt himself grow hard and had to bend over from the throbbing. When he straightened up again, he held the bikini to his nose. By God, it smelled like her. Dammit, he was in pain again.

Ah, man, this was killing him. Until he fixed himself. Now he needed to clean up with some tissue. Maybe he'd use her bath towel. He went over and grabbed it off the rack.

He needed to get going before he got caught, so he stuffed the bikini into one of the bags. It wouldn't be a good idea to clobber someone in the head and have the police come in again. Just as he turned to get the hell out of Dodge, he noticed a necklace hanging on her bedpost and decided to take it too, along with two books on her nightstand. He shoved them down in the bag, then he zipped it up and hurried out of the apartment.

When he got to the end of the walkway, he saw the guy he'd clobbered walking toward him, holding hands with some other guy. Ah, he was a gay boy. How special. At least he didn't have to worry about him having a thing for Beth Ann too.

"Good morning," the shorter guy said. "Isn't it a beautiful day?"

The boyfriend just gave him a long, hard stare and said nothing.

"Sure is." He nodded and pasted on a smile as he hurried past them with his hands full.

Okay, that was too close for comfort. He'd better not come back now that they'd seen him. And the way the tall one had been glaring at him, made him nervous.

* * * *

Over the next few weeks, it seemed to Beth Ann that she had almost no time to do anything. Everything happened so fast after Gram and Nicky's wedding, like the restaurant's grand opening that was a huge success, her birthday had come and gone and now she was only six years from being thirty. Did that make her old? They had also had a small party when Mitch had brought her Tony award. It had been fun to spend time with some of the old cast that had been in her first Broadway show.

Today would be her first day of rehearsing for the new show. Not to mention, trying to find her missing things had become a monumental pain in the butt. She leaned down and searched the bottom of her closet once again.

"How the heck can I lose my shoes?" she complained aloud.

Kaylob waltzed into the closet. "Baby, I think it's time to start unpacking your suitcases from the honeymoon."

She put her hands on her hips. "I will when I get time. And that doesn't explain my missing shoes."

With a slow arch of his brow, he asked, "how can you find anything when you're living out of your bags? Not to mention that you have at least two hundred pairs of shoes."

"You're right. I like shoes." She bent down again and picked up a pair of sneakers. "I guess these will just have to do."

Kaylob placed his hand over his heart and staggered against the wall.

Beth Ann rushed to his side. "Kaylob, what's the matter?"

"My … heart's in shock. Did you just say I was right?"

"Very funny." Holding up the shoes, she scrunched her nose. "These are just so ugly." She frowned and breezed by Kaylob then plopped down on the bed. She knew he was watching her, so she halfway opened one eye and peeked at him standing with his arms crossed over his chest.

"Why did you buy those shoes if they're ugly?"

She gave a half shrug. "I don't know."

"Wait, I think I know where your missing shoes vanished to," he said with an impish grin. "Maybe the fairy shoe mother came in and stole them while we were gone."

"I don't think so," she said with a frown. "See? You and my fairy godmother think they're ugly. She wouldn't even take them."

"Elizabeth Ann Rose, I never said they were ugly, and I never said fairy godmother. I simply asked why you bought ugly shoes — you said it, not me. And I said fairy shoe mother." He laughed, then bent over closer to her face. "In other words, if you think they're ugly, why did you buy them?"

"Go away, Kaylob Shawn O'Brien. You're not helping." She pushed on his forehead, but he caught her wrist and pulled her off the bed into his arms.

"I know how I can take your mind off those ugly shoes." He nibbled her neck. "I mean, the ones *you* think are ugly."

"Kaylob, I have to get ready." She had to be at work in three hours, so she pushed him away, although she felt like doing something else.

"Okay, but just wear the shoes. I think they're fine. Or you could stop and buy a new pair. It's not like we can't afford it, even though God knows you don't need more shoes." He went over to the dresser and pulled out a shirt. Once he slipped it on, he gave her a sexy smile. "Or don't go in today and we can go back to bed and forget all about shoes."

Beth Ann laughed. He was so darn sexy. "Funny, Mr. O'Brien, but we both have to go to work." She walked over and started buttoning his shirt while giving him her best seductive smile, then she stood on her toes and gave him an inviting kiss. "I'll let you make me forget about my shoes tonight." She ran her hand down his pants. "Whoa, Mr. O'Brien, you weren't kidding, were you?" She moved her hand in a way she knew drove him wild.

"Grrrr …" He growled like an old bear and bit her neck. "I want to eat you for breakfast." He took her hand and lifted it up to his lips. "Don't tease me like that or I'm seriously going to miss work today. I can't go in like this, can I?" He looked down at the front of his pants.

She grinned and backed up to the bed again, slipping off her clothes. "Come here, Mr. O'Brien, and I'll take care of that issue for you." She lay back with an invitation he obviously couldn't refuse.

He leaped onto the bed, and there was no mention of ugly shoes the rest of their time together.

* * * *

Beth Ann managed to leave on time and wasn't late when she dropped Carol off outside Disneyland a few hours later. Carol had switched her hours around so they could still ride together. Just before she stepped inside the gates, Carol turned and waved. Her dark mocha skin matched her brown outfit today, and her hair was cool too. Her afro was shorter than Beth Ann had seen it in a long time, but it looked amazing.

While she drove to the theater for rehearsal, her mind drifted to the way Kaylob had made her feel that morning. He always took his time, making sure she was happy. He had a three-time rule, and she had no complaints, because he knew just how to get her there.

As soon as she walked into the theater, she recognized Alberto; he was a tall man with thick black hair. There were three guys on the stage who were obviously trying out for the lead role. Alberto turned to pick up something and saw her.

"Ah, Elizabeth, I'm so glad you're here." He strode toward her with his hand outstretched. "Come on stage and watch while we decide who will be your love in the show." He lifted her hand to his lips and gave it a light kiss. *Sei ancora più bella.*

Beth Ann had no idea what he'd said, but she smiled and nodded. Off to the right were some other cast members who were stretching and warming up their bodies. After each of the guys had auditioned their lines, she thought the man named Leo on the far left had done a fantastic job. His voice was beyond marvelous and so powerful that it gave her chills. He was tall, handsome and danced well, and he said the lines perfectly even though his French accent was pretty thick. She was happy when Alberto ended up choosing him for the part.

The other two guys shook Leo's hand before they left. Beth Ann felt sad for them, but understood that only one person could get the role. She remembered her first tryout for the lead role in the music review and how nervous she was, but she got the role.

"Elizabeth," Alberto said. "I'd like to introduce you to Leo Simon. He will be the man you love in the show."

She moved across the stage and held out her hand to Leo. He took it and also brought it up to his lips. "*Prise de souffle*. Nice to meet you, and I look forward to our working together." His brown eyes were friendly and his smile was warm.

Beth Ann smiled. "I'm thrilled to be a part of this show and to be working with you." She glanced between Leo and Alberto. "But I'm going to feel very short around such tall men."

Leo winked. "*Sqaut vers le bas.*" He squatted down and made Beth Ann laugh.

"You and Leo will be rehearsing the songs today," Alberto said. "And tomorrow you will practice the scenes. You are in love with him, but you are engaged to another man. You want Leo, but you don't want to break the other's heart."

Beth Ann felt a lump in her throat at how close that was to her real life experience.

A couple of stagehands pulled the piano out to the stage, then a balding guy sat down and started flipping through the music. He began to play, and Beth Ann knew it was time to get to work.

The morning elapsed into late afternoon, with new songs and new dance moves. Leo was a nice guy and easy to perform with. Overall, it was a great day. Beth Ann also met her understudy, Nicollette Chevalier, who was beyond stunning and talented. In fact, Beth Ann couldn't help but wonder why she hadn't gotten the main role.

She was still thinking about that and other things when she picked up Carol at Disneyland. Carol must have noticed because after they'd been driving for a few minutes, she reached over and touched Beth Ann's arm.

"Okay, you, what's up? You're far too quiet."

"Nothing." Beth Ann tried to change the subject. "Look at your skin, it's so beautiful. I wish I had your complexion, and I love the shorter afro on you. I could never get away with that."

"Well, of course not." Carol laughed. "Number one, you're a white girl. White girls rarely look good in afros. Now stop changing the subject. What's up?"

"I'm just going to miss Kaylob so much, and he doesn't seem to care that I'm leaving." Beth Ann sighed.

"Don't be ridiculous. Of course he cares. Would you rather he threw a fit?"

"Maybe," she said and meant it. "At least I'd know he didn't want me to go."

"Honey, you know Kaylob is just being supportive." Carol shook her head. "He loves you so much that he doesn't want to tell you how bad he's going to miss you. He doesn't want to take away your dreams."

"I guess. I just wish he'd say that though."

"Well, maybe you should rethink leaving him alone with all the single women in town. You know they'll be coming on to him faster than a hummingbird hums."

"And just how fast is that?" Beth Ann cocked her head.

"Damn fast, that's how fast." Carol chuckled.

By the time she dropped Carol off and pulled into the parking garage, Beth Ann felt better and was glad to be home. But the minute she stepped out of the car, a chill ran down her back. Why did she feel danger lurking?

She thought she heard a noise in the corner, so she whipped her head around. "Hello, is someone there?"

A second later, one of her neighbors walked into the garage. "Hi, Beth Ann, it's just me, Wanda."

"Oh, good." Beth Ann placed her hand over her pounding heart. "I thought I heard a noise over by your van."

"That's why I'm here. Toby got out again, and that little guy loves to hang out down here." She bent over and called, "Here, Toby. Here, kitty, kitty." She got a meow as an answer, then he came running out. "You silly boy," she said, scooping him up. "You're not supposed to be out here." She scratched him under the chin then glanced at Beth Ann. "I keep telling him he's an inside cat, but he refuses to listen. At least he just comes down here and hangs out."

Beth Ann was almost as happy to see the kitty as she was to see Kaylob's truck parked in his spot. She was also glad she had someone to walk with her.

"See you later, Wanda, and thank you for walking with me." She petted Toby's head.

"No problem." Wanda smiled. "Sometimes that garage gets a little spooky at night." She waved goodbye with Toby's paw.

Beth Ann waved back and thought, *okay, that's it. I'm taking that self-defense class*. There was no way she'd go on living her life in fear. Once she opened the door, her wonderful husband was waiting for her with dinner cooked. She rushed into his arms and kissed him passionately.

"I missed you so much today." She found her eyes filling with tears and had no idea why.

"Baby, you okay?" He backed her up and studied her face.

She nodded and went back into his arms, breathing in his scent. "I just missed you so much."

"I missed you too." He kissed her forehead. "Now, how about we eat dinner and you tell me about your day? Oh, the school called and wondered if you could fill in over the weekend. They said a little girl named Cathy has been asking for you, and her father said if you could work with her, he'd pay extra." Kaylob arched a brow. "You're popular, that's for sure."

"I'll do it next weekend, but not every weekend." Beth Ann sighed with a frown. "I want to spend as much time as possible with you before I leave."

"I want that too." Kaylob took her hand and brought it up to his lips. He kissed her knuckles, then turned it over and kissed her palm.

While they ate, Beth Ann filled him in on her day and told him how talented Leo was. She was excited and wanted to do the show, but deep inside she wished Kaylob would ask her not to go. What was wrong with her?

Even the restaurant was going to be hard for her to leave, because she'd fallen in love with the place. When she'd met Chef Andria Marino, she had been impressed with how she kept the guys in line in the kitchen.

Andria had this motherly way about her, going so far as to scold them when they "misbehaved." And she knew how to bite back even harder than they did. It was easy to tell she had been in kitchens all her life, because she could yell loud and had a quick wit.

Weeks later, Beth Ann had picked out a band and thought they were really good. For fun one afternoon, she'd sung with them. All the people eating had loved it and had given her a standing ovation. The whole experience had actually been a surprise. After Broadway, she hadn't expected to love doing that so much, but it had warmed her heart in a way she couldn't explain.

Things were definitely getting busier at the restaurant. They were booking parties months in advance, and the new manager had started negotiating with the hotel across the street to use some of their parking lots. Beth Ann felt so much pride with all that Kaylob was doing, but that only made it harder to think of leaving, and she had to fight to shake off the sadness that rolled over her.

The following Sunday morning, Beth Ann woke up and couldn't resist just watching Kaylob sleep in the bed beside her. He'd taken the entire day off because she was down to the last week before she had to leave for the six-month tour. A pain stabbed at her just thinking about being away from him for that long.

Broadway had been her dream since childhood, so there was no way she should be feeling sad. Her parents had paid for all her training, and that was the only reason she and Kaylob had left Novato. It had been exciting when she'd been accepted at Lakeside School of Performing Arts, so she should be thrilled about this tour.

This was her second Broadway show, and this one was even bigger than her first. Winning the Tony had been exciting and maybe a second one was in her future. She closed her eyes and imagined getting the award, but felt nothing. What the heck? Maybe she should slap herself upside the head.

The phone's loud shrill scared the heck out of her, and it only got worse when all she heard was breathing after she said hello. She said it again and was about to hang up when she heard a man's low voice.

"I love you, and very soon you're going to be mine."

A chill raced down her spine and she hung up the phone as fast as she could. When she turned back around, Kaylob was awake and staring at her.

"Who was that?" He folded his elbow and propped his head on his hand.

She shrugged and climbed back into bed. "Someone playing a joke."

"Someone?" Kaylob's eyebrows furrowed. "Someone we know?"

"No, I don't think we know him. He said I would be his soon, but it's probably just some creepy paparazzi, the same one that called me in the past. We've changed the locks, but maybe we should get our number changed too."

Kaylob nodded. "We'll do that first thing Monday morning." He pulled her closer, slipping off her teddy and moving his hands in a way that made her shiver. "But for now you're all mine."

What this man did with his fingers drove her wild.

"Oh, Kaylob ..."

"Yes, Mrs. O'Brien." He explored her and made her call out his name as he did things only he could do. She soared so fast to the finish line that her body went limp afterward, completely spent.

"Kaylob, how do you do that?" She pushed him onto his back and started raining kisses down his chest.

"I know your secrets, baby girl, just like you know mine," he said with an aching in his voice.

Armored with that knowledge, she led him to paradise almost as fast as he'd led her.

Two hours later, after many trips to the finish line, they somehow found enough energy to get showered and dressed. As they sat, eating their breakfast, Beth Ann savored the omelet Kaylob had made. Just as she took what would be her last bite because she was too full to finish, they were interrupted by a knock on the door. Kaylob got up to go answer it, and she heard Frankie's voice.

"Hey, am I disturbing you guys?"

"Not now," Kaylob said then laughed. "My wife already seduced me this morning, so we're good for a few minutes."

"Kaylob Shawn O'Brien!" she yelled and heard them both crack up.

"Hey, that smells good." Frankie walked in smiling. "Got anything left over?"

Beth Ann handed him half her omelet since she'd taken her last bite, and Kaylob got him some coffee and toast.

"I came over to see you guys because I know Beth Ann is leaving this week, right?" Frankie said with his mouth full.

Kaylob poured himself another cup of coffee and Beth Ann nodded, trying to hide the tears that sprung to her eyes.

"How long are you going to be gone?" Frankie asked.

"Six months." She looked up at Kaylob, but saw no emotion on his face.

"Don't worry." Frankie reached over and patted her hand. "I'll only bring a few girls over while you're gone."

Kaylob smacked him with a towel. "You trying to get me killed?"

"Hey, she's leaving you for six months. You deserve something."

Kaylob sat down next to Beth Ann and put his arm around her. "In all seriousness, I'm very proud of my wife." He kissed her cheek.

Frankie nodded. "Yeah, I'm proud of her too."

"Thank you both." She smiled at Frankie and leaned her head on Kaylob's shoulder.

The phone rang and Kaylob answered it. "Oh yes, he's here." he said, then he put a hand on his hip and wiggled over to the table. "Frankie darling, it's Bernadette for you." He ran his fingers through Frankie's hair.

Frankie punched him in the arm before going to pick up the phone. "Hello, Bernadette. No, I knew I'd be here that's why I left you this number. He's my best friend, or was up until a minute ago." He paused to laugh. "No, he's very happily married."

While Beth Ann listened to Frankie flirt on the phone and watched Kaylob chuckle at Frankie's comments, the reality hit her that she would be gone soon and would miss out on mornings like this for the next six months. She took a deep breath and knew she was going to be homesick, and it made her wonder about everything. What if she didn't go? How would her family feel about it?

Stop it! You've worked your whole life to be on Broadway. You can't disappoint everyone like that.

Maybe if she kept scolding herself, she'd stop wishing she could just stay home.

Chapter Eight

Beth Ann's last week of rehearsal proved to be grueling. With late night sessions and last minute changes, Beth Ann just couldn't make time to work with any of the children from school. She felt awful about it, but she was too tired.

Two days before she was supposed to leave, Beth Ann stepped inside their townhouse and noticed right away how wonderful everything was. There really was no place like home.

When she walked into the living room, she froze when she saw Kaylob passed out on the couch, sound asleep. He was in his shorts, and his marvelous legs were stretched, dangling off the end. Her heart did a double thump when she noticed that he was holding Beary Bear, the stuffed animal he'd won for her at a carnival when they were kids.

The TV was on, and there was a pizza box on the coffee table, along with an open soda. Being very quiet, she picked up the mess and carried it into the kitchen. As she emptied the can into the sink, she took a long deep breath. Could she really leave this incredible life? *Holy bear, I can't do it.* After everything they'd been through together and being apart for two years, while he fought for his life to protect this country. There was just no way she was leaving him.

This tour was a mistake, and she knew she had to do something to fix it. She wanted to be with her husband, to support him while he worked at the restaurant. What on Earth had made her think she could be away from the love of her life after just getting married?

She made up her mind that she would go to work the next morning and let her understudy take over. Nicollette was talented and would be able to step right in. Alberto would just have to understand. Maybe he already suspected something was up since Beth Ann hadn't signed the contract yet. She kept putting it off, because inside she'd known the truth all along.

Her life was right here, lying on the couch, holding Beary Bear. She loved every minute of her world just the way it was. Everybody would just have to accept that.

She went back and sat on the coffee table, watching Kaylob sleep while she pondered everything she'd need to do and imagined her future spread out before her, singing in his restaurant, working with the kids at the school, maybe even having children of their own.

Wait, where did that come from? No, that was pushing it a bit too far.

She rose from the coffee table and noticed that his shirt was exposing his bare belly, making her want to take advantage of him while she had the chance. Moving her hand ever so slowly, she slipped it inside his shirt and touched his muscular chest and abdomen.

"Better be careful," he whispered with his eyes closed, grabbing her hand and pulling her closer. "If my wife catches you, she'll break your fingers, call you a floozy and rip off your head. Even worse, she'll kill both of us with flying pillows."

Beth Ann smacked him when he laughed. "You're really a smarty pants, you know that?"

He opened his eyes and had an impish smile. "I'm not wearing any pants right now."

She picked up the stuffed bear and kissed its nose. "What are we going to do with this man?"

He took it back and held it behind the neck. "See, I told you she missed us too."

Beth Ann grabbed it away. "Beary Bear, you can't watch what I'm going to do to my husband." She took the bear over to the chair and set him down, facing the other direction. Then she slipped off her shirt and wiggled out of her skirt, leaving on just her tiny panties, and went over to turn on some music, dim the lights, and grab a bar stool. Feeling Kaylob's gaze on her, she turned to see a slow, sexy smile spread across his handsome face as he removed his shorts and waited for her to start.

They had a new rule. While she put on a show for him, he had to put on one for her. That was their little secret they'd discovered after they were married, it drove them both wild.

Neither of them got much sleep that night.

* * * *

Slick waited until Kaylob left and knew he was taking a big chance, but wanted to get a look at his redheaded beauty. Once he opened the door to their townhouse, everything was quiet, so he tiptoed down the hall into the bedroom doorway. Instantly his body responded when he saw her bare legs. He pulled out a small camera from his suit pocket and snapped a couple of pictures. Beth Ann shifted on the bed, Afraid he'd wake her with the clicking sound, he put the camera away.

With ease, he moved closer to the bed and shivered from the visions of things he wanted to do to her, he ached from his head down to his toes. Maybe he could touch her and that would tide him over until he took her.

He inched his fingers closer and touched her silky hair, then being as quiet as a snake, he leaned down and inhaled her scent. Oh damn, he needed her and wanted to slither between her legs. He could tie her up and take her, but that would wreck his entire plan. With little effort, he pulled the sheet down and studied her hot body. Hellfire and brimstone, he was burning up. Maybe just one touch, he thought as he stared at her with lust that was about to overtake him. Just as he reached his hand closer, the goddamn phone rang and he had no choice but to dart into the closet. Shit, he was going to get caught. He hid behind Kaylob's clothes and hoped like hell she didn't find him. Had he locked the front door back? Yes, he was pretty sure he had, the last thing he wanted was for her to find it open.

Now, he needed to stay still and quiet so she wouldn't find him.

* * * *

Beth Ann heard the loud shrill of the phone. Man, she didn't want to wake up. She felt a chill run through her, but realized it was because she had lost her covers. Luckily for her, the other actors were rehearsing this morning due to some glitches in their performances. That gave her an extra three hours and time to think about how she was going to tell

Alberto her plans.

She jumped up and finally answered the phone.

"Hi, sweetness."

"Gram, where are you calling from? The background is so noisy I can barely hear you."

"We're down at this Perklin's Café on Main Street." She was practically shouting over the noise. "Nicky and I finally started our honeymoon/vacation and decided on Disneyland first. I couldn't go there without stopping to see my wonderful granddaughter. Can you meet us for breakfast?"

"Sure I can! That's just right down the street. I have to get showered and dressed, but I'll be quick."

"No hurry. We'll drink some coffee and read the newspaper while we wait."

Beth Ann hung up the phone and darted into the bathroom. The minute she started shampooing her hair, she jumped. What the heck? She thought she heard the front door open and close. "Kaylob?" She turned off the shower and listened. "Kaylob is that you?" She called out again. Everything was totally silent. Holy crap, she needed to see her therapist again. She was having issues.

Ten minutes later, with her curly hair still damp, she hurried out of her townhouse and out to her car. A movement caught her eye when she got to the garage. Was someone behind that large truck? She listened and didn't hear anything once again, so she shook her head and told herself to get over it. That did it. She was calling and making an appointment first thing tomorrow morning. Heck, her therapist might lock her up if she talked about seeing men with pink dresses and shadows lurking behind cars. It was starting to make her feel crazy.

As she opened her car door and climbed inside, she glanced at the wall in front of her.

SOON was written in big red letters.

A bolt of fear shot through her. Had that always been there? Glancing around, she did see other writings on the walls. She'd have to remember to ask Kaylob if he'd seen it before. She felt relieved when one of her neighbors got out of a car two spaces down and waved at her. Oh brother, she had to stop with all this paranoia. That word had probably been there all along.

"Kung fu classes," she whispered to herself. "Here I come."

When she pulled up at Perklin's Café, she felt lucky to find an empty space. The place was always packed for breakfast. She walked inside and was greeted by the aroma of cinnamon and maple syrup, which made her think of pancakes. She saw Gram and Nicky sitting in a booth next to the window and waved at them. They had to be the most adorable newlywed couple ever.

"How is my famous granddaughter doing?" Gram and Nicky both got up to hug her when she arrived. "I'm just tickled pink to see you and hear about the role you got in another Broadway show."

Nicky nodded. "I can't wait to see one of your shows."

Beth Ann couldn't bring herself to tell them right now that she'd decided not to go, so she just smiled and unfolded her napkin to place it on her lap.

Thirty minutes later, while she ate her pancakes with scrambled eggs, they talked about Disneyland and all the sights around the area, such as Beverly Hills and Knott's Berry Farm. Gram and Nicky said they were going to check them all out. Beth Ann looked up from sipping her coffee and noticed Gram studying her. After Nicky excused himself to go to the men's room, Gram reached across the table and put her hand over Beth Ann's.

"Sweetness, what is it?" Gram asked. "Something is on your mind. I know that look."

"I can't do this anymore, Gram. I can't go on this tour." Beth Ann let out a deep sigh. "I feel so bad because Mom and Stanley paid all that money for my training and now I don't want to do it. I want to be home with my husband and sing in the restaurant and work with the children."

Gram didn't say anything for a minute. She took a sip of her coffee, then looked into Beth Ann's eyes. "Is this really what you want?"

Beth Ann nodded and felt a lump forming in her throat. "I don't want to leave my husband. I love my life here with all our dreams."

"Don't you mean *his* dreams?" Gram set down her coffee cup harder than Beth Ann expected. "How dare Kaylob expect you to give up your dreams. That's selfish." She picked up her napkin and dabbed the side of her mouth. "I have a good mind to march over to his restaurant right now and tell him a thing or two."

Beth Ann was taken aback by her grandmother's words. She'd never seen her so agitated before over anything. Well, except maybe her son's shenanigans.

"No, Gram. Kaylob has been nothing but supportive, and he doesn't even know I've decided not to go." Tears burst from her eyes and slid down her cheeks. "I know I've disappointed everyone. I'll pay back my parents all the money they spent. Actually, we were going to do that anyway."

Gram turned to stare out the window, the look on her face was anything but pleased. Beth Ann had been prepared to get a lecture from her mom and maybe even from her brothers, but not from Gram. When she finally cleared her throat, Beth Ann knew she was about to hear more.

"I just want to be sure that you're not being pressured to do this. I know all too well what it's like to give up a dream because someone is pushing you." She paused and her lip trembled. "You've talked about being a star since you were old enough to talk. I don't want you throwing it away just to make Kaylob happy. I love Kaylob, but I won't let him do that to you."

Beth Ann gasped. "Kaylob would never do that. I'm not sure he's even going to understand my decision. He might be upset like you." Her voice cracked. "Or … he might be disappointed in me too."

Gram tilted her head, then reached across the table and held Beth Ann's hand. "Oh, honey, no way am I disappointed in you. I just want you to be happy, and I don't want anyone mapping out your future." She squeezed her hand. "Be a team with Kaylob, but never let anyone have dictatorship."

It took a minute, but Beth Ann got it. Gram's dreams had been stolen when she was young because her parents had forced her to write a Dear John letter to Nicky. They'd even gone as far as to stand over her and tell her what to say. They had dictated her future and even chosen her husband. Because of them, she had missed out on all those years with Nicky, her one and only true love.

"Gram, I promise you and swear with all my heart that this is my choice and mine alone." She looked into Gram's blue eyes. "I can't stand the thought of missing six months with Kaylob or the children I love working with." She waved her hand around. "I love my life and my job here in Riverside. I want to sing on the stage that Kaylob built for me and help bring in customers to *our* restaurant. This is my *new* dream, and I finally realized that last night."

She paused and touched her wedding ring.

"I came home and Kaylob was sleeping on the couch with Beary Bear." She looked up and smiled. "When I saw him like that and I envisioned us apart, I knew I couldn't do it. I finally knew what I wanted, and it wasn't Broadway anymore."

Gram gave her hand another gentle squeeze. "If that's what you want, then it's what you should do. That's all I need to hear. Well, there is one other thing. Who's Beary Bear?"

Beth Ann giggled. "Oh, he's the stuffed bear Kaylob won for me when we were young."

"I see." Gram chuckled.

Nicky came back to the table and Gram patted the seat for him to sit down beside her.

"Darling, Beth Ann has some news to share."

After she'd told Nicky about her decision, Beth Ann said, "I'm so glad to have your support, Gram, but I don't know how my mom's going to take the news. She might just stop talking to me."

Gram shook her head. "She's going to be just fine. Believe me."

"Are you sure?" Beth Ann asked. "They spent a lot of money on me, and Mama always had dreams for me. I am going to pay them back though."

"I don't think they're worried about that," Gram said. "You won a Tony, and you teach at a prominent school. They couldn't be any prouder. Besides, your mom already mentioned that she was surprised you were leaving Kaylob for six months."

Beth Ann felt her heart expand. "Really?"

"Yes, really."

Nicky cleared his throat. "Can I say something?"

"Of course," Beth Ann and Gram said in unison.

He took a drink of water, then looked right at Beth Ann. "I want you to know that it's okay to change your dreams. As we grow older, sometimes our desires mature and take on different meanings. They say we should follow our heart, and that's true." He glanced at Gram then back at Beth Ann. "I never wanted to be a farmer when I was growing up. I had all these plans, but as I grew older, I had to accept that what I thought I wanted wasn't what I wanted at all. Being a farmer was my future and became my new dream. I loved raising animals, and raising food from the earth gives me joy. It became the second love of my life."

He leaned over and kissed his wife on the cheek.

"I say let the seasons of life guide you, and let your heart lead you on the journey that fits for who you've become, not for who you were." He took Beth Ann's hand. "There's no law that says you can't do more than one thing in life. You've done one tour and won a Tony, so now it's time to fulfill your new dreams. And only *you* can write that new chapter of your life."

"Thank you, Nicky." Beth Ann's eyes filled with tears. "I will most certainly listen to my heart." Her lip trembled and she was truly touched by his words. Her new step-grandfather was a wise man, and she loved him already.

They spent another hour talking about the next stage of her life and laughing over memories from her childhood. Finally, Beth Ann looked at her wristwatch. "I wish I could stay and talk to you both all day, but I guess it's time for me to break the news to Alberto and make sure the understudy can take over for me." She looked back and forth between the two of them. "How long are you staying?"

"We're staying at the Disneyland Hotel through Thanksgiving," Gram said. "I've never stayed there before, and we booked the honeymoon suite." Her cheeks flushed and she chuckled. "Well, I've never been to Disneyland before, you know."

"Would it be okay if Kaylob and I join you this weekend? We'll book a room there too, if he can get away for a night." Beth Ann wanted to see Gram having fun in Disneyland.

"We'd be thrilled." Gram's eyes lit up. "We actually talked about inviting you before we left, but we knew you were leaving soon. We can all spend Thanksgiving together."

Beth Ann nodded and was beyond happy that she'd be home for the holidays.

Nicky wrote down the phone number and room number at the hotel. "Call us after you talk to Kaylob. We sure hope you both can make it."

Driving down the highway to Beverly Hills after she left, Beth Ann's stomach fluttered at the thought of breaking the news to Alberto, and she prayed he would take it well. When she got to the theater and walked in, one of the dancers on the stage named Jamie saw her and waved.

"Hey, you're early. We should be done in about an hour."

"I came to talk to Alberto. Do you know where he is?"

"I think he's in his office. He had a phone call to make." Jamie turned back and started watching the other dancers.

Beth Ann crossed in front of the stage, waving to a few people as she headed to the doors that led down a long hallway. When she got to Alberto's office, her stomach flipped and turned as she knocked lightly.

Alberto opened the door. "Elizabeth, you are early."

"Can we talk?"

"Sure, sure." He waved for her to enter.

She told him everything and waited nervously for his response. He was quiet for a moment, and it was giving her a stress headache.

Finally, he asked, "Are you sure this is what you want?"

"I'm very sure." She nodded. "I'll work with Nicollette if you need me to, I know there are only a couple days before you leave, but I won't expect any payment."

Alberto shook his head. "Not necessary. She is all ready. You see, we were feeling your heart wasn't here." He grinned. "I saw it in your eyes. You didn't want to leave your husband behind. I understand, and there is no need for you to worry."

Beth Ann breathed a sigh of relief and stood up. "Oh, thank you so much!" She wanted to turn and skip out of the building so she could get home and tell Kaylob, but she restrained herself.

Alberto walked around the desk and embraced her. "You're a very talented young lady, and maybe someday you change your mind."

"Maybe," she said, but she knew it was a fib. Her days of touring were behind her.

* * * *

An hour later Kaylob stood in the restaurant kitchen with Andria,

81

talking about the upcoming menu and the parties for the holidays they had scheduled. Andria was an amazing cook, and Kaylob was actually learning things from her. It was nice to meet someone who had loved cooking even longer than he had. She was at least ten years older, so her experience surpassed his. Plus, she had a special talent for turning recipes into something out of this world. In fact, her talent was making his stomach get a tad round. He'd better start working out or finding something to do besides eat.

He'd also been eating too much because it helped take his mind off Beth Ann leaving, and he thought he deserved to win an award for pretending to be fine with it, even though he didn't want her to go. Broadway was her dream—he'd known that since childhood. Besides, he was damn proud of her, and at least this time he'd get to see her on stage.

"Kaylob, get your mind back here right now," Andria said. "I know you're sad about Beth Ann leaving, but you have to pay attention if you want me to show you how to do this."

"Does it show that bad?" he said. "I thought I was doing a good job of hiding it."

"I'm sure you do a fine job of acting around her, but I can see the sadness in your eyes. Now let's get your mind off your worries and teach you how to make the best mousse in the world."

"All right, but I can't eat too much." Kaylob touched his stomach. "I've put on at least ten pounds."

"Oh, pooh." She laughed and pulled him beside her. "Look, when you're making this, it's really quite magical. Watch, I break the chocolate into bits and melt it over a pan of simmering water, then I stir in the egg yolks. Whisk the whites to soft peaks and then gently, ever so gently, fold in the chocolate mixture, adding a tiny bit of rum. Then refrigerate until set." She held the bowl up to his nose. "It's so fluffy and light, it almost melts on the tongue." She kissed her fingers together like a typical Italian, then she kissed his cheek.

Kaylob threw back his head in laughter at her theatrics as he watched her walk away toward the freezer. When he turned around, he saw his beautiful wife standing at the door.

"Hey, baby. What a nice surprise! I didn't know you were getting off early." He rushed over to kiss her.

"I wanted to surprise you."

She smiled, but it looked a little strained to Kaylob. Something was up, he could feel it.

Andria walked out of the freezer. "Kaylob, do you want to learn how to make coffee mousse next? Oh, hello, Beth Ann. I didn't know you were here."

"Hi, Andria." Beth Ann turned to Kaylob. "Can we go somewhere and talk?"

"Sure," he said, still wondering what was up. "Andria, Ralf will be here in a few, will you be okay? The prep chefs are on break. I can send them in if you want."

"No, I'm fine. I love the peace and quiet, even if it's only for a few moments." She waved Beth Ann and Kaylob off. "You two lovebirds go and have some time together."

"Thank you, Andria." He pulled off his apron and took Beth Ann's hand. "Where did you want to go?"

"I'd like to go home," she said. "I can bring you back to your truck later if you want to take my car."

"Okay, we can come back for my truck later," he said with a worried frown. "Is something wrong, Beth Ann?"

"I'll tell you when we get home."

The drive home was silent, and Kaylob began to wonder if Beth Ann could be jealous over Andria. Maybe she'd seen the kiss on the cheek and was letting her mind run wild again. She didn't really seem mad though. And she was always friendly to Andria.

When they walked into their townhouse, he half expected her to start puttering and talking a mile a minute the way she usually did when she was nervous, but she just walked over to pick up Beary Bear and sat on the couch.

"Kaylob, I need to talk to you about something."

"What is it, Beth Ann? You're making *me* nervous." He sat down in the chair, facing her.

For a few seconds she just looked at him and held Beary Bear against her chest. Finally, she cleared her throat and took a deep breath.

"I'm not leaving, Kaylob. I don't want Broadway anymore, and I don't need another lecture either." She got up and began pacing. "I want to sing on the stage you built me at the restaurant, and I want to stay home. I love my life here, and my dreams have changed. My old dreams were okay before, but I have new ones and I have the right to follow my own desires."

"Beth Ann, I—"

"No, let me finish," she said. "Don't even try to tell me I can't change my mind, because there's no law that says I can't. People grow up and make other choices. So don't you dare try to tell me what to do!"

Kaylob watched her and wondered what had happened to that puttering little girl who threw pillows and stomped around then he answered his own question. She'd grown into a magnificent woman.

"Elizabeth Ann Rose, when did you—"

"This is my home, and I'm not leaving! Just like you made a choice to go back to the war the second time without talking it over with me, I made *this* choice alone. There's no use trying to talk me out of it, because it's a done deal. I already quit, and the understudy is taking over." She stopped pacing and stood in front of him with her hands on her hips.

He couldn't help himself. She looked so cute and sexy standing there, trying to look tough with Beary Bear still tucked under her arm, he started laughing.

"What is so funny, Kaylob Shawn O'Brien!"

"I'm sorry, Beth Ann, but you're just so darn cute. And I'm not gonna try to stop you. I couldn't be happier that you're not leaving." He got up and put his arms around her. "I love you, and if this is what you want, I support your decision. You're a smart lady, and I trust your choices."

"Really?" She looked up at him, her eyes wide. "You're not disappointed in me?"

"How could I ever be disappointed in you?" He held her at arm's length and looked into her eyes. "Beth Ann, you're the biggest and brightest star in the universe, but not just because of Broadway or your Tony. Because of *who* you are. I couldn't be more thrilled that you're not leaving, but even more, I couldn't be any prouder of you. Baby, I love you."

"I love you too," she whispered. "And I'm also proud of you." She put her hand on his chest where his heart was, then she opened his shirt to kiss him there.

Jesus, how did she do that to him? One minute he was laughing, the next he wanted to devour her. He picked her up, and as he looked into her eyes, he wondered again how he'd gotten so lucky to have her for his wife.

Then he carried her to their bedroom so they could celebrate her staying home.

Chapter Nine

Slick stood staring at Beth Ann's car. She was home early today.

He wasn't worried about anyone seeing him anymore, because every time he parked his car in the visitor area, he made sure to wave to the neighbors like he belonged there. He'd pull out his briefcase and act all businesslike. So far, they all seemed to buy it.

He looked up at his handiwork on the garage wall with a proud smile. At least he'd let her know she was going to be his soon, and he'd also told her that on the phone more than once. Now it was written on the wall above her car, he had marked his territory. She should be getting the message by now.

Damn it to hell, he wanted to sneak up there and watch her again, but something felt off. He'd told himself he was going to stay away after seeing the two gay boys, but he was hooked on her. Even more so since he'd been so close, while she lay naked in bed. *She was so hot.*

He'd try for tomorrow morning. He was starting to learn her schedule and knew she always stayed in bed after Soldier Boy left for work. He had to have one more look at her, up close up and personal, to relieve the pain she caused.

Meow.

That damn cat was at it again. One of these days, he was going to kill that thing. It had almost gotten him busted the other night.

He walked over to his car and slid inside, glancing at his new haircut in the rearview mirror. He was a handsome devil, and his brown eyes matched his brown hair. Once again, he waved to that same chick picking up the stupid cat. She looked disgusting with her sleazy bellbottoms and her frizzy hair. But he smiled and waved. Oh gag, she was wiggling her skinny ass at him. No thank you! He had way higher standards than that. He started his car and was surprised when he saw Soldier Boy come out and get into Beth Ann's car. The asshole didn't even look his way. What a dumbass. He was big and stupid, and he was going to lose his wife forever.

Slick pulled out behind the S.O.B., following him down Main Street until he turned into some Chinese restaurant. The guy was a loser and had nothing to offer Beth Ann except that pathetic townhouse. Wait until she saw what *he* had to offer. Yeah, Blake Tanner had given her the moon and stars, but Blake was a pansy and didn't know how to treat women right.

Now, Slick was going to treat her good. And someday, she'd give herself to him willingly.

This whole thing was taking way longer than he wanted. He was hoping to have her for Christmas, but there would be no way to do that now. Those damn construction workers were asking him questions like, *Why do you want the basement walls done in cement?* He'd told them he was going to have a recording studio and wanted complete privacy with no outside noises. They'd appeared to buy it.

Yes, he was ready to make his move as soon as they got the damn house finished. The library had been a big help when he'd looked up how to use chloroform. She was tiny, so he had to be careful not to use too much. He really didn't want to kill her.

* * * *

Two days later, Beth Ann knew she needed to wake up, but kept slipping back to sleep. Kaylob wouldn't know how long she'd slept in, because he'd already left for work. She felt so decadent, but finally forced herself out of bed, and a shiver immediately ran through her.

What was wrong with her? Was she going to live in fear for the rest of her life? The locks had been changed, and Kaylob was going to get a new phone number soon. It had been quiet lately. She was becoming one big ball of paranoia, and needed to take those self-defense classes, along with some therapy.

She glanced around and everything appeared normal, so she shook off her worries and told herself that today would be a happy day. This weekend they were going to meet Gram and Nicky at Disneyland, not to mention spending the holidays at home. No commute to rehearsal and no traveling on the road for six months. She'd have to call the school and see if they'd rehire her, because she truly loved working with the kids. On her way to the closet, the phone rang and she went back to pick it up.

"Hello?" Nothing but breathing. "Hello, is anyone there? Who is this!"

The phone went dead.

What the heck? She slammed it down and stood there a few seconds, trying to calm down by telling herself it was probably just a wrong number or the paparazzi. Anyway, the calls would stop as soon as Kaylob got the number changed. After a few deep breaths, she went to her closet to get dressed.

Today, she knew exactly what she wanted to wear. Some casual jeans along with a cute white sweater to match and her slip-ons. After she was dressed and went to slide her foot inside her shoe, she felt something jab her toe.

"Ouch!"

What was that? She took off the shoe and shook out a gold and silver cufflink. Where had that come from? When she held it in her hand, she saw it had the word *Texas* engraved on it, so she knew it must be Blake's. He must have lost it when he'd packed up her stuff. She turned it over in her fingers and admired the beautiful craftsmanship. Blake had always had expensive tastes.

Now she had the fun job of returning it to him. She went to her nightstand and took out the beautiful stationary with her and Kaylob's names on it. His Aunt Lillian had sent it as a wedding gift, along with some amazing Waterford crystal. Beth Ann found a pen and sat down to write a note to send with the cufflink.

Dear Blake,

I found this cufflink in one of my shoes and wanted to return it to you. I guess you lost it when you were packing up my things. I do hope you are happy and life is treating you well. Blake, I saw you at my wedding and don't know why you came, but if it's you who's been calling me and hanging up, please stop. And if you are having me followed, please stop that too.

I know that deep inside you're a good man, Blake Tanner. You have to move on with your life, and I wish you only the very best.
Sincerely, Beth Ann

She put the note and the cufflink in an envelope and put it in her underwear drawer. She'd mail it later.

The phone rang again, and she picked it up in exasperation. "Hello, and don't just breathe into the phone!"

"Hello, is this Beth Ann?" said a woman's voice that sounded like silk.

"Oh, I'm sorry. Yes, this is Beth Ann. Who is this?"

"This is Aunt Lillian. I was wondering if Kaylob is there."

"No, he's not here right now. How funny that you called. I was just thinking about you and wishing you had been able to come to the wedding. Thank you for all the beautiful gifts."

After a few seconds of silence, Aunt Lillian said, "You're most welcome, and I'm sorry I couldn't be there. Could you have Kaylob ring me when he gets a chance? No pressure."

"Sure," Beth Ann said and took down the number.

When she hung up with Aunt Lillian, Beth Ann called the school and was thrilled when they agreed to take her back. They had to keep her replacement for a few more weeks, but seemed pleased to have her return. They also asked if she had gotten the message from Cathy's dad about working with her on the weekends. She apologized for not following through on it, and promised to call him right away.

When she dialed the number, she was startled to hear a woman answer with, "Tanner Real Estate, how can I help you?"

Oh, she wasn't expecting them to answer the phone like that, since Peter worked at a different office. She identified herself and asked to speak to him. After a few seconds on hold, his friendly voice answered.

"Hello, Beth Ann! I'm so glad you called."

"Hi, Peter. I wanted to let you know that I can do that extra time with Cathy on weekends. I'm not going on tour after all, but I'll have to wait until after Thanksgiving."

"That's great, but what happened? Not that I'm complaining. Cathy will be so pleased. She talks about you nonstop."

"I really like her too. She's such a sweet little girl—just adorable and so talented. The truth about the tour is I just didn't want to be away from home again."

"Well, that's understandable. I heard you got married."

"Yes, I did." Because he worked with Blake, she didn't want to say much about Kaylob. "So when after Thanksgiving would you like me to work with her again? I won't be back at the school for a while, but if you want, I could work with her at my house. I have a nice music system and plenty of room for training"

"That's very kind of you. But are you sure that will be okay?" He sounded hesitant.

"Yes, if you'd like, you can come visit me to see my home. If you feel comfortable leaving Cathy in my care, then I'd be happy to work with her."

"Sure, that would be great. How about Wednesday at noon, the week after Thanksgiving?"

"Sounds good. Let me give you my phone number in case anything changes." She gave him the number and they hung up, then realized she hadn't given him her address and he hadn't even asked. Well, he'd call her back before the lesson to get directions, there was plenty of time.

As she put the pen and stationery back in the drawer, she noticed an invitation. Oh, man, she'd completely forgotten about being invited to Dana's birthday event. She was Blake's housekeeper, but she had always been good to Beth Ann, and she wanted to go.

Maybe Blake wouldn't be there. She remembered that they'd had to miss the one party that Dana had invited her to when she was still with Blake. He always had business trips and events that took precedence over everything else. Dana was so sweet and loved Blake like a brother, so she always made excuses for his absence. She'd told Beth Ann that he always did something extra special for her instead.

And if she went to the party, she could give Dana the cufflink and note for Blake instead of mailing them. That settled it. She was going.

* * * *

A few weeks later, Blake sat at his desk, trying to focus on his job. He was trying to get things in order so he could leave and go back to

Texas, but every time he turned around another crisis happened that held him back. Maybe someone was trying to tell him something.

He hated being in Palm Springs. It was too damn close to Beth Ann, and even though he was trying like hell to get over her, it wasn't easy. He'd loved her since they were kids, but what an idiot he'd been for letting himself fall even harder for her when she was a heartbroken girl still in love with her dead fiancé. And when Kaylob had proved to not be dead after all, Blake still had ignored the logic that told him to stay away from her. Now he was walking around with a bleeding heart, and it was way too late to cry over burnt turnips.

Everything seemed to remind him of her. That's why he'd sold that townhouse. The damn place was haunted by memories. Sleep there was impossible, unless he got so drunk that he passed out. He'd gotten really good at that, to the point that every damn time he walked through the door, he headed for the booze like a dog going after a bone. At least he'd stopped all that nonsense after selling the place, and he was on the wagon now.

As he stuffed the last papers in his briefcase, there was a knock on the door.

"Hi, Blake." Melissa poked her head inside and smiled. "It's five o'clock. I'm taking off unless you need something."

"No. I'm gonna surprise Dana this year and show up for her birthday party. I'll be leaving soon."

"Really? I'm on my way there now."

"All right, I'll see you there." He waved her off and rose from his desk. "I have to go by and pick up Dana's gift. It should be all wrapped and ready to go."

She came all the way into the office, her head tilted as she looked at him. "I'm speechless, Blake."

"Why?"

"You're really going to Dana's party? She told me you've never made it to one before. She's going to be surprised."

"Good, that's what I wanted."

"Okay, I'll see you there." She turned to leave, but stopped at the door. "Blake, do you want to go together?" Her eyes sparkled.

"No, I have some things to do first, but thanks."

She stared at him. "You know you could ask me out sometime."

"Look, little darlin, you're a knock out, but you need to be asking guys your own age. I am not dating seriously and I might not ever again."

The phone rang and saved him from any more of the conversation. After she left, he decided to let it go into voice mail. He was done and wanted to go pick up the gift. Maybe some fun at Dana's party would take his mind off anything to do with his broken and battered heart.

Chapter Ten

"Kaylob, I can't do a thing with this mop!" Beth Ann yelled over the blow dryer. When she'd done everything she could with her wild, curly hair, she walked into the bedroom. "So are you going to tell me what you and your Aunt Lillian talked about?"

He looked up at her with an impish grin. "Baby, you know I love your mop. And we didn't get to talk long because there was almost a fire in the kitchen."

"A fire?"

"Between two of the cooks, not a burning fire." He laughed and shook his head. "I thought I might have to fire both of them, but they cooled off."

"Glad everything turned out." She frowned at her hair again in the dresser mirror. "I'm cutting it all the way off."

He walked over and gave her a scolding look. "Don't even think about it. And don't tell me I'm not the boss of you either."

"How did you know I was ... oh, never mind."

He laughed again. "You look amazing, and I love your hair. It's like a crown of gold that circles you."

He picked up the pink dress she had laid out to wear, then he lifted her arms above her head and slowly pulled it down over her body. After he zipped it up, he turned her to face him, scanning her from top to bottom.

"You are such a fox." He growled and went for her neck.

"Honey, don't mess up my hair."

He threw back his head and cracked up. "I thought you couldn't do a thing with it and had given up." He took a ringlet and curled it around his finger. "I would be sad if you cut off your hair."

"Okay. I won't cut it off. Yet." She laughed.

A few minutes later as they got ready to leave, Beth Ann remembered the cufflink and stopped when they got to the door.

"Wait, I have something of Blake's I'm giving to Dana. I meant to call her right after Thanksgiving, but with Disneyland and all the fun, I forgot."

"What is it?" Kaylob furrowed his eyebrows.

"Just a cufflink. It was mixed up in my shoes." She went back to get the envelope from her drawer, then they went to the garage and got in her car.

It took twenty minutes to get to Dana's lovely little house, and Beth Ann was delighted as soon as she saw it. There were flowers that bordered the white picket fence and a big California sycamore tree in the middle of her yard. The front porch was decorated with live plants, some that were blooming. It was picture perfect.

Six cars were parked along the fence, and Beth Ann felt relieved when she didn't recognize any of them. She and Kaylob stepped out into the cool, breezy evening, the smell of fall tickling her nose. When Kaylob put his arm around her as they walked toward the house, it really helped with her jitters and the chills from winter being right around the corner.

"Oh, we forgot the gift." She stopped and pointed at the trunk.

Kaylob jogged back to get the package wrapped in flowery birthday paper with a big yellow bow and a card on top.

"What is it?" he asked when he handed it to Beth Ann.

"Some handmade soap, lotions, and a beautiful silk scarf."

"Sounds nice." Kaylob smiled and put his arm around her again. "Are you gonna be okay?"

She nodded, but he still squeezed her a little tighter as they reached the front porch. Before she could knock on the door, Dana opened it, her smile widening as soon as she saw Beth Ann.

"You made it!" Her eyes filled with tears and she threw her arms around Beth Ann. "I'm so glad you're here."

Beth Ann hugged her back the best she could with the gift in her hand and whispered, "Me too."

Dana stepped back and smiled at Kaylob, so Beth Ann introduced them.

"Nice to meet you," Kaylob said. "I've heard all good things about you."

Dana's hand went across her heart as she glanced at Beth Ann. "Oh, it's nice to meet you too. Please come in." She seemed flustered as she opened the door all the way.

Beth Ann handed her the gift with a smile. "This is for you."

"Thank you. That's very sweet." Dana placed the gift on a table with others.

The aroma of Italian food was intoxicating. Because of her husband, Beth Ann recognized the fragrance of oregano, basil, and fresh tomatoes.

"Wow, something smells good," she said and got a nod of agreement from Kaylob.

"Cass did it all. Isn't it enchanting?" Dana waved a hand at the candles set up along with birthday flowers. There was a knock at the door, and Dana said, "Go introduce yourselves to everyone while I get this."

Beth Ann glanced around and saw that the new arrival was Melissa. It felt strange to be surrounded by some of Blake's friends.

"Hi, Beth Ann," Melissa said when she walked over with Dana. "It's so good to see you again." She gave her a tiny smile and grinned at Kaylob.

Beth Ann introduced him again and he nodded as he shook her hand.

Melissa cleared her throat. "I hate to have to say this, but I think you both need to know." She swallowed a gulp of something, Beth Ann thought looked like nerves. "Blake is on his way."

"What?" Dana's eyes widened. "He's never come before, but I'm sure everything will be fine." She smiled but didn't look convinced.

"Maybe we should leave." Beth Ann glanced at Kaylob. "What do you think, honey?"

He squeezed her hand. "I'm okay if you are."

She nodded and touched Dana's arm. "If anything bad happens, we'll leave. This is your special day, and we wouldn't want anything to spoil it. Everything looks beautiful, by the way."

"I want you to stay and I want to introduce you to my best friend, Cassie." Dana took Beth Ann's hand. "We just call her Cass. She and Melissa did most of the decorating yesterday, and Cass did everything else today."

"I'll be back." Melissa smiled and headed towards the living room.

The front door opened just then and Johnny, Blake's former or current bodyguard, came walking in the door with two other guys. He didn't even knock, but he'd always been a bit bold. When he walked toward them, Beth Ann started to fidget, and her palms began to sweat.

"Hi, Johnny." Dana's cheeks looked a little flushed.

"Hi, Doll." He winked and gave her a small kiss, then looked at Kaylob and Beth Ann. "Hi, Beth Ann." He nodded towards Kaylob. "And you are?"

Kaylob stood a little taller and held out his hand. "I'm her husband, Kaylob."

Johnny shook his hand. "I'm Johnny."

Dana pulled on Beth Ann's arm. "Come on, let's go find Cass."

Beth Ann glanced at Kaylob and he nodded, so she followed Dana through the dining area close to the kitchen.

"Dana, are you dating Johnny?" she asked as they walked.

"Yes, he's taken me out a few times." Her cheeks flamed this time. "He's such a dream."

Beth Ann couldn't help but laugh. "He is very handsome. And big." Dana was so tiny, much shorter than Beth Ann. "Well, so long as he treats you good, I'm happy for you. Oh, by the way, I have something I'd like you to give to Blake for me if you don't mind. It would be better if you gave it to him after the party." She took the envelope from her purse. "It's a cufflink I found in my stuff and wanted to return it to him. There's also a note."

"Okay, sure." Dana took it and stuck it in her very large purse that was hanging on a chair.

"So how serious are you and Johnny?" Beth Ann put her arm around Dana's shoulder.

"I like him a lot, and he does treat me wonderfully. But ... he hasn't kissed me yet. I mean not a real kiss."

"Johnny's a good guy. And when he does kiss you for real, you have to promise to call me and give me updates." She chuckled.

Dana laughed with her. "Okay, and speaking of good guys, Kaylob sure is good looking. And his voice is well ... hot." She smiled. "Does he make you happy?"

Beth Ann nodded. "Happier than I ever thought possible, but he always did."

When they entered the kitchen, Beth Ann noticed a tall, round brunette stirring something in a pot on the stove.

"Cass," Dana said. "I want you to meet someone."

Cassie turned, wiping her hands on her apron with eyes that glowed with kindness. "This must be Beth Ann." She smiled and reached out to greet her.

Dana introduced them and Beth Ann felt very welcomed by Cass, especially when she offered to let her sample the food. They spent the next few minutes laughing and having a good time.

"It's been so nice talking to both of you," Beth Ann said. "But I need to go find Kaylob. He doesn't know anyone here."

"Of course. We'll talk more later," said Dana.

When Beth Ann got back to the living room, she scanned the small groups of people gathered here and there and spotted Kaylob laughing with Johnny and his friends. Melissa was sitting on the couch talking to a girl who looked very young. With all the activity and laughter, she finally started to relax as she walked towards Kaylob.

Then a typhoon blew in the front door.

Blake instantly caught her eye, and the look on his face made her want to find somewhere to hide. It was full of pain and anger, all mixed into one giant ball of trouble. She saw him spot Kaylob and knew this wasn't going to be pretty. Kaylob hadn't seen Blake yet because he had his back to the front door in the formal living room and the music had been turned up, but he'd know he was there any second.

Blake strolled over to Beth Ann. "Well, isn't this special? Come to dig the knife in a little deeper?" He walked past her and headed to the bar where he poured something into a glass. He stared at her for a moment, then he slammed down the drink in one gulp.

Beth Ann walked toward him hesitantly. "Blake, we didn't know you were coming until we got here. Normally you never had time to come to Dana's parties."

He chugged down another drink, then glared at her. "You've got some nerve coming here. These are *my* friends."

Beth Ann felt a little irritated at his comment. "I didn't crash the party, Blake. Dana invited us."

He filled his glass a third time, then looked her up and down. "So why would you come here with Mr. Perfect?" He pointed in Kaylob's direction. "Nobody knows him here."

"Because I care about Dana and wanted to see her," she countered. "I've missed her."

"Oh, how sweet." He downed his drink then laughed bitterly. "You care about her. Is it supposed to make me feel better to know you have more feelings for my housekeeper than you do for me?"

"Stop this, Blake. You know that's not true. And please don't do anything to spoil Dana's birthday."

She turned and walked over to Kaylob who still hadn't seen Blake. Kaylob put his arm around her out of habit when she walked up, and she heard Blake make a loud derisive noise behind them. Kaylob turned around, and Beth Ann saw the minute their eyes connected. Kaylob broke the stare and looked at Beth Ann.

"You okay? Do you want to leave?"

Beth Ann didn't know what to do, but she didn't want to hurt Dana's feelings. "Maybe we could stay for a bit, if things stay calm."

She stayed in the room with Kaylob, and Blake disappeared somewhere, thank God. She and Kaylob sat on the couch and talked for a long time with a couple they met who were going to have a baby soon. Beth Ann was just beginning to think everything would be okay when, out of the corner of her eye, she saw Blake at the bar again, slamming down more drinks and giving her looks that made her stomach flip upside down.

Kaylob drained his own glass and started to stand. "I need a refill. Do you want one?"

The last thing she needed was for him to run into Blake at the bar. There was no doubt in her mind it would get heated.

"Let me go get it," she said, pulling him back down to the couch.

He looked a little surprised, until he spotted Blake at the bar in the other room, then leaned close to whisper to Beth Ann. "He looks pretty drunk."

"I know." She nodded. "He's been drinking nonstop since he got here."

Fortunately, nobody else seemed to notice how wasted Blake was getting. The music played at a nice level now that allowed for conversation, and everyone was too busy laughing and sharing stories. Johnny had taken Dana by the hand a few minutes earlier and they'd vanished somewhere. Beth Ann made her way to the non-alcoholic beverages. When she turned with the soda pops in her hand, Blake blocked her path, clearly unsteady on his feet.

"You're such a phony," he slurred. "You never loved me."

"Blake, you should go lie down in one of the bedrooms, or get Johnny to take you home." She tried to slip by him, but he grabbed her arm.

"Come back to me, Beth Ann. You know you belong with me. I love you and I'm never gonna let you go!"

She pulled her arm away. "Blake, please don't do this." When he pulled her closer and tried to kiss her, she pushed him away. "Let me go!"

"No, I'll find a way to have you again if it's the last thing I do!" He stuck his nose into her hair and pulled her back into his arms.

"Blake, stop! I'm sorry you're hurt, but it's over."

"God, I miss you." He ran his fingers up her arm to her neck. "Everything about you."

"Blake!" She slapped his hand away and dropped one of the cans of pop, but he grabbed her again.

The room went silent for a second, then Kaylob's angry voice rang out. "Get your hands off my wife!"

"Who's gonna make me, asshole?" Blake released Beth Ann and turned toward Kaylob as he rushed over to them, his face red with fury. "She still wants me, you know!" Blake taunted him. "I bet I made her feel better than you ever will!"

Kaylob reached out to grab him, but Johnny hurried over and pulled Blake away by the arm just before Kaylob got his hands on him.

"Come on, boss," Johnny said. "Let's go see Dana in the kitchen and get you some food."

"Let go of me!" Blake jerked his arm free. "I'm gonna tell them something they need to hear!" He swayed and tried to turn around again.

Kaylob placed his hand on Beth Ann's back. "Let's go, sweetheart."

She nodded and could feel tears sliding down her cheeks. It only got worse at the sight of Dana's face when she stepped out of the kitchen and saw Johnny still trying to pull Blake away. Beth Ann couldn't help but blame herself for his behavior. Why had she come tonight? She should have known better.

Melissa tried to help Johnny with Blake, and Beth Ann noticed she had tears staining her cheeks when she looked at him. Oh God, she was crazy about Blake. How awful for her to see him acting this way.

"Why didn't you just stay dead!" Blake yelled at Kaylob. "She belongs to me, not you!" He managed to pull loose from Johnny and ran over to slam shut the door they had just opened to leave. "She's mine and she's staying with me!" He grabbed Beth Ann's arm and yanked her away from Kaylob.

Kaylob pushed Blake away, making him stumble backward. "Touch her again and you'll wish you were the one who was dead!"

Johnny rushed over and grabbed Blake again. "Come on, boss. You need to take a load off and sober up."

Blake knocked Johnny's hands away. "Get off me or you're fired!"

He tried to walk toward Beth Ann again, but suddenly his knees buckled, his eyes rolled back in his head, and he went down with a loud thud.

Beth Ann dropped to the floor and touched his face. "Blake, oh my god is he okay?"

"He needs help in more ways than one," Kaylob leaned down and checked to see if he was still breathing.

"He's just drunk," Johnny said, pulling Blake up to help him walk. "I'll take care of him. Come on, boss. You need to stop all this crazy shit."

Blake's eyes fluttered. "Did you see, Johnny? Beth Ann touched my face. She was worried about me. I heard her. She's gonna come back home soon. I know she will."

Johnny looked at them apologetically. "Sure, boss. Let's get you somewhere to lay down." He led him out of the room with Melissa trailing behind.

Beth Ann and Kaylob hurried out the door without saying goodbye to anyone. Beth Ann felt horrible and prayed that Blake would get the help he needed. Before they reached the car, Dana came running up behind them.

"Beth Ann, I'm so sorry. This is all my fault."

"No, it's my fault." Beth Ann turned to hug her. "Go back inside, and please don't let this spoil your party."

"Neither of you are at fault," Kaylob said as he opened Beth Ann's door. "Blake was drunk and put on a show all by himself."

"Can I see you again?" Dana asked. "I've missed you so much."

Beth Ann nodded. "Call me and I'll take you to lunch or dinner for your birthday." They embraced again before Dana went back inside.

Once they were both inside the car, Kaylob leaned over and kissed her cheek. "I'm sorry all that happened, sweetheart." He rubbed her arm. "Did he harm you?"

"Not physically." Beth Ann choked back the tears.

"I didn't hear everything he said, but I'm sorry if he said hurtful things to you."

She put her head on his shoulder. "I know he'd never hurt me, but his words were filled with hate and venom. I'm just sad for him."

"Well, I'm glad you trust him not to hurt you, but I swear if he ever touches you again, I'll kill him."

"No, Kaylob." Beth Ann felt her stomach clench. "Neither of us want him dead. We just wish he'd get better so he can move on."

He sat in silence for a minute, staring out into the darkness. "You're right."

As they drove home, Beth Ann knew one thing for sure: it had been Blake calling her on the phone all those times. She didn't believe he was the one who'd hit Jack over the head—that must've just been a burglar. But Blake had said some of the same things as the mystery caller. He had clearly lost it, and she felt her heart sink. He'd meant a lot to her, but there was no way they'd ever be friends again, not now.

Chapter Eleven

The Wednesday after Thanksgiving, Beth Ann realized Peter still hadn't called to get directions for Cathy's private lessons. She wondered if it was because he'd heard about the incident with Blake. Maybe he wasn't going to let her train Cathy. After all, he worked for Blake and ran one of his main real estate offices. She hoped not, because she really loved Cathy and wanted to work with her.

The things Blake had said to her at the party really hurt her deeply, and not just because of the words. The way he'd looked at her with so much hate in his eyes had made her want to cry for their lost friendship. Beth Ann also wondered if he even knew that Melissa was crazy in love with him. It showed all over her face, but he was probably too blinded by his hatred to see it.

A knock at the door startled her, and she was surprised when she peeked out the security hole and saw Peter and Cathy standing outside.

"Hi, Cathy. Hi, Peter," she said when she opened the door. "I was waiting for a phone call asking for directions."

He waved his hand with a little laugh. "I'm a real estate broker, remember?"

"Oh, of course." Beth Ann shook her head. "No wonder you didn't need directions."

"Daddy," Cathy said, looking around. "We've been here before."

Peter nodded. "Yes, I listed one of these townhouses in the past for some old friends." Cathy looked as if she wanted to say something else, but he touched her nose and laughed. "You're very smart and have a good memory."

Beth Ann smiled at Cathy. "I have some homemade cookies out on the breakfast bar if you want one before we start." She pointed and the little girl's face lit up.

"I love cookies!" Cathy took off ahead of them.

"Don't be rude, Cathy," Peter called after her.

"No problem," Beth Ann said. "Come back about two o'clock. We should be done by then."

Peter nodded. "Cathy, I'll be back to get you in two hours."

"Okay," she mumbled with her mouth full of cookie.

Peter laughed. "I hope she doesn't eat them all."

"I'll keep her busy enough that she won't have time." Beth Ann chuckled and led Peter to the door. When he said goodbye, his eyes seemed to gleam with pride for his little girl.

The two hours went by quickly with voice lessons that included new songs. Cathy had done really well, so after they were finished, Beth Ann offered Cathy another cookie while they sat at the bar and waited for Peter to come back.

"My daddy says you're a famous star and I'm very lucky to have you as my teacher."

Beth Ann smiled. "Well, I don't know how famous I am, but I love being your teacher."

"I'm so glad you're my teacher." Cathy scooted over and took Beth Ann's hand. "Maybe someday I can sing good like you, but I'll never be pretty like you."

Beth Ann squeezed her hand. "You're already prettier than me."

"No, I'm not pretty at all," she said matter-of-factly.

"You're beautiful, Cathy." Beth Ann felt sad that Cathy would think that.

"But my daddy—" She stopped when there was a knock at the door.

"I bet that's your daddy now." Beth Ann stood and hurried over to open it.

It wasn't until after they'd left that Beth Ann realized she'd forgotten to tell Peter what Cathy had said about not being pretty. Her parents needed to make sure and tell her that more often.

Later that afternoon, Beth Ann was in the worst pain she'd ever been in. It was that time of month, and this one was horrible. She called Kaylob to tell him she would be in bed, then she crawled under the covers and fell into a deep sleep. She didn't know how long she'd slept when a kiss pressed against her forehead and the familiar smell of ginger, cloves and garlic hit her senses.

"Kaylob, you're home." She sat up and hugged him, then pressed a hand to her stomach. "It's that time of the month, and it made me sick this time."

She didn't miss the sad look and little frown that formed on his lips. He touched her stomach before going to the kitchen to do what he always did—get the Midol, a glass of water, and a heating pad for her tummy. Could she ask for a better husband?

* * * *

Christmas had passed and she and Kaylob had shared it together, alone. It had been wonderful and romantic. They'd opened their gifts by candlelight, had wine and played soft music. With all the romance in the air, they had made love all night. Thank goodness he had brought dinner home from the restaurant, because they had slept in and ... the phone jarred her from her lazy daydream.

"Hello."

"Hi, Beth Ann. It's Dana."

"Hi, there. How are you doing? I've thought about you and wondered how your party turned out. I hope you had wonderful holidays."

"Everything calmed down and yes, thank you, it was great. The night of my birthday, Johnny stayed on the couch because Blake was passed out the entire night. I wanted to say thank you so much for the beautiful gifts. I loved everything. I should have called sooner, but with the holidays things got crazy."

"You're welcome and I totally understand. Dana, I still want to take you out to lunch."

"Actually, I was hoping we could get together today or tomorrow since I have two days off," Dana said.

"Great! I just happen to know a fantastic restaurant with the absolute best lunch menu in the world."

They made plans to meet at Seven Nights and Seven Roses at noon. Beth Ann decided to wear a blue cotton dress with matching shoes. Now that she had unpacked everything, she was even more perplexed about so much of her stuff missing. She reminded herself to call the resort in Hawaii to see if she'd left some items behind. It had been so many months ago, they may have donated them or something.

After she finished her makeup and did her hair in a French braid, she checked her reflection in the mirror one last time before grabbing her purse and keys then leaving for the lunch date. The minute she entered the restaurant, she saw Kaylob behind the bar, laughing with one of the guys. When he spotted her, he waved and pointed to the main dining room. Beth Ann blew him a kiss and took off to look for Dana. The hostess named Julie came over and smiled at her.

"Hi, Beth Ann. Your friend is here waiting for you. Follow me."

Beth Ann spotted Dana as soon as they rounded the corner. She looked so cute dressed in yellow with her dark hair flowing freely. She had always been so adorable.

Dana stood up to hug her. "Hi, I'm so glad to see you, Beth Ann."

Julie smiled at both of them as they sat down. "Would you like something to drink while you look at the menu?"

Beth Ann nodded. "Some sweet tea would be great."

"I'll take the same," Dana said.

"I think Kaylob knew." Julie grinned. "He made a special batch of sweet tea today."

After Julie left, Beth Ann reached across the table and took Dana's hand. "How are you? I feel so bad about what happened at your party."

"Don't feel bad, please." Dana shook her head, but tears misted her eyes. "I was so happy to see you. I've missed you so much. You were always like a sister to me."

"Thank you, Dana." Beth Ann's heart melted and warmth soaked through her. "You're very special to me too."

Julie brought their drinks and they both took a sip.

"Wow, this is really tasty," Dana said.

Beth Ann grinned. "Everything my husband makes is good." She took a couple more sips then sighed. "How's Blake?"

"Oh, I have something for you. I know I should have given this to you sooner. I hope it's okay that I brought it." She reached in her purse and pulled out a blue envelope. "Oh no, I forgot to give Blake his cufflink and the note you sent." She held up the envelope that Beth Ann had given her at the party.

Beth Ann took the letter Blake wrote to her. "It's okay, it's not like he's going to be missing it anytime soon. And, maybe it's best if you do wait a few weeks to give it to him."

"Okay," Dana agreed. "This is the first time I've used this purse since that night. I'm sorry, I forgot."

"It's okay. Should I read this now?" She held up the envelope and wondered how Kaylob would feel about her getting a letter from Blake.

Dana nodded. "Blake let me read it. I think you'll be pleased."

Beth Ann opened the note and read it silently.

Dear Beth Ann,

I was such an ass the night of Dana's party and I don't expect you to ever forgive me. I'm going away for a month or so to get my head on straight. You didn't deserve what I said, nor should I have put my hands on you. I am truly very sorry. Please don't blame yourself for any of this, I'm the idiot, and I need to stop acting like a crazy man.

I will always love you, and I think you are the most beautiful, kind and loving woman in the world. I know you made a choice to be with the love of your life, and that's your right. After all, it was your radiant sunshine that guided him home. I finally see the truth. As they say, "The truth will set you free."

I wish you and Kaylob the very best. I know that might be hard to believe, but darlin, I always wanted you to be happy, so please be happy and I'll find my happiness again someday. I'll always cherish our memories, but it's time for me to move on, let go and accept what is.

With love always,
Blake

By the time she got to the end, tears were building. She would always love Blake and have him tucked away in a special place. He had been so good to her, and although she had never been *in love* with him, she loved him as a friend. She folded the letter and put it in her purse, then she looked up and saw Dana's lip trembling too.

"Thank you for bringing me that lovely letter." Beth Ann reached across the table and covered Dana's hand with hers. "You're right. It makes me happy."

The lunch ended up being everything she'd expected. Kaylob made them lobster with a creamy garlic sauce that melted in their mouths, and the salad was amazing. Once they finished eating all they thought they could, he brought them the most incredible coffee mousse.

"No wonder he's the love of your life," Dana said as she took the last bite, and they both laughed.

After Dana left, Beth Ann went to Kaylob's office and found him on the phone, booking a wedding party. She stood in front of his desk to wait for him to finish.

"It's okay if you end up inviting twenty more," he said. "We can still handle it. We have a good-sized reception area. Thank you, and we look forward to hosting your party." He filled in the appointment book and wrote everything down so he could transfer it all up front for them to charge the deposit to a credit card.

"Thank you for the wonderful lunch," Beth Ann said as she walked around the desk. "But now I think Dana is crushing on you for your cooking."

"Is that so? Well, sadly for her I'm a happily married man." He touched her leg and she sat on his lap. "Oh, baby, you're teasing me." He groaned and shifted her weight.

"I'm not teasing," she said, wiggling her bottom a little. "It's an offer for when you get home tonight."

His eyes rolled back in his head. "I can't wait that long. Go lock the door."

"No, you can wait." She kissed him then stood up. "I'll be in our bed, waiting when you get home. Right now I have to run by the travel company and pick up some brochures for Ireland, then I'm taking my fourth Kung Fu lesson." She arched her foot and showed him her stance.

He chuckled. "Wow, you're scary." He pulled her down again and kissed her senseless, his eyes heated with desire. "We really could lock the door. I'll make you feel so good you won't mind missing your lesson today. I'll even let you practice on me."

"I love you, honey, but I think we can wait until you get home." She giggled. "You know we'd both be so embarrassed if someone knocked on the door and caught us naked. Besides, I'm really enjoying learning martial arts."

"I'm glad, Beth Ann, and you know you can beat me up anytime." He kissed her again, causing her head to spin.

She wiggled out of his arms and left his office while she still could. The last thing she heard was a growl.

She spent a few minutes at the travel agency, grabbing every brochure she could find that had anything to do with Ireland, then she headed out to her lesson. Her instructor taught the students a new kick, and Beth Ann had no problem kicking her leg over her head, and she loved the way all of it gave her a sense of power. When the lesson was over, she sprinted out to the parking lot with a new feeling of independence.

She and Kaylob had decided to go to Ireland in April and spend it with his relatives that he didn't know at all. There was so much to plan and she needed to get busy. At least her family had been excited and supported them going. They couldn't go to Novato for Easter, then to Ireland too, not with the restaurant being so busy. As it was, they'd be away in Ireland for at least three weeks.

Actually, Beth Ann was more excited about meeting his relatives than she had imagined. While Kaylob had been in the hospital after being in a POW camp for over two years, she'd overheard his mom talking to his Aunt Lillian and had been confused when Jackie kept saying something was unfair. More than once, Jackie had said that Lillian had the right to see Kaylob, and Beth Ann had been wondering ever since what Jackie had meant by that.

Besides, it would be nice to see where his gene pool came from and where he'd gotten his blond hair and blue eyes. Jackie had dark hair and dark eyes, and Kaylob looked even less like his dark-haired dad. Harold was a short, heavy man who was always grumpy. Kaylob was never grumpy after getting over his stress disorder from the war. Every now and again, he'd have a nightmare, but that was rare. However, loud noises and stress still got to him, and she wondered if that would ever stop.

When she got home, Beth Ann decided to soak in a hot tub and use her bubble bath that Kaylob always said made her smell like luscious, ripe strawberries. Entering the tub felt so good, and it also felt wonderful that she didn't have any rehearsing to do. She had loved it so much when she was young, but after doing the first tour and winning the Tony, she'd loathed all those camera people stalking her. That wasn't the life she wanted.

She lay back in the tub, thinking about everything she and Kaylob had been through. It sure had been rocky when he first came home from Vietnam. He'd been tortured in that horrible POW camp and was lucky to have survived, but look how well he was doing now. She slid deeper into the water, letting it flow over her shoulders and neck. The warmth rolled over her like a warm blanket, soothing her to sleep. When the clock chimed the hour, she realized she'd dozed off.

"Brrr ..." She jumped out of the now-chilly water and threw on her clothes, but once again, she was hit with a spine tingling chill, which had nothing to do with the water being cold. Why was she feeling as though someone had been watching her? She had made an appointment with her counselor for next week. She'd put it off far too long. She picked up her new book from the nightstand and wondered where she had left the other one. She was usually careful not to lose her books.

Although, it wasn't a big deal to buy the book again. She'd found the new one down the street at a little bookstore—*Once Is Not Enough* by Jacqueline Susanne. The reviews were amazing, and the story was certainly living up to them. The girl's obsession with her father was a little odd, but Beth Ann still loved the story.

She fixed herself a cup of tea and went into the reading area, her special space in the family room that Kaylob called her 'bookworm room.' The blanket Gram had crocheted was thrown over the back of the chaise lounge, so she picked it up and wrapped it around her shoulders. Ah, even after all these years, it was still so soft and cuddly. This was the first chance she'd had in a very long time to pamper herself.

It was a beautiful day, so she opened the window and kicked back on the chaise. A burst of wind brought in the aroma of the roses. Gosh, she loved that smell, winter crisp. This was her favorite spot in the entire house. Well, maybe her second favorite, because the bedroom was number one.

The sun had started its descent behind the far off hillsides, and the last rays of sunlight spilled radiance across the flowers. She'd always thought this was the loveliest time of the day because the dusk made everything look so elegant. She pulled her eyes away from the splendor and got lost in her book. What a story it was. The author baited it with a big hook, and Beth Ann took hold and didn't want to let go.

When she finally glanced up at the clock, she couldn't believe it was only two hours before Kaylob would be home. Holy bookworm, she'd been reading forever. Time to get up and do a big stretch. She touched her toes, then lifted her arms above her head. With a long, deep breath, she exhaled and gazed at the memorabilia table with all her special trinkets that she'd put together with love.

What the heck? Some of my stuff is gone!

She walked over and searched the table, even looking underneath and all around. She proceeded to throw off the chaise cushions and looked under everything. Nothing. The items were gone.

How could that be possible? There was no way she had taken the Bible anywhere. Gram had recorded the dates of every special occasion—her first steps, things she'd said, the solo at church. That Bible meant everything to her. Even the silver cross and the picture with the engraved frame of her and Gram was missing. It was taken on Easter Sunday when she was ten, in her new pink dress with Gram holding her hand. Tears slid down her face from the realization that it was gone. How could everything just vanish? As she stood there trying to make sense of it all, reality slammed her upside the head like the missing baseball bat.

Someone had come into their home and taken them. But when, and why?

She remembered picking up the picture and planting a kiss on it before she and Kaylob left for their honeymoon, and she knew it had been there after the intruder situation with Jack, because she had dusted everything on the table that day she had tried to cook spaghetti.

How had they gotten in? She glanced around the room, panic slamming into her and making the room spin. With wobbly legs and feeling faint, she made it over to the drawer to get the new keys. None were missing, so how was it possible?

The last few months rolled through her mind, like a movie playing

110

out all the details.

She refused to believe it was Blake, so who was it? A stranger or someone she knew? Who had access to her keys to make a spare, which is the only way they could have done it? She needed to tell Kaylob everything so they could alert the police and have the locks changed again, but first she had to get out of the house. She was there alone, and someone had a key.

She grabbed her purse and ran to the door, but she had to stop to keep from hyperventilating. After a few seconds of gaining control, she headed out the door and hurried to the garage. Standing beside her car, she glanced up at the wall and knew for sure that word was meant for her.

Her mind was whirling with thoughts of everything that had been happening. She couldn't seem to get enough air in her lungs, and a lump formed in her throat. No way could she let herself pass out, not now! She bent over and put her hands on her knees, trying to get control of her breathing as she told herself to stop panicking. Her head was thumping from her worst fears.

Finally, she straightened up and fumbled with the keys, trying to find the right one, but her hands betrayed her. Before she could get the key in the lock, she heard a noise from the darkened corner. Fear blinded her as she tried to focus on the lurking shadow.

Her insides warned that danger was looming. Sweat slid down her back. "God this can't be happening again," she said just above a whisper. Her hands trembled and caused her to drop the keys. The sound seemed to echo through her, and tears blurred her vision.

Once again, she heard a noise. "Who is it?" she said, praying it was just the neighbor's cat again like it had been so many times before. "Hello, who's there?"

Out of the shadows, a figure emerged and made her flinch back with a shriek, then panic choked her like a thick fog stuck in her throat.

"Oh, it's you. God, you scared me." She put her trembling hand across her heart and inhaled. "I didn't know you were coming over. Is something wrong?"

He didn't answer.

She'd been relieved when she'd seen who it was, but now something didn't feel right. Why was he just staring at her like that, and why were his hands behind his back?

"Why are you here, Peter? Is something wrong with Cathy?" He stepped closer to her and she backed up against the car. "What are you doing?"

"You belong to me."

Oh, God. It was the voice and the words from the phone!

"It's been you all along." She looked around and saw his car sitting in the guest parking. "That's the car that's been following me. You hit Jack over the head and stole my things." She wanted to punch him in the face. "You've been in my home, you asshole! I'm going to turn you in."

He had a familiar gleam in his eyes, but she knew now that it was evil.

"Yes, I've watched you for a very long time," he said with a sick grin. "I'm in love with you, and in time you'll love me back."

Bile rose in her throat. Why hadn't she noticed his twisted look before?

"Get away from me!" She turned and tried to unlock her car again, but he wrapped his arms around her. She remembered what she had to do, knock him to the ground and kick him in the balls! She squirmed around to face him, then took a swing at his head and missed, but she'd get him the next time.

He ducked the second attempt and said through clenched teeth. "Now, now, don't make me hurt you." He grabbed her wrist and pressed a rag across her face.

Beth Ann swung again, but felt disoriented and knew she was losing consciousness.

"Oh my God …"

Chapter Twelve

While Mike worked on inventory, Kaylob hurried to finish up his work so he could leave the restaurant a little early to surprise his wife. Man, had she teased him today or what? The memory of the way she'd moved on his lap was planted in his brain. Yes, tonight would feature a special dessert.

Who knew they could be so open with each other. That was something he'd never imagined when they were growing up. Beth Ann had been so innocent he couldn't have known she would ever be so sultry with a dash of hot spice.

That was one reason he was looking forward to their trip to Ireland. They'd be staying in a resort for the first week with no interruptions and no work, and he planned to make the most of their time alone together. Plus, it would be good to get away from all the stress.

Memories of what Blake had done at the party assaulted him. That guy had almost pushed past the point of no return and he was lucky to be alive, especially since there had never been any love lost between him and Kaylob. Of course, if the truth be told, Kaylob couldn't see himself killing anyone. There had been enough death in Vietnam to last him a lifetime. Walt had been his best friend and had died right in his arms. Death really sucked, and he hoped he never had to witness it again.

One thing Kaylob knew was that Beth Ann didn't like to admit when she was wrong. Blake had been the one calling, but she continued to defend him. Kaylob had suspected all along it was him, but after their wedding and then the party, he knew it was the truth. Which led him to another thought. They might have to get a restraining order. He suspected Beth Ann wouldn't like that and he might end up in the doghouse, but he intended to put all the cards on the table tonight and have a long talk about her ex.

But all that would have to wait until after dessert. He laughed to himself and Mike gave him a knowing grin.

"Kaylob, I can finish up here if you want to get home to your lovely wife."

"Are you sure?" Kaylob felt bad leaving him to close up.

"No problem. That's what you pay me for." He chuckled. "You've been closing a lot lately anyway, and besides Beth Ann canceled her tour to have more time with you. I can see that makes you a happy man, so go."

"Thanks, man." Kaylob pulled off his apron. "I'm going home to my wife and taking some of that lasagna Andria made with me. That woman is truly a culinary genius."

"No shit." Mike nodded and touched his stomach. "I've put on too many pounds since I started working here."

Kaylob laughed. "I think I've put on a few too."

He decided to take an entire tray of lasagna so they'd have leftovers since Andria had made plenty to serve the next day. When he got home and parked, he noticed something lying on the ground next to Beth Ann's car and walked over to see what it was.

"How the hell did she drop her keys?" he said as he looked around. She must have had her hands full when she got home, but how did she get in the house? Something didn't feel right, and a seed of worry sprouted.

He ran to their townhouse and almost crashed into the front door. It was locked so he used his key to get inside, shouting her name as soon as he opened the door. The silence was deafening.

"Beth Ann!" He called as he set down the lasagna, then jogged through the house. There was no sign of her. He ran through every room and found nothing, not even her purse. The only thing that seemed odd was the chaise cushions were on the floor, a cup half full of cooled tea was still sitting on the small side table. What the hell was going on?

He ran to the neighbors' and knocked on their door. He knew it was late, but something wasn't right and they had been keeping an eye on Beth Ann since the intrusion. Jerry answered the door and looked at him with concern.

"What's wrong, Kaylob?"

"I'm sorry to bother you, but Beth Ann is missing." He held up her keys. "I found these out by her car. Did you hear anything odd tonight?"

"I know Beth Ann was here earlier." Jerry's eyes widened. "I saw her coming up the stairs carrying what looked like a bunch of brochures. Have you checked the workout room or the pool? I've seen her there at night a few times."

"Thanks, I'll go check there now." Kaylob's heart sped up with hope.

He headed to the workout area, but there was no sign of anyone. Quite a few people were hanging out by the pool, none of them Beth Ann. Kaylob recognized a lady he'd seen Beth Ann chatting with once. He hurried over to talk to her.

"Excuse me, but have you seen Beth Ann?" Kaylob asked.

"No," the lady said and stood up. "Is something wrong?"

Several people stopped talking and stared, probably because of the panic in Kaylob's voice that he couldn't hide.

"She's missing." He held up her keys. "These were down by her car."

Nobody had seen her or saw anything suspicious, so he tore away back to his place to call the police. He was in full run mode when he passed by Jerry's again.

"Did you find her?" Jerry called out.

"No, I'm calling the police."

"Shit. I'll help look for her. Let me know what the cops say."

Kaylob thanked him and ran inside to grab the phone. As soon as the dispatcher answered, his words came out in a flood. "My wife … I know she was taken because I found her keys down by her car and she's nowhere to be found! Her tea wasn't finished, her purse is missing, and the cushions were on the ground! I looked everywhere and—"

"Sir, calm down and take a deep breath," the lady said. "Now explain to me again what happened and why you think someone took your wife."

Kaylob took a deep breath and tried to explain everything more calmly, then he gave her his address and phone number. The dispatcher informed him they were sending officers to his home right away.

When he hung up with the police, he called all their friends and also Beth Ann's mom and dad, but none of them had heard from her or knew where she was. Frankie insisted on coming over right away, and her parents were coming down too. Jean was going to contact the rest of the family, which he really appreciated. He couldn't bear the idea of having to tell Gram and Nicky. The last time he'd seen them was at Thanksgiving and they were headed to other destinations for their honeymoon.

Kaylob paced while he waited for the police to get there, feeling his pulse race in his throat. Beth Ann had been feeling nervous and was sure someone was watching her. Damn him, he had dismissed everything, thinking it was just the paparazzi or …

"Blake!" A light went on in Kaylob's head. "He's got her. I need to find his number." He frantically started searching through all Beth Ann's things for his phone number and finally found it in her old address book.

"Hello, Tanner residence. Dana speaking."

"This is Kaylob, Beth Ann's husband. Is Blake there?"

"No, he's gone away for a month or so. Is something wrong?"

"Where the hell did he go?" Kaylob demanded.

"I can't divulge that information," she said, sounding shocked. "What's the problem?"

"He has my wife, and I want to know where the fuck he is!"

"He has Beth Ann?" Dana gasped. "What do you mean? I was just with her today."

There was a knock on the door. "That's the police. They'll be heading over there, because Beth Ann is missing and I know damn well Blake took her!"

He slammed down the phone and ran to the door. It was the police with Frankie right behind them, looking stressed.

He pushed by the police and came inside. "What the hell's going on, Kaylob?"

He held up the keys and looked between Frankie and the police officers. "She's missing and I found these on the ground by her car. Somebody took her!"

One of the officers said, "You shouldn't have touched them."

"I thought she dropped them!" Kaylob snapped. "And I know who has her. If we find him, we'll find her."

"She hasn't been missing for twenty-four hours, so there's nothing we can do right now." The cop's nametag read Officer Vincent Deluca.

"Nothing you can do? She's been kidnapped!" He studied the officer and remembered him from when Jack was attacked. "You were here before. Remember when our friend was hit in the head? Now my wife's been taken, and we can't wait twenty-four hours!"

Frankie nodded. "Beth Ann wouldn't just leave and drop her keys on the ground. She told me about the phone calls she's been getting. Obviously, she has a stalker, and that's serious."

"You're damn right it's serious!" Kaylob said. "And the stalker/kidnapper is Blake Tanner! I know he's got her."

Officer Deluca arched a brow, and Frankie tilted his head.

"What makes you so sure it's Mr. Tanner?" the officer asked.

"We ran into him at a party just before Thanksgiving and he made it clear he wanted her back. He was also at our wedding dressed as part of the catering staff. We know he's been calling and hanging up, and I'd bet he somehow got a key to this apartment." Kaylob took a deep breath. "There are witnesses who saw me have to pull the idiot off my wife at the party."

"Jesus Christ, the guy has lost it." Frankie shook his head. "I thought it was him calling and hanging up, but Beth Ann got furious when I said it."

"Weren't they engaged at one time?" Officer Deluca looked from Frankie to Kaylob.

Kaylob nodded. "Yeah, but what's that got to do with the price of tea in China?"

"Well, maybe she took off with him willingly."

Kaylob was so mad that his hands were shaking, and he could feel his skin heating up. He wanted to scream at this stupid ass police officer, but Frankie spoke up first.

"Look, officer, I'm her best friend, and she wouldn't do that. She's crazy in love with this guy." He placed his hand on Kaylob's shoulder. "They haven't been married all that long and—"

He stopped when the other policeman walked through the open door. His name badge read Andy Morrison.

"I talked to some of the neighbors," Officer Morrison said. "One of them said she talked to Mrs. O'Brien a few days ago and that she was spooked because she thought she'd seen someone hiding in the garage. And, sir, did you see the writing where her car is parked? The lady I spoke to said it hadn't been there long."

"What writing?" Frankie and Kaylob said in unison.

Morrison waved for them to follow. "Let me show you."

When they got to the garage, he shined his flashlight on the wall so they could see the single word: SOON.

"Somebody wrote this on the wall where her car is parked," Morrison said to Deluca. "Now I'm no expert, but I'd say someone was sending her a message."

"Okay." Deluca nodded. "The first thing we do is put out an APB, then we talk to Mr. Tanner." He pulled out his notepad. "Do either of you have his address?"

Frankie shook his head. "He moved back to Palm Springs last I heard. I've never been there."

"I don't know it either," Kaylob said. "But I have his home number. I was on the phone with his housekeeper when all of you got here. She said he's away for a month or so."

Deluca held up his hand. "We'll find him. Give us the phone number and we'll see what information we can get. Have you contacted any of her friends?"

Kaylob nodded. "Everyone, including her parents. They're on their way here." His throat tightened and he felt his stomach knotting up.

"Blake loves her." Frankie must've guessed how he was feeling, because he put a hand on Kaylob's shoulder. "He'd never hurt her."

"I hope you're right, Frankie." Kaylob rubbed the back of his neck with sweaty palms. He wanted to believe what Frankie had said, but inside his heart, he knew things were bad. He couldn't explain it, but he felt a deep nagging that Beth Ann was in danger, just like the time she'd been attacked.

"Come on." Frankie clutched his arm. "Let's get back to your place in case she gets a chance to call."

"Good idea." Officer Deluca agreed. "We'll be in touch after we find out about Tanner. Let us know if you hear anything before then."

When Kaylob and Frankie got back to the townhouse, Frankie pulled the phone over to the couch and waved for Kaylob to sit down.

"You look pale, buddy. Want some tea or coffee?"

"Coffee and water." Kaylob's mouth felt like a desert. "I have a feeling it's gonna be a long night, and I'm so stressed that I feel dehydrated." He leaned over and held his head in his hands. "I can't lose her, Frankie."

"You're not gonna lose her, buddy. She'll be back tonight." He went to the kitchen and came back a couple of minutes later with a glass of ice water. As he handed it to Kaylob, the phone rang and Kaylob snatched it up.

"Kaylob, this is Dana. Have you found Beth Ann yet?"

"No!" Kaylob snapped and knew he was taking it out on the wrong person.

"Listen, I know this is a hard time, but I wanted to let you know that Blake is on his way home to Riverside. I told him what was going on, and he spoke to a police officer. He doesn't have Beth Ann."

"Bullshit! He has her somewhere and I know it."

"No, he doesn't. He was frantic when he heard she's missing, and he's on his way back in his private plane. If he had her, he wouldn't be coming back." She paused to sigh. "Kaylob, he was really upset and wanted me to tell you to stop wasting time looking at him instead of other leads."

"Yeah, I bet he'd love that!" Kaylob hung up the phone, then threw a magazine off the coffee table. "He's full of crap!"

Frankie dodged the magazine. "Hey, what did she say?"

"Blake's on his way home and swears that he doesn't have her, which of course he'd say. He probably has someone watching her while he comes back." Kaylob dragged his fingers through his hair. "I can't stand this sitting around. I feel like I should be doing something." He stood and started pacing.

Two hours later, Frankie was sitting in the chair trying to keep his eyes open and Kaylob was still pacing. Every time the phone rang, he'd pick it up before the first ring ended. Friends were calling non-stop, and Jerry stopped by to let them know that he and his wife had driven around for hours, scanning the area with no luck.

After Jerry left, Kaylob noticed Frankie watching him.

"What?" he asked, knowing Frankie had something on his mind.

"What if Blake is telling the truth? Maybe he didn't take her and we're wasting time on him."

"I know he took her, Frankie," Kaylob said. "You didn't see him the night at the party. And look at what he did at our wedding. He was stalking us for Christ's sake!"

Frankie got up. "Well, he's going away for a long time if he did. Kidnapping is a felony and comes with a lot of years in prison." He walked into the kitchen and poured himself another cup of coffee. "Want a refill?" he asked, holding up the percolator.

Kaylob nodded. "Yeah, thanks. Look, you should go home and get some sleep. No sense in both of us being up all night. I'll call and let you know what's going on."

"Forget it. I'm not going anywhere." He handed Kaylob another cup of coffee. "You have a spare room, so I'm using it until she comes home. For tonight, I'll sleep in this damn chair until we hear something, if I sleep at all."

Kaylob sat back down. "Okay, I'm glad you're staying." Just as he started to take a sip, a bang on the door made him jump.

Frankie hurried to open it, and it was Officer Deluca.

"I'm sorry to say this," he said, looking at his notebook when he came in. "And I know it's not what you want to hear, but we have no leads. From everything we've found out, we can't arrest Blake Tanner. Witnesses said he boarded his private plane alone and has not been seen with anyone."

"I know …" Kaylob paused, trying to catch his breath. "I know he found another way to sneak her out of town. I know he has her."

"I'm sorry, but we can't take him in without proof." Deluca sighed. "We have an APB out and we're on the lookout for her, but that's all we can do until we get more leads." He tucked away his notepad. "We'll be back in the morning. Officer Morrison has interviewed all your neighbors, and nobody has noticed any strange people hanging around. The only person mentioned was a man with a little girl about eight who was seen coming to your place. Do you know who that is?"

Kaylob nodded. "The little girl is one of Beth Ann's students. She's known the dad for years and just started giving his daughter private lessons here a few days ago."

"Well, we may want to interview him and see if he noticed anything," Deluca said. "Although, I doubt he did since he doesn't live in one of these townhouses. But I thought the lady said she'd seem him here more than once."

Kaylob rubbed the nape of his neck and felt like punching something or someone. "Look, I know Blake Tanner has her. You didn't see him at the party. He was nuts."

"We plan on doing some extensive searching of Mr. Tanner's properties, and he's agreed to let the Texas police search his house there tonight." He looked at his wristwatch. "Or should I say this morning. They're doing that right now, so we should hear back in the next hour." Deluca put his hand on Kaylob's shoulder. "Look, if he has her, we'll find her."

Another knock sounded at the door, and Frankie went to let in Jack, Lenard and Carol.

Jack rushed in and hugged Kaylob. "Don't you worry, honey. We're going to find her." He glanced at Deluca. "Aren't we, officer?"

Deluca nodded and left.

With his friends gathered around him, Kaylob fought to control his emotions, but it was no use. As soon as Carol wrapped her arms around him, he broke down and sobbed.

"I can't lose her. She's my whole life …"

Chapter Thirteen

Blake watched out the window as his private plane started descending altitude. He wanted to get off the damn thing and find out who had taken Beth Ann. What the hell was everybody thinking? He would never take Beth Ann against her will. Someone had kidnapped her, and it sure as hell wasn't him. He needed to search for her himself. Just thinking about where she might be, tied his stomach in a knot.

After giving her that note, he was surprised that he was a suspect. He'd wished them happiness forever, and that hadn't been easy. Not when his heart was in shreds and he was still deeply in love with her. Luckily, the police had cleared him because he'd been able to prove he was in Texas when she was abducted. That was a relief, but he still didn't like people thinking he'd done something so terrible.

If truth be told, he *had* made an ass out of himself at the party, and it didn't take a rocket scientist to see that he'd acted like a crazy fool capable of who knows what. But there was no way he'd hurt the girl he had loved since childhood. Other than losing his parents, nothing had ever been as bad as his breakup with Beth Ann. He'd fallen apart—no denying that fact. Maybe he'd gone off the deep end by showing up at their wedding in a disguise with plans to stop it, but he hadn't been ready to let her go.

A question hit him. Would she have dumped him if they had already been married when Kaylob came back?

He knew the answer to that. Kaylob had always been her number one guy. Blake had never stood a chance. When Kaylob had come back from the dead, or everyone thinking he was dead, Blake had known he'd lost her. He'd fought it, but all the fighting in the world wouldn't have kept her from Kaylob.

So where in the world was she now? The police had asked him if he thought she had just taken off with no word. There was no way she' would've done that of her own free will. The big question was, who the hell would do this? Who would just take her? He racked his brain, trying to think of anyone who would want to hurt her, but there wasn't one person he knew who didn't like her. Everyone loved Beth Ann.

He rubbed his sweaty hands on his slacks, and a memory flashed through his mind, making the hair on the back of his neck stand up. Beth Ann's words rang in his ears, and there was no way to hide from the echo. She had asked him if he was having her followed and if he'd been calling and hanging up. He'd gotten mad and accused her of being melodramatic. He'd even gone as far as to tell her she had an overactive imagination.

He bent down and squeezed his head. How could he have been so arrogant and self-centered? Someone really had been following her. Shit, her voice had even sounded shaky, and she'd almost been crying. If only he had listened to her, this might not be happening. Maybe Kaylob was right to blame him, because right now he was sure as shit blaming himself.

He felt the plane tilt slightly as it began a slow and steady turn. Down below, the ground looked like boxes of maps. He couldn't make out anything, but gradually everything began to come into view. The long dark highway with car lights going in every direction made him feel lonely and sick. Somewhere out there, maybe on that road or in a house, somewhere, Beth Ann was being held against her will, alone and frightened. Tears gathered in his eyes and his stomach turned. Jesus, he couldn't let himself throw up.

He felt a bump that meant the landing gear had been released, then he felt the pressure on the brakes as the plane slowed down. He was up and out of his seat the second it stopped.

"I called before we took off," the pilot said when he came to the back, "Johnny said he'd be here waiting."

Blake picked up his bag. "Thanks, Tom. I'll see you later." He rushed off the plane and spotted Johnny standing out by the limousine.

"Hey, boss."

"Hey, Johnny. Take me to 3459 Springfield Lane as fast as you can get there." Blake handed him the suitcase and got inside the vehicle.

Blake hoped the trip to Riverside wouldn't slow to a crawl from the traffic. He looked at his wristwatch and prayed that the early morning hour would mean most people weren't up and about yet. Maybe they could make it in an hour. He leaned his head back against the seat and tried to clear his thoughts of worry, but it was to no avail.

"Beth Ann," he whispered, feeling his heart sink.

Minutes passed, giving him a chance to try and piece any part of the puzzle together. The only one he had was that day she'd called him from Salem awhile back. She had mentioned that she was being followed around by someone in a dark car, but he couldn't remember anything else. He closed his eyes again and tried to relax.

A little while later when he looked out the window, he was surprised to see they were getting close to Riverside. The town lights were glistening, and a few cars were out on the road. Once they pulled up to the town house on Springfield Lane, everything looked quiet. Not a soul out and about.

Johnny jumped out and opened the car door. "Let me go with you, boss. You might not get a warm, fuzzy welcome here." He glanced in the direction of the townhouse.

"You're right," Blake said. "Let's brave this and go forward."

When Frankie opened the door for them, his eyes widened and he shook his head. "What the hell are you doing here, Blake? This is no time for you to show up."

"Who is it, Frankie?" Kaylob asked as he stepped up to the door.

As soon as their eyes met, Blake knew this had been a bad idea.

"You son-of-a-bitch! Where is she?" Kaylob dove at Blake, his fists pounding his face as they both tumbled to the ground.

"Kaylob, stop!" Frankie yelled. "This isn't helping anything!"

Johnny pulled Kaylob off, but not before Kaylob managed to land another punch that filled Blake's mouth with blood and made it impossible to speak. It took both Johnny and Frankie to keep Kaylob from attacking Blake again.

"I'll kill you, Tanner!" he yelled, his face a dark red. "I know you took her! I'm gonna pound you into the ground if you don't tell us where

124

she is, you bastard!"

"I didn't take her!" Blake managed to choke out, splattering blood on the sidewalk.

Frankie yelled at Johnny. "Get him the fuck out of here, now, before he gets killed!"

Johnny wrapped his arms around Blake's chest and pulled him up. "Come on, boss. Let's get you home."

Blake struggled to get free. "I don't have her, O'Brien! I'd never hurt her. You guys are wasting time when you need to be searching for her!" He kept shouting over his shoulder as Johnny dragged him away.

* * * *

Beth Ann rolled over and felt her head thump inside her skull. She needed to get up and get some aspirin. The dream she'd had was awful. She snuggled down in the comforter and wondered if Kaylob had left for work yet.

Wait. When had Kaylob come home? She didn't remember anything.

She sat up and tried to focus, but everything was so hazy. Where the heck was she? A rush of trepidation moved through her as she glanced around and noticed almost everything looked like her bedroom. Even the comforter and pillowcases were the same—but it *wasn't* her room. The smell was different, and the air felt foreign. And why was her head exploding with pain? She massaged her temples, trying to understand what was going on.

Wait. She opened her eyes wide and glanced around. It hadn't been a dream. She remembered now, she had been taken!

"Oh my God, did he …?" She put her hand down below to see if there was pain, but it would be hard to tell because it was that time of the month.

"Hi, love," Peter said as he waltzed into the room. "No, I didn't do anything to you. I would never hurt you." He smiled as he carried a tray of food and acted as though it were normal for her to be there. "Here you go, my lovely. Fruit with eggs over medium, and toast with your favorite strawberry jam."

"I want to go home right now!" she demanded. "My family will be worried, and you're going to get in trouble with the police. And what about Cathy?" She studied his face and noticed that he didn't even flinch. She tried to stand, but her legs wouldn't hold her steady.

He shook his head and set down the tray. "Don't be silly. You *are* home, and my little daughter is fine. Here's your breakfast, and don't worry your pretty little noggin about Cathy."

"I want to go home now, Peter." She tried again to stand up.

"Don't you listen? You *are* home." His brows furrowed as he frowned. He went to touch her cheek, but she slapped his hand away.

"Touch me and I'll stab you to death!" She picked up the fork and jabbed at him, but he caught her hand and took the fork away.

"You don't want to make me teach you a lesson. I don't want to start off our life together in a fight." He squeezed her wrist, and his face drained of any kindness. Cold eyes glared back at her, and she knew what she had to do.

"I'm sorry, Peter. I guess this headache is making me cranky." She touched her head and pasted on a smile. Something in her gut told her to act nice and pretend to be grateful. "Thank you for the breakfast."

His face lit up like a jack-o-lantern. "You're most welcome, my love."

"Peter, is there any aspirin?" She tried to look at him but was afraid she'd throw up.

"Everything you'll need is there in your bathroom." He pointed. "Well, I know you do need some personal items."

What felt like bugs started crawling up her spine. How did he know? Had he looked at her?

He must have read the look on her face, because he said, "I only know because I've kept track of that time and found things in the garbage cans. He sat down on the edge of the bed. "You want me to help you change or bathe?"

"No." She shook her head and gulped. "I can do it. Thank you though."

"You know, the bathroom is actually larger than your old one, and it has a soaking tub." He wiggled his eyebrows, and she almost upchucked.

She plastered on another smile and drenched her voice with sugar. "That's nice, Peter. This breakfast looks very good." She picked up the plate, and he handed her back the fork.

126

"I have to be gone for a while, but you shouldn't be lonely. You have your own reading room." He nodded to the left. "There's also a fully stocked little kitchen, even though I'll be taking care of most of your meals. So just relax and enjoy yourself, and try not to burn the house down. We both know you can't cook at all." He chuckled. "I have to go make some appearances so nobody thinks anything fishy about me."

"Peter …" Beth Ann made her voice sound small.

"Yes, love?"

"How long are you keeping me?"

"Why, forever of course." He moved closer and touched her cheek. "I've loved you since the first time we met. In time, I'm going to show you how good it feels to have a man love you like I do."

She grinned and nodded. "Okay. But, Peter, I'm shy and you know—"

"It's fine, Beth Ann, even though I know you're not all that shy. We have all the time in the world." He stood up and stared at her. "The most important thing is that we're together. And no one can bother us."

Screw him! I'll never let him touch me!

She told herself there would be that moment when he wouldn't be looking, and she'd find a way to kick his ass and escape. How long had he stalked her? Maybe she could take a page out of his stalking manual and observe everything he did.

He walked over to the closet and opened the door. "Everything you need is hanging up or in the drawers. Your personal feminine items are in the bathroom. If I forgot anything, just let me know. I want you to be happy."

She was sure as hell glad she was an actress, because she had to give the performance of her life.

"Thank you, Peter." She hated even saying his name. *I'm going to get away from you, and when I do, you better watch out!*

She looked inside the closet and spotted the pink dress, and she also recognized other items that must have vanished without her noticing. Kaylob was right; she had too many clothes to keep track of them all.

He stared at her a few moments longer, then turned and exited the room. She heard him lock the door, then heard footsteps going upward followed by another door closing. That had to mean she was in a basement somewhere, but where was the house?

When all the sounds vanished, she rose, but almost fell when the room started spinning. Plus there was a jackhammer inside her head.

"Ugh, I need those aspirin." She hung on to the wall and stumbled into the bathroom. How in the heck was she going to get out of this situation? At least he didn't seem violent—she'd been there and done that. He was clearly disturbed, so she'd play him good. Whatever it took to stay alive.

Once she found the medicine cabinet with the pills inside, she glanced around in shock. The bathroom was almost identical to the one in her home, only larger with a soaking tub. It even had the same monogrammed towels, only instead of a K there was a P. How long had he been planning this?

She noticed a faint smell of paint still lingered in the air. Holy crazy man, he was disgusting and clearly obsessed. She shuddered at the thought of him trying to touch her, and a chill went up her spine.

There had to be a way for her to get out of this. She had to believe that. No, she did believe it. She swallowed the pills and inhaled deeply.

"Kaylob," she said. "Please feel me and know I'm okay."

With pure determination, she managed to stumble back and collapse on the bed. What in the world had he given her to make her react like this? She had to figure out how to escape, and in order to do that, she had to sleep and get strong. She forced herself to eat the food since she knew she would need every bit of energy and brain power to get away from this lunatic.

"Don't worry, honey," she whispered before she drifted off to sleep. "I'm coming home."

Chapter Fourteen

Two days later, Kaylob sat at the kitchen table surrounded by his friends and family. His parents and Beth Ann's mom and stepdad were staying at the townhouse. His mom and dad had gone downtown to pick up some groceries. Lisa and Denny had been calling daily, and today Carol was helping Jack cook breakfast. The support around him had touched him deeply, and he needed it to hang on to his sanity.

The news stations were going to air a report about Beth Ann's disappearance, and Kaylob hoped with all his heart that someone would come forward with information. Maybe someone had spotted her or seen Blake take her away. He had to have an accomplice who was watching over Beth Ann. The only piece of good news was that Kaylob could feel her alive. The connection they'd had while he was in Vietnam had been strong, and thank God, it was still there between them.

The police said they couldn't find anything in Blake's Texas home. What the hell difference did that make? Just because they hadn't found anything didn't mean a thing. They'd searched his townhouse in Palm Springs too, and said Blake had been out of town when she'd vanished. Somebody was missing something, like a hidden room, or another house, or someone who was holding her for him.

But what if Blake didn't have her? Could he be telling the truth? That stupid idea made his chest hurt. It had to be Blake—look at the insane way he'd acted at the party. Of course, he was trying to make himself look innocent now. No telling how long he'd been planning this.

Kaylob's stomach growled as the aroma of breakfast filled the air. All the good smells and people around him couldn't help with the worry though. He couldn't bear not knowing what Beth Ann was going through. Was she hurt? Did she have food and water?

Jean was trying to be optimistic and kept saying that Beth Ann would be back soon, but the look in everybody's eyes was shaded with fear. Kaylob was starting to get irritated by the questions people were alluding to, like if Blake really had her, why wasn't he in hiding, and why was he helping the police? Maybe Kaylob should go investigate Blake himself.

"I can't take this anymore," he said, standing up. "I'm going to find her, and I know where I need to go look!"

Jean rose from the couch, her face pale and her lips trembling. "Kaylob, honey, I think you should stay here. What if she calls?"

"You can't go around flipping out on people." Frankie looked up at him from where he sat at the table. "You'll get thrown in jail for assault, and that's the last thing anybody needs." He took a sip of coffee. "Sit your ass back down and stop this. Beth Ann is going to reach out to you. You said that yourself." He gave Kaylob a pointed look.

"I can't just sit around doing nothing." Kaylob paced back and forth. "I know he has her. None of you saw how he acted at the party. And look what he did at our wedding. The guy is crazy!"

Stanley walked over and put his hand on Kaylob's shoulder. "Son, you know if she gets a chance to call, she'll need to hear your voice on the phone. We have to wait for her to contact you."

Kaylob's parents came walking in the door with groceries.

"Any news?" his mom asked.

Kaylob shook his head then sat down again with a deep sigh. When the phone rang, he snatched it up on the first ring.

"Kaylob, it's Blake. Please don't hang up. The cops just left, and they'll tell you she's not here. I don't have her. I wish I did."

"You're full of shit! Where is she, Tanner? You don't fool me just because they can't find her." He felt like his heart might explode from anger. "Bring her home, you asshole. Now!"

"Kaylob, I do not have Beth Ann, but someone does. We need to find her, and as long as you think I have her, you're keeping the police from looking in other directions." He paused for a minute. "Let me help with the search and I'll use all my resources to find her, but these damn cops are following me around when they need to be looking other places."

"Go to hell, Tanner! We all know you have her hidden somewhere."

Kaylob hung up and felt a stabbing pain in his jaw. He couldn't catch his breath, and his heart was racing like crazy. Sweat poured from his forehead as he tugged at his collar.

"It's so hot in here," he said. "I can't breathe …" He could feel the air being sucked out of his lungs. and his ears were ringing.

"Kaylob, what's wrong?" Frankie jumped up, letting the chair fall backward as he rushed over. "Are you okay, buddy?"

"I don't know. I think I'm having a heart attack."

Kaylob could feel everybody surrounding him while he melted off the chair and fell to the floor. He heard voices all around him, and when he opened his eyes, his dad and Stanley were leaning over him.

"Just relax, Kaylob," Stanley said. "Paramedics are on their way. I just called them."

Frankie's face appeared with Carol beside him, her eyes full of worry.

"You're okay," Frankie said, touching his head. "You're gonna be fine."

Muted voices were circling all around, and he could hear his mom crying. He knew he was about to pass out and said a quick prayer: *Please, God, don't let this happen. I have to be here for Beth Ann.*

* * * *

Peter was gone, so Beth Ann took that time to soak in the tub. She was feeling stronger since she'd been eating everything that lunatic brought to her. Right now Peter was acting nice and seemed to be doing everything he thought would make her happy. Thinking about it made her sick, but she had to play it cool and try to gain his trust. Her goal was to escape and make it home. Nobody was going to rescue her, because nobody knew where she was. This time she had to save herself.

The way he talked about the new home sounded like they weren't in Riverside anymore. He had dropped some hints by saying things like *I had this house built for you. But not to worry, it's not in my name so nobody knows I have this place. Not even my ex-wife. And it's isolated. We have no neighbors, so nobody can find us.*

He also mentioned that it was in some corporation's name overseas.

Not even the title company knew he was the owner. He had done up the deal like he was the realtor and gotten some legal paper saying he was an attorney in fact, or something along those lines. Beth Ann had no idea what all that meant, but she knew he was smart enough that he had covered all his tracks.

When she'd told him how smart he was, he'd fluffed up like a skunk tail. That had been two days ago. He'd left both days for work and had come back about five hours later. She was making mental notes of his routine.

She knew Blake would be under suspicion by everyone, but it wouldn't take long for them to figure out that he didn't have her. And she also knew Blake would be searching for her too. However, she didn't think he'd look twice at Peter, because he'd appeared so together and acted like such a good father.

Her mind traveled back to the first time she met Peter. On tour in Chicago, she had gone on a date with Blake because Kaylob was missing and presumed dead. Thinking about it now, when Blake had introduced them, Peter held her hand for just a little too long after he kissed it, and she remembered feeling uncomfortable. Why hadn't she thought about that? Why hadn't she noticed the sick look in his eyes?

The answer was clear. You never suspect a man wearing a business suit, with a charming smile and appears to be a dedicated father. That's not what society tells you a creeper looks like.

She also remembered Cathy saying that she would never be as pretty or as good as her. Did she say that because it's what she heard from her daddy? Had he put Cathy in the school to get closer to Beth Ann? He had played at being surprised when he'd run into her and she had believed the whole show. No, it was an act—all part of his twisted plan.

Peter had been planning and scheming for no telling how long. He'd built a house with a private prison just for her and tried to make it look like her bedroom. That must have taken a year at least. She wanted to ask him when it had all started. Now she knew it had been him spying when she would hear the bumps in the night? And what about the time she'd heard the door open and close when she was taking a shower, but no one had been there when she called out to Kaylob. She'd blamed her paranoia, but had it been Peter all along.

How did he get inside the townhouse? Oh, god. He'd probably gotten the key from her purse at the school. He must have taken her Bible, picture and cross. But where were they? Would she ever see them again? She'd fight like hell to make sure she got those things *and* her life back.

She closed her eyes while she lay in the warm tub, and the next thing she knew she was standing in front of her townhouse, only someone had put a big picture window where the front door used to be, and she could see her family inside. She started pounding on the glass, but nobody paid her any attention.

"Kaylob, Mom, Stanley!" she yelled. "Let me in!"

Her heart pounded so hard that it was echoing through her head. She needed to get inside before he came looking for her. Through the window, she could see tears streaming down her mom's face. Stanley wrapped his arms around his wife, and Kaylob had his head in his hands, not even looking in her direction.

"Please hear me," she cried. "Why won't you let me inside?"

Then she heard someone coming and everything started to get dark. Her hands trembled, and sweat poured out of her skin, leaving her standing in freezing cold water.

"Mom. Someone, please let me inside."

She shouted over and over again as the footsteps got louder and closer. It was the bogeyman and she knew it. She had to get away, but the fear captured her and left her paralyzed. She needed to run and hide, but where? He would find her and take her back to the prison. She whipped around, ready to dart away, when she heard him laughing.

"You'll never get away from me. I'll never let you go." His evil eyes filled with something black that started oozing down his face.

She let out a bloodcurdling scream. Her eardrums were assaulted by her own squeal, which woke her in the tub that was now filled with cold water.

"No ... I want to go home." She got out and slid down to the floor, sobbing as she wrapped her arms around her legs. "Kaylob, I need you."

With no clock, she had no idea how long she'd been crying. Everything was so quiet. All the sounds of buses, brakes, and car horns were absent. Not even a knock on the door or the sound of a TV. Funny, she'd never thought that a quiet life could be so lonely. Just a chirping bird or a dog barking would have made her feel less alone. She'd even be happy to hear that annoying loud shrill of her phone again. She began to sing "Somewhere over the Rainbow" in hopes that it would cheer her up, but her heart felt so heavy that she had to stop.

Snap out of it, Beth Ann! Enough of the pity party. She looked in the mirror at her red, puffy eyes—the face of a poor little victim. And that's *not* what she was. She needed to get tough, right now! If all she did was cry and give into the pain, she'd never find her way home.

She went into the reading room and found a pen, then she picked up one of the books the slime had stolen from her nightstand. There were some empty pages in the very back, so she decided to write up her plan there. She sank down onto the sofa and started jotting down his every move, How many steps he took before he locked the second door, and the sounds she heard from above. She could hear when the water was turned on or the toilet flushed, so she knew when he was in the bathroom. That might come in handy later.

She smirked as she thought how the tables had turned. She would listen, watch, and observe everything he did, the way he'd done to her all those months. The difference was that she didn't love him and had no emotions to get in the way. Well, other than hatred for the bastard, but she'd even curtail that. She needed a clear mind to do what needed to be done.

That was the moment she knew she could outsmart Peter and find a way to take him down.

* * * *

Blake stood staring out his window at the townhouse when he heard Dana's voice. "An Officer Deluca is here to see you."

Blake turned. "Show him in." He prayed inside that they had some good news.

When he saw the look on the police officer's face, he knew something wasn't right. He felt the room start to spin and Dana came and stood next to him.

"Mr. Tanner. We found a purse belonging to Beth Ann. It had her Driver's license and," he held up a letter. "A note from you. I wanted you to verify you wrote this letter before we show it to her husband."

Blake examined the letter. "Yes," he nodded. "I wrote this."

"Oh heavens." Dana spoke up. "I gave that to her and she gave one for me to give to Blake, and with everything going on, I forgot." She headed to the closet and pulled out her purse, then reached inside and took out a large envelope. "It has your cufflink in it. It was in some of her stuff."

Blake opened the letter and Deluca stepped closer. When he shook the envelope, the cufflink spilled onto his hand. "Wait a minute, this is not my cufflink. I bought these last year for one of my top brokers, Peter Steel."

The officer stared at the cufflink and gave Dana a pointed look. "I wish you would have remembered this sooner."

"I'm sorry," she cried. "I thought it was Blake's."

Blake reached out and touched her arm. "What's important is we have it now. We need to go tell Kaylob. Maybe he'll finally believe that I don't have her."

"I need to use your phone," Officer Deluca said. "We need to send a team over to his house. Do you have his address?"

"My office manager knows." He ran to the phone and dialed.

Chapter Fifteen

Kaylob was released from the hospital after twenty-four hours and was glad to be out of there. He'd seen enough damn hospitals to last him the rest of his life. He also couldn't stand being away from the phone in case Beth Ann called or there was any word from the police on finding her. They told him he'd had a bad anxiety attack and his blood pressure had spiked. The doctor had also explained that because of what he went through in Vietnam he had low tolerance for stress.

They'd given him blood pressure pills and told him to take one daily until things calmed down, but nothing would calm down until Beth Ann came home. The doctor had ordered him to rest and he was doing the best he could, but there was no turning off his brain.

He'd finally talked his parents into going home, and Jean and Stanley had gone back to San Francisco so Stanley could get some things done with his business, but they'd be back tomorrow. Gram had called several times in tears, and that had broken Kaylob's heart. She'd also given him some ideas on how to bring down his blood pressure naturally and had made sure to tell him to do both treatments while he was under so much stress.

Gram and Nickolas were in Nashville visiting friends and relatives for two weeks, but of course, when Gram had found out about Beth Ann, she wanted to come back to Riverside right away. Kaylob had pleaded with them to stay and promised he'd call twice a day with updates, but Gram insisted on coming back.

It worried Kaylob for them to return with no rest. It was a long drive for two seniors, so he'd copped a plea, as Frankie would say. He told Gram that the last thing he needed was to worry about them and add to his stress, so she had finally agreed to wait at least two days before they left.

"Hey, buddy," Frankie said after Kaylob hung up the phone. "You want some of this chicken Andria brought over? Man, that woman can cook. I wish she was single. She's a fine-looking woman, too."

"She's a good lady. But I'm not hungry right now. Maybe later." Kaylob was unable to conjure up even a small smile. "I don't understand what the hell is going on. Why can't the police bring Blake in, at least for questioning? Maybe he'd break down and tell them where she is."

Frankie just swallowed and looked at the floor with a shrug.

"Look at me, Frankie," Kaylob said. "I can tell something's up. What is it?"

Frankie put down the piece of chicken he was eating, then reached for a pop on the coffee table and took a big gulp before answering.

"Actually, Blake's been working with the police. He hired two top investigators, and even took a polygraph test to prove he was innocent."

"What?" Kaylob stood and headed towards the phone. "Can't those idiots see that it's all a ruse? He found a way to trick the machine."

"He's covered all the costs for the investigation, and he really seems worried, Kaylob." Frankie's eyes showed doubt. "The guy had tears in his eyes the last time I spoke to him."

"To hell with Blake. He doesn't fool me. I'm going to the police station." Kaylob went into the kitchen to find his car keys. He hadn't been able to think straight since this had started and had no idea where he'd put anything. "Where did I put my damn keys!" He pulled open the junk drawer and threw everything on the counter.

"You're not going without me," Frankie said. "I'll call someone to cover the pho—" Pounding on the front door interrupted him.

"Jesus, are they trying to tear my door down?" Kaylob asked as he went to answer it. He swung it open and couldn't believe his eyes. "What the fuck? Tanner, I'm gonna break you into tiny pieces and feed you to your horse!"

"Wait a minute, Mr. O'Brien." Officer Deluca pulled Kaylob's hands off Blake's shirt and held up Beth Ann's purse. "This was brought in from the sanitary department and there is a letter inside. When the garbage men saw her name on the IDs, they knew it was the missing girl.

You need to read this letter. The waste that it was with, all came from this building."

"I see you brought an officer for protection and trying to plant letters to cover your ass!" Kaylob wanted to punch Blake between the eyes. "Smarter than I thought you were!"

Frankie appeared behind Kaylob in the doorway. "Don't do this now, Officer. Kaylob just got out of the hospital and doesn't need more stress. Blake, just go away."

Deluca stepped between Blake and Kaylob. "I'm sorry, but you both need to read this letter and listen to what's going on. We might have a break in the case, and we wanted to come and talk to you about it."

Kaylob reluctantly opened the door wider. "Fine, but I don't know why *he* needs to be a part of this."

When they got to the living room, Blake handed Kaylob an envelope. "Here, look at this. Beth Ann found this inside a shoe and thought it came from my house and gave it to Dana to give to me. With everything going on, Dana forgot about it until this morning."

Kaylob unfolded the letter and read it, then he looked at the cufflink imprinted with *Texas*.

"What does this have to do with anything, and how is it a break the case?" He glared at Blake and stepped closer, but Frankie held onto his arm.

"Kaylob, read this letter they found, I wrote this to her right after the party situation," Blake said.

Kaylob opened the letter and his heart took a dive. Sure enough, it was Blake saying how sorry he was.

He handed the letter to Frankie. "That still doesn't prove anything. So you felt guilty and said you were sorry and wished us well. What the hell does that prove?" He glared at Blake and Officer Deluca.

The officer nodded towards Blake. "Listen to what he has to say."

"Kaylob, I know who this cufflink belongs to. Beth Ann found it in her stuff and gave that note to Dana with the cufflink inside. I bought those for my employee Peter Steel while I was in Texas after he closed a very large commercial account for me. There's no way it should have been in Beth Ann's stuff. He's never even been to my house." Blake had a sick look on his face. "We've tried to contact him, but the neighbors said he's hardly ever home anymore."

Deluca held up a photo of Peter. "I'm sending my partner around with this to ask your neighbors if they've seen him around here."

Kaylob felt his stomach turn and had to brace himself against the wall. "He's the one I told you about that's been bringing his daughter here to meet with Beth Ann for private lessons. Jesus, he was very persistent and even offered her more money." Kaylob rubbed the back of his neck.

Deluca nodded. "I want to find out how often he's been here. From what we understand, your wife had a black car following her around, and we know this Peter Steel has one fitting that description. Someone might have seen him or his car here the night she vanished."

Kaylob nodded. "I saw that car, but thought it was the paparazzi."

Deluca pulled out his notepad. "Steel drives a black 1973 Lincoln Continental with tinted windows. Is that the one you saw?"

Kaylob rubbed his forehead. "Shit, I didn't notice what kind of car it was, but it could have been."

"I'm going outside to talk to my partner. I'll let you know if we find out anything."

After Deluca left, Blake said, "We have a call in to Peter's ex-wife and hopefully we'll hear back from her soon." He swallowed hard. "I hope you don't mind, but we gave her this number."

Kaylob looked at the worry and anguish on Blake's face and finally believed that he didn't have Beth Ann. Plus the letter and the cufflink made it seem pretty clear.

"No, that's fine," he said, then the room suddenly began to spin and there was a high-pitched ringing in his ears.

Frankie saw him stumble and took his arm. "Do you need one of those pills?"

Kaylob shook his head. "I took one already. I'll be fine."

They all sat down in silence for a minute while Kaylob tried to calm himself down.

Deluca came back, his eyes showing worry and something else Kaylob couldn't read.

"What's wrong?" Kaylob heard his voice go up in pitch.

"Several officers are at Mr. Steel's house right now. He's there with his daughter. There are no signs of Mrs. O'Brien, and he offered to let them search. He said he might have lost the cuff link the day he helped her with a heavy suitcase. He said she had wanted to take it out of the closet and put it on the bed to unpack."

Kaylob nodded and felt his world spin out of control. She had unpacked, but he didn't know that Peter helped her lift the suitcase, but it made sense because it was so heavy.

"Where the hell is she then?" Kaylob glanced at Blake with some lingering suspicion, but he knew in his heart that Blake didn't have her.

Blake's face suddenly went as white as his shirt. "Can I use your bathroom?" he said as he dashed down the hallway.

As much as Kaylob hated to admit it, he knew Blake was in love with Beth Ann too, and they were feeling almost the same things. But nobody could feel as bad as he did. She was his wife and the love of his life.

Officer Morrison arrived and filled them in on what they'd learned from questioning the neighbors. "Several people reported seeing Peter Steel around here." He handed Kaylob the picture they'd shown the neighbors. "They reported seeing him dropping off his little girl at your place." He looked down at his notes. "A few people reported seeing him alone, but they assumed it was to pick up the little girl or just visiting. They didn't notice any suspicious behavior. He was always friendly and waved."

Deluca nodded and turned toward Kaylob. "I'm sorry, Mr. O'Brien. We'll continue to search for leads and do everything in our power to find your wife, but we're hitting dead ends here. It's been a week now."

After the officers left, Blake came back to the living room, wiping his mouth with a handkerchief. His eyes met Kaylob's, and for the first time, there was no bitterness or hate, just mutual fear and pain with a touch of spewing anger. Only this time not at each other.

Frankie put a hand on both their shoulders. "Try not to worry so much, guys. We'll hire a posse if necessary to get her back home. My parents have offered to help financially, and I'll do whatever I can."

Blake shook his head. "No need for your parents to spend their money, Frankie. I'm gonna hire a special team to start investigating every detail. I'll cover all the costs."

For the first time in his life, Kaylob was glad Blake was there.

"I have funds too," Kaylob said, swallowing back tears. "Together we'll find her. And I really appreciate the help from both of you."

"We can offer a big reward too," Blake said.

"And put her picture on every news station locally and far away," Frankie added. "Someone has to have seen something."

Kaylob nodded. All he wanted was to bring his life back to him. Yes, his life was a tiny and stubborn redhead with a fiery personality. Having her back was the only way his heart would beat normal again.

* * * *

Beth Ann didn't know what time it was when Peter came in carrying food on a tray, but from the sound of her stomach growling, she knew it was later than normal. She could also see that it was dark outside through the small window in the bathroom. She'd already given up hope on trying to escape through it since it was up so high and way too small to squeeze her body through.

Peter seemed uptight and not in a good mood, so she kept quiet when he turned and walked out without saying a word. After eating everything on her plate, she put it by the door with a thank you note that read *Thank you, Peter. That was very good.* She hoped he wasn't thinking about murdering her or doing anything else since she was trying to stay on his good side.

Ten minutes later, while she was reading her book, she heard footsteps and knew he was picking up the tray. She wondered why he was in a bad mood, but she couldn't help being thankful that he wasn't bothering her or even attempting to come in and try to talk. Tomorrow she'd count the seconds it took for him to gather things. He always left the door open while he did it, so maybe that would be a way to escape. She'd also take notes from the moment the shower came on until he came down to check on her again.

Her mind raced with different ideas of how she could get away, everything from bashing his head in with the lamp, strangling him with the cord, or breaking down the door and leaving while he was at work. She sketched out plan after plan, no matter how far-fetched. One of them had to be a way she could break free and escape the creep holding her prisoner.

For the next few days, Peter hardly spoke. He just delivered her food them rushed away. Something must be going on, because he was staying away for long periods of time. She wished there were a TV or something to watch. Maybe they were showing her picture on the nightly news like she'd seen them do with other people who vanished.

The good news was that she'd counted anywhere from fifteen to twenty seconds that it took Peter to pick up the tray and set it back down. That wasn't a lot of time, but she might be able to make it work with one of the plans. She had to figure out some way to get the heck out of there. How long had she been locked up? She thought about ten days, but wasn't sure. It was hard to keep track of time when you were cut off from the outside world.

The aroma of food made its way down into her dungeon, so she knew he was cooking. When he entered this time, he had a smile on his face and a white rose on the tray. Did he know what the color meant? Beth Ann knew many flower meanings because it was something in which she'd always been interested. White meant purity and innocence, silence or secrecy, also reverence and humility. The silence and secrecy fit, no doubt about that.

"Hello, Peter. That smells wonderful." She glued on a smile.

"Thank you, my love. I made it just for you and I have a big surprise for you." He set it down on the small table and put a spoon and pink napkin beside the bowl. He went to the cabinet and pulled down a vase that he filled with water. He had his back to her while he did it and was gathering something out of a box. She thought about walloping him then, but she tensed up and didn't move.

"Here you go my love. I wanted to show you how much I love you. I know these mean a lot to you."

Beth Ann swallowed the burning tears. It was her Bible, the picture of her and Gram and the cross from her house.

"Thank you, Peter. This means the world to me." She clutched the bible to her chest.

"I know and I wanted you to have them."

Crazy jerk she wanted to say, but instead asked, "Are you joining me tonight?"

"I wish I could, but as you may have noticed, I've been gone a lot and working long hours." He didn't even look at her. "Are you lonely?"

"I just wish I had a little TV or a clock, for when I work out. Oh well, at least I have my bible and all the other memorabilia." She took a bite of soup. "This is very good, Peter. Thank you."

He nodded. "I'll bring you down a clock, and I'll give the TV some thought." He turned and started to exit the room but glanced back. "I'm sorry for not thinking of those things already. I want you to be happy here."

"That's okay," she said. "You've had a lot to remember, and I know it can't be easy taking care of me." Using her best acting ability, she gave him an innocent glance. "If you ever trust me enough to help you, I can make kitchens sparkle."

He stared into her eyes and said nothing. But when he shut the door, he must have stood there thinking, because she counted to forty before she heard him go up the stairs.

That night she dreamed of her honeymoon in Hawaii. She and Kaylob were on the beach, running through the sand. When they stopped, she noticed a boat in the distance, and someone on it was watching them with binoculars. Was that Peter? Had he been watching her in Hawaii on her honeymoon? She had pointed to the boat and told Kaylob it had been out there for days. He waved toward the area, thinking it was another couple or someone living on their boat. Now, even in her dreams, she knew it must have been Peter.

The next morning as she pushed away the sleepy haze, she heard footsteps and tried her best to keep her eyes closed and feign sleep. A few minutes later, she felt him sit lightly on the bed, so she pulled her blanket up around her face.

"Beth Ann ..." He leaned close to her ear. "Guess what I have sitting outside the door for you."

Sticking her nose out from under the cover, she took a deep breath and asked, "What?"

He went to the door and opened it. When she peeked at him from under the covers, she saw him setting up a small TV. He put rabbit ears on top, then he turned and smiled at her.

"You can get about four stations with the antenna." He switched the channels and played with some type of knob on the rabbit ears. She heard the sound come on and he laughed. "There you go, love. It's all set up." He turned the TV off, then walked over and smiled down at her. "Now you can stop your sulking, because you got what you wanted."

Yeah, right. What she wanted was to go home and leave this craziness, but she knew asking would just set them back. Right now, he was acting as if he were beginning to trust her. He turned to leave, but stopped to look back when she said his name.

"Peter, thank you so much for spoiling me."

His face lit up like a Phantom on Halloween.

"You're welcome, and there's more where that came from. You have a good day, and I'll make sure to be home in time for dinner."

She wanted to play it right, so she forced a smile. "Promise?"

He nodded. "Of course, love."

As soon as he shut the door when he left, she almost threw up. Being nice to him made her want to scream. She needed to get home to Kaylob and everyone she loved. Tears flooded down her cheeks to think how worried Gram must be.

She jumped out of bed and ran over to turn on the TV. It greeted her with the sound of other voices, which were a warm welcome. Even the commercials she had hardly ever watched were golden to her ears now.

Having the TV was nice and all, but still, the morning was dragging. Beth Ann was grateful for that because she was not looking forward to Peter coming back and having dinner with her. She had some snacks and a hot plate with a few cans of soup that he'd brought down, so she could make do until dinner time. He'd pretty much stocked the kitchen with everything she needed. She picked up one of the cans and thought about what a good weapon it could make. Maybe she could knock him out with it. She could just see the headlines: *Tony Winner Kills Kidnapper With Can Of Vegetable Soup.* She had to laugh at that, but her mind still raced with thoughts of how she really could take him out.

One way or another, she was determined to get away. And it would be soon.

Chapter Sixteen

Kaylob sat on the couch, waiting for Blake to call. He watched the dark, ominous clouds outside his window. His mood matched the storm that was getting ready to break. Beth Ann had been gone for over a week, and he was riddled with worry. There had been no leads and nobody coming forward with any information. It was a miracle he was still able to stand. Now he had a glimpse of what Beth Ann had been through when he was missing and later declared dead. If he lost her, he would want to join her.

Frankie had been with him the whole time, spending hours studying so he wouldn't fall behind. The books he studied seemed like another language to Kaylob. Frankie was going to make a great attorney and had to be smart to be able to understand any of that stuff. Frankie walked into the room just then with his head down in one of those foreign things.

"Do you really enjoy that?" Kaylob pointed to the book.

"Hell, yes." Frankie nodded. "I've been thinking about Beth Ann though, and my mind keeps drifting. Do you think she's okay?"

"Yes, I know she is. I can't explain it, but I can feel her thinking about me. Last night I even heard her whisper when I was dozing off."

There was a light knock at the door, then Lenard and Jack walked in, Jack's eyes were full of worry. "Any news?"

"Not yet." Kaylob stood and hugged them both.

"It's just a matter of time before they find her." Lenard squeezed Kaylob's arm and turned toward Frankie. "How are you doing?"

"I'm okay. Just really worried and having a hard time keeping my mind on my studies."

Jack and Lenard both sat on the couch. "I wish we could do something to help," Jack said, brushing the hair from his eyes. "We heard that Blake is working hard with a top team of investigators."

Lenard nodded. "We saw him on the news. And he spoke well about you, Kaylob. He said you refused to give up hope and were diligent in waiting for a call from her."

Kaylob sat in the chair across from them. "Blake's been working hard at trying to find any clues since I'm stuck here waiting on her call. The police don't think I should leave either. I want to be out looking for her, but I also want to be here so if there's that one moment when she gets to a phone, it'll be me she hears first." His voice broke and he straightened his shoulders. He couldn't let himself fall apart.

"Anybody want some coffee or pop?" Frankie asked, no doubt trying to change the subject.

"Sure," Jack said. "I'll help get it." He turned to Lenard. "Pop, honey?"

"Yes, please."

"Kaylob, you want something?" Jack asked.

"No, I'm okay."

Jack and Frankie went to the kitchen and came back with drinks and chips. Lenard cleared a spot for them on the table and picked up the picture of Peter the cops had left.

"Holy shit," he said. "We saw this guy here!" He gave the picture to Jack. "He was carrying all those bags, remember?"

Jack studied the photo and nodded. "I said good morning to him." He looked at Lenard then back at Kaylob.

"He was just bringing his daughter to see Beth Ann," Kaylob said. "She's one of her students at the school and wanted private lessons. Peter works for Blake as one of his top realtors. That's how he met Beth Ann in the first place when she was with Blake way back when."

Lenard shook his head. "No, you guys were at Gram's wedding and not even in town when we saw him." He took the picture back from Jack. "He was here while we were watching your house, so he couldn't have been here for his daughter."

Kaylob stood up. "Are you fucking serious? Beth Ann didn't start working privately with his daughter until after we got back from Gram's wedding." Kaylob felt his heart start to race.

"He was here carrying some bags." Jack nodded. "I thought he lived here."

"I didn't like the guy as soon as I saw him." Lenard shook his head. "He gave me the creeps, so I watched him go to his car. It was black with tinted windows."

"We need to call Blake and the police right now!" Frankie ran to the phone and started dialing.

"That bastard must have her!" Kaylob started pacing the room. "But the cops searched his house and found nothing."

Lenard's eyes got wide. "If he's a real estate agent, I bet he has another house or maybe a house that's vacant and one of his listings."

"Shit, shit, that's why he's never home!" Kaylob rubbed his hand through his hair. "The neighbors told the police, he's hardly ever around."

"Frankie," Lenard almost shouted. "Tell Blake to find out what other houses this guy owns or has listed that might be empty."

Frankie covered the phone. "Dana's trying to find a number where we can reach him." He tapped a pencil on the table nervously while he waited.

"What can we do while we're waiting?" Jack asked Kaylob. "Want us to go to a neighbor and call the police while Frankie's on hold?"

"Yes, please." Kaylob was feeling sick. "Damn it, why didn't we dig deeper? And how the hell did this guy get a key to our house?"

"Maybe he stole it from Beth Ann's purse at the school," Lenard said.

"Christ, I bet you're right." Kaylob took deep breaths, trying to calm himself down as Jack and Lenard rushed out the door.

After what seemed like an hour, Frankie hung up and the phone rang again. Frankie answered it, then handed it to Kaylob. "It's Deluca."

"Peter Steel has her!" Kaylob said into the phone. "Our friends saw him here when we were out of town!"

"Yes, they just called us," Deluca said. "We're heading back over to Steel's house. I'm getting a search warrant as we speak and we'll check it from top to bottom this time."

Kaylob exhaled. "You have to find that maniac!"

"We will," Deluca said. "I'll call you back as soon as we know something."

Lenard and Jack came bursting through the door and glanced around at everyone.

Jack rubbed the back of his head. "I realized that bastard is probably the one who hit me upside my head." He looked at Kaylob then back to Lenard. "Blake will know how to find him, so we can find her."

"Blake is headed to Peter's office now," Frankie said. "He called the secretary and told her to pull every transaction Peter has done this last year—every house, every commercial account, every property he's managing."

"We have to find out where he has her!" Kaylob needed a minute to process it all, so he left them in the kitchen and went back to the living room. Staring out the window at the storm, he fought to control the one raging inside him. Man, when he got his hands on that asshole, he was going to make him regret being alive.

The most important thing right now was he had to keep a clear head so they could figure out how to find Beth Ann. They knew who had her, so they just had to figure out where.

Please, God. Keep her safe until we get there.

* * * *

Beth Ann knew evening was approaching from the darkness she could see gathering outside the small window. Peter had said he'd be there for dinner, and dread crept through her, holding her breath captive. Closing her book, she leaned her head against the cool cover and tried to memorize every plan. It was said that time will tell, but in her situation, she couldn't take the time. All she wanted was to escape.

She got up and hid the book on the shelf with all the others. She couldn't stand the silence any longer, so she flipped on the TV and was stunned to see a picture of herself and Peter on the split screen. Holy midnight, they were talking about him being a possible suspect, and there was a reward offered for information.

"When did all this happen?" she whispered to nobody.

Next, the camera scanned over to Blake. *Oh my god,* she placed her hand over her mouth as tears filled her eyes. He looked so tired and

148

ragged. She turned up the sound so she could hear better.

"Yes, we're offering one hundred thousand dollars to anyone who helps bring her home," Blake said, his voice breaking. "Her husband is at home waiting by the phone and hasn't left since she vanished. Please, if you have any information, contact one of the two numbers."

They scrolled the contact numbers across the screen. One was her home phone and the other she didn't recognize. Just before they cut back to the news person, Blake swiped away a tear.

The emotion caused sharp pains in her stomach, just knowing that Kaylob was waiting for her day after day. It also touched her deeply that Blake and Kaylob seemed to be working together to bring her home, when they hated each other so much. They were both hurting and didn't know if she was alive or dead. She definitely knew how painful that could be.

They were both good guys. She was madly in love with Kaylob, but Blake would always hold a special place in her heart. She'd known all along that he would never hurt anybody, even though at times she had wondered if it was him calling.

Peter, on the other hand, was the psychopath who had hit her dear friend Jack upside the head and left him for dead after he drugged him. The guy was pure evil and wicked. Who takes someone away from their loved ones and didn't have one ounce of remorse? A sick bastard like Peter, that's who.

Blake's words soared through her again. Kaylob was sitting there waiting for her. Rage burned through her insides, and her face got hot.

"I hate you, Peter, and I *will* get away!"

Angry tears coursed down her cheeks. She struggled to breathe, and with each gasp of air, another sob escaped. At that moment, she wanted to kill Peter and easily imagined bashing his brains out. She sank down to the couch and tried to collect herself, because she needed to be able to play out her plan.

Once the sobs finally stopped, she got up and walked into the bathroom. The mirror didn't lie, and there was no missing the red rings around her eyes. When she touched them, the skin underneath stung. She opened up the medicine cabinet to grab some aspirin, and that's when she noticed the bottle of cough syrup. The label said it contained codeine and included a warning: *Do not drive. May cause marked drowsiness.*

Perfect! Peter had put some wine in the cabinets. What if she poured the whole bottle of cough syrup inside? It was cherry flavored, so would it taste funny or would the flavor of the wine hide it? She ran to the kitchen and opened a bottle of the red wine to take a swig. Wow, it tasted pretty darn good. She poured some into a glass to make room in the bottle for the cough syrup, then she emptied the whole bottle of it into the wine and shook it well. When she tasted it again, she smiled.

"Not bad, not bad at all. This just might do the trick."

She set the table and dimmed the lights, then she lit a candle. Maybe tonight would be her freedom night. Her idea of Independence Day would be to watch the asshole fall to the floor and break his neck.

"Jesus, I'm getting a bit twisted." She laughed, but stopped and decided she needed to focus on prayer instead. But what should she say? She thought about Gram and how she might pray, and the words in their song came back to her: *It is no secret what God can do.*

Beth Ann took a deep breath, folded her hands and spoke to God. Maybe he would cause Peter to leave the door unlocked so she could make a run for it.

Chapter Seventeen

Another hour passed and Peter was still not there. Beth Ann began to imagine that he'd been arrested. If he was, it wouldn't take long for them to find her. However, her fantasy ended when she heard the clunking of his footsteps vibrating through the house. A few minutes later ,he opened the door and came in carrying food on a tray. His lips curled down with a scowl, and his eyes slanted when he looked at her. He placed the food on the table silently, then tugged out of his wet jacket.

"Hi, Peter. How was your day?"

"Not good. They found out about us, and now I won't be able to work anymore. Luckily, I have enough money saved that I don't need to." He lifted the two styrofoam containers that held the food from the tray to reveal steak, green beans and some type of potato. "The good news is we're going to be spending a lot of time together now." His smile sent a cold chill up her spine as he set down the steak knives.

"Is that such a bad thing?" Beth Ann pretended to like the idea. "Don't you think we need to get to know each other better?"

"Yes." He nodded. "But now I won't be able to see my daughter."

His face went into a frown, and for a second Beth Ann thought he was going to cry. How could he be so sweet about his little girl and still be a psychotic kidnapper? She sat down at the table and poured wine into the glasses, he handed a steak knife to her.

"Well, how about tonight we just relax and enjoy our dinner?" She picked up her napkin and spread it on her lap. "Peter, this food looks wonderful." She picked up the wine glass and put it to her lips to make him think she was taking a sip.

"You're right, my love. Tonight we'll just have fun." He sat down and spread the napkin on his lap. "I'll figure everything out tomorrow. I may just show up at my house to prove I don't have you."

"Are you sure you should do that? They might arrest you." She dabbed at her lips daintily. "We don't want that. Besides, I would worry about you."

She took a deep breath and placed a small piece of steak in her mouth, praying she could swallow. "How do you know they suspect you?"

All he did was stare at her with a creepy grin, so she concentrated on her food and did her best to avoid making eye contact. He picked up his glass and chugged the entire thing, then he refilled it. "I overheard Janice telling another worker today that Blake wanted them to pull every transaction I did this year. I knew something was up, so I slipped out the back door and got the hell out of there. I ran by my house, packed a few things and got dinner."

"Good thing you overheard that." Beth Ann tried to smile, but it was a chore. Then a thought occurred to her. The food was still warm. That was a big clue.

How long would it take for the cough syrup to work? He hadn't reacted to the taste, so that filled her with hope. Had she put enough in? There was no way to know because she'd never done anything like that before. It wasn't even in one of her plans, but this seemed better.

When the wine bottle was empty and Peter was still awake, her heart sank. It hadn't worked! But maybe it just hadn't had time, so she continued to observe him as she nibbled at her food, feeling her stomach twist into knots. What if he tried to touch her tonight?

Why had she set this dinner in motion and made him think it might get romantic? Maybe this wasn't such a good plan after all, because now he was staring at her with silent concentration. His eyes stalked her, and her palms began to sweat.

The man was creepy with a capital C.

When she finished her dinner, she rose to do the dishes and Peter stood with her. He moved closer and caressed her arm, then pulled her to him.

"I love that you would worry about me, Beth Ann." She could smell the alcohol when he leaned close to her ear. "I want you tonight."

His lips grazed her neck and she flinched. Her eyes shot down to the fork on her plate and made her think about stabbing his eyes out, but what if she missed and he got angry?

She backed away from him with the plate in her hand and set it down. "You're drunk, Peter. This can't happen tonight."

"Why?" He slammed his fist on the counter. "You're the one who got me drunk. You can't just tease me!" He moved toward her again, his gaze crawling over her. "We're gonna make love tonight. I've already seen you naked, and I know I can make you feel good."

"Get away from me, you sick bastard!" Her body convulsed at the thought.

"You've been playing me, haven't you?" He yanked her into his arms. "I'm taking what's mine tonight, and you're gonna like it!"

He tried to kiss her, but she managed to push him backwards, then picked up the plate, hurling it at his face and nailing him right in the forehead. A gash appeared as blood splattered and started running down his nose.

He wiped off the blood and stared at his fingers.

"I'm gonna teach you a lesson for that. You're my woman now, so you'd better get used to it." He darted over and grabbed her wrist, glaring at her. "I'm tying you up, and you'll only get to do what I allow you to do. You won't shower, sleep, or go to the bathroom alone. You're gonna be punished." He paused to cackle. "And spanked."

"Go to hell, Peter. You're not going to touch me!" She balled up her fist and threw a punch that landed under his cheekbone, then she kicked him in the balls the way she'd learned to do in class.

He groaned and bent over, holding his crotch. "Goddamn it, you're a spicy little redheaded bitch, aren't you?"

She stood in her stance, ready to fight the way her self-defense instructor had taught her. "Fuck you, Peter!" She was ready to kick his ass.

"You're funny, Beth Ann." He lunged at her then clamped his sweaty hands on the back of her neck, forcing her to look at his twisted face. "I told you, you're mine now." He dragged her to the bed and shoved her down onto it. "I want you, and now I'm not gonna wait for you to be ready. I'll make you fall in love with me if it's the last thing I do!"

He fell on her and invaded her mouth, making her heave with nausea. She bit down on his lip and hit him again on the side of the head.

"Goddamn you, stop fighting me!" He grabbed her wrist. "Let's make this nice. I don't want to hurt you."

Still holding her wrist with one hand, he reached underneath the bed for something, and she didn't want to wait to see what it was. She had to take him down now. With all her strength, she raised her foot and launched it right between his eyes, throwing him backward to fall on the floor with a loud thump. She jumped off the bed to look, hoping the fall had knocked him out, but then she saw the fury in his eyes.

"You'll be sorry for doing that!" he snarled at her.

She ran to the table and grabbed the knife, holding it up in front of her. "Stay away from me or I'll stab you!"

"Like hell you will." He charged at her again.

With every bit of power she had, she plunged the knife deep into his neck and heard a horrible crunching sound. Blood went everywhere—on her shirt, hands, and it even splattered onto her face.

Peter's eyes went wide and he covered his neck, but the blood poured out over his hand. Slowly his legs buckled and he went to the floor with a thud. It was like watching a horror movie to see the blood ooze from his neck as he tried to stand, but he kept falling down.

"Why, Beth Ann?" He stared at her and struggled to his knees. "I didn't want to hurt you. I *love* you." He coughed and blood dribbled from his mouth too. "You'll die out there if you leave." Tears flooded his eyes. "I can't believe you stabbed me."

With no other thought but escaping, she ran to the door, but it was locked, so she went back and grabbed Peter's jacket. She whispered a silent prayer of thanks when she heard the keys jingling inside one of the pockets. "Thank God," she uttered, and could almost taste freedom, but there were so many keys! How would she ever find the right one?

"Beth Ann, you can't get away." Peter's voice was faint. "I take apart the car every night so it won't start. You'll never find the parts." He winced while still trying to get up. "We have no phones, and we're surrounded by hundreds of miles of wilderness. If you leave, you'll just have to come back, or I'll have to come and find you." His threats seemed ludicrous with the knife still in his neck.

"At least I'll be away from you, and that's all that matters!" She grabbed a bottle of water to take with her and kept his jacket.

"Beth Ann, please. Something's not right. Help me …"

With the keys in her hand, ready to flee, she froze at the door and reluctantly turned to look at him. He was either bleeding to death, or the cough syrup was finally kicking in. Every time he tried to get up, he'd stumble and fall over again. A part of her felt she should save him. He did have a daughter, after all. But the thought of being locked up again, made her decide against it. Once she got to safety, she'd tell someone she stabbed him and he needed help. Right now, escape was all that mattered.

For what seemed like an eternity, she fumbled until she found the right key that unlocked the door. When it opened, she pushed it so hard that she dropped all the keys, then made a fast decision to run and get her Bible. She was at least going to take that with her. With her heart in her throat, she snatched up the keys again, and ran like hell. As she rushed through the house, she didn't take time to check for a phone. The place was dark, and she was too afraid he'd come upstairs and drag her back to that dungeon. The second she stepped through the front door into the rain and wind, she screamed at the top of her lungs.

"Help me! Someone please help me!"

Not one sound. Only her heart jackhammering against her ribs.

"Help!" She yelled again and again, but it was clear there was nobody around.

She bent over, trying to catch her breath and saw the car, the one that had been following her all those months. She had to at least see if it would start. The rain was blinding her with unexpected fury that made it even harder to find the right key, but luckily she found a tiny flashlight on the key ring that helped her spot what appeared to be a car key.

Please, God, let that be the right one, and please let it start!

The key worked on the door, but nothing happened when she tried the ignition. Not even the lights came on. "Damn you, Peter!" She tried it one more time to no avail, then she pounded the steering wheel with her fists and lay her head against it, tears streaming down her face.

But there was no time for crying now. With the tiny flashlight's small beam of light, she examined the inside of the car and spotted a blanket, some snack bags and a newspaper, then she saw the best find of all—a leather overnight bag. She scooped everything up, including her Bible and put it all inside the bag along with the bottle of water and the jacket she'd brought with her. She didn't know what she'd do with any of it, but she took it all anyway.

The minutes were ticking by and she needed to get the hell away from there, so she slid out of the car into the wet, stormy night. All she could concentrate on was getting as far away as possible from the prison Peter had built for her. Rain pelted her face, but she didn't care. She took off running and ran for her life.

The road was full of potholes, so she sparingly used the flashlight to guide her. She couldn't risk falling into one and twisting her ankle or letting that maniac find her. Saving the battery was also important because she had no idea where she was or how far she needed to go. She knew it was risky to keep running as fast as she could, but it gave her a sense of freedom.

After running nonstop for what felt like hours, she had to stop for a short break. Gasping for air, she tried to get a look at her surroundings. It was dark and spooky, plus she was soaking wet and her legs were shivering. When her teeth started chattering, she knew the temperature had plummeted. As much as she hated to wear anything of his, she slipped on Peter's oversized jacket. Her stomach clenched with repulsion, but at least it warmed her.

So far, she hadn't seen a single house, car, or any sign of life, just one sign that said for sale, with a phone number and it was nothing but empty raw land. He had brought her out to the middle of nowhere. Her breath became ragged as fear slammed into her. The question kept plaguing her, what if Peter recovers enough to fix his car and comes looking for her. Maybe the anxiety was playing tricks on her, because shadows seemed to be lurking everywhere.

That knife hadn't seemed to be very sharp, so there was no way to know how far it went into his neck. He'd been struggling when she left, but that might have been from the cough syrup. How long before that would wear off? What was codeine anyway—a sleeping drug?

She decided to get off the road in case he came after her. Maybe she should have tried to lock him in the room, but all she could think of at the time was getting out of there and getting the hell away from that monster, dropping the keys hadn't helped either.

With that in mind, she headed towards the side of the road, lined with thick bushes and rocks covering the ground. She tried her best to survey the area, but couldn't make out anything but dense vegetation ahead. It must be a forest, but how big and deep was it? As she scurried through the night like a wild animal, she kept looking behind her, expecting him to be there. Every now and again, she'd hear something and would crouch down behind a tree, but it would turn out to be just the shadows in the night, maybe from the passing clouds or trees she moved passed.

Her pace didn't slow much despite having to navigate the forest. Bushes scraped against her legs, and she kept tripping over boulders that sent her tumbling to the wet ground. At any rate, it was better than being killed or even worse, getting raped and tortured. She stood and brushed off her soggy pants and was glad she'd put on jeans and a long-sleeved blouse, even though right now she was soaked and chilled to the bone.

Her stride eventually slowed as she continued going deeper into the unknown. At times, the wind would slow her down, but her will was strong and she pushed forward. After what seemed like forever, her legs would hardly move. How long had it been? One, two, three hours? She had no clue. The only thing that made her feel better was that there had been no sign of Peter.

She was trembling when she finally came to a stop and glanced around. "I have to get warm," she whispered, and pointed the flashlight to the far right and saw a large tree, so she made her way underneath the branches. The rain no longer hammered her, and she was happy to find it was almost dry. At least she'd have shelter. Using her foot, she cleared the area and spread out the blanket on the ground.

Once she climbed into the center of it, she wiggled out of Peter's jacket and grabbed the corners, wrapping herself up like a cocoon next to the base of the tree. She huddled inside for as much warmth as she could find. Her soaked clothes chilled her, but that wasn't all that made her shiver. It was the unknown things that lurked out in the darkened night.

"I'm coming back to you, Kaylob," she stammered. "I won't stop until I get back home."

Slowly she warmed up a bit, and just as she was starting to doze off, the sound of a loud crack and rustling made her jump. She froze and listened, moving closer to the tree. It had sounded like a tree branch falling, so she closed her eyes and prayed that nothing landed on her. Somehow, while listening to all the nighttime sounds, she drifted off to sleep and dreamed that instead of being wrapped in a thin blanket in the woods, she was wrapped in Kaylob's arms in their bed.

Chapter Eighteen

The morning light made its way through the wool material of the blanket, pulling her reluctantly from her wonderful dream. Her eyes took a moment to focus, and her mind was absorbing all that had happened the night before. She jumped up, ready to run and was relieved to find that Peter still hadn't found her. In fact, the only sounds she heard were birds singing and a woodpecker pecking. When she saw a giant tree branch lying on the ground to her left, she knew that had to be what she'd heard the night before.

Once she surveyed the surroundings, she let out a deep sigh. Thank God, she was even deeper into the forest than she'd thought. Somehow, she had made it far away from the road. Now she had to figure out which direction to go and how to find help.

There was no way she'd venture back to where she'd come from. If Peter had survived, he'd be searching for her for sure. She reached above her head and did a big stretch, trying to get the kinks out of her neck. It was time to hit the trail again. She shook off her blanket and picked up the coat, tucking them away in the leather bag. She would examine the contents later, but right now the further away she got, the better.

As the small trail weaved its way through thick bushes, she glanced around for any sign of life—a broken bottle, newspaper, empty can, but there was nothing. It was as though nobody had ever passed this way before. That couldn't be true, could it?

She swatted at the flies that tried to land on her. "Get away," she demanded, but they weren't listening, so she picked up a fallen branch and decided that would be her flyswatter.

As the morning turned into afternoon, the sun came out and the temperature warmed. It helped that the rain had stopped, even though moisture was everywhere. The little trail was leading downward, and she could only hope she was heading in the right direction. Surely, she'd stumble across something soon, like a person hiking or a cabin.

As she marched on, she continued swinging at the bugs that swarmed around her. That's when she noticed Peter's blood was still on her hands, she realized that was attracting the insects. That wasn't good. She'd already attracted an evil snake that she'd had to stab with a steak knife. She didn't need any more pests.

What she did need was to figure out where she was. What kind of forests were in Southern California that you could get lost in? Well, that was a silly question.

"The one I'm in right now," she said, shaking her head.

Wait, she'd heard of Big Bear and some other mountain areas. Sadly, for her, considering her current situation, her musical studies and Kaylob's restaurant life had kept them from exploring the mountains. Any chance they got to take some time away for a day was usually spent at the ocean or on a picnic. And when she'd been with Blake, they'd stayed in five-star hotels, and the only mountains they'd seen were the Swiss Alps. That wasn't going to help her now.

While she trudged down the trail, dust clung to her clothes and water dripping from the trees soaked her hair and face. The bugs were getting worse by the minute. Up ahead, she spotted a wider path that appeared to be more than just an animal trail. She headed toward it, but something made her stop and listen. What was that? Could it be …

"All right!"

She hurried toward the little waterfall coming from a hillside nearby. It wasn't much, but it would be enough to wash her hands and clean up some. And if it smelled fresh, she could refill her water bottle. As soon as she placed her hands in the stream, ice almost formed on her fingers. It was freezing, but refreshing. It was way too cold to bathe in, but at least she was able to rinse away that bastard's blood from her hands, and that definitely made her feel better.

Glancing down at her shirt, she frowned when she saw how much of Peter's blood was on it too. The thought of the knife sticking out of his neck flashed through her mind, causing her to gag. Never had she imagined doing harm to another person like that, even if that person was a crazy man.

She found two rocks and used them with the water to remove as much of the blood stains as she could. While she scrubbed, she realized she'd learned to do that from the Indians on the reservation, they'd lived there when she was small, and she was pleased as heck that she remembered it. Thank God for that.

Now, so long as the shirt dried before the sun went down, hypothermia wouldn't get her. And being on a wider path gave her hope that she would be found. Maybe she'd run into someone that way. She didn't want to sleep out in the elements again. Besides the weather and bugs, there might be bears or mountain lions. Wait, what kind of wild animals lived in the forests in California in January? Didn't they hibernate during those times? At least she was sure there were no alligators, she could be thankful for that. Right?

She continued down the trail, listening to the birds singing and scurrying noises in the bush. That made her think about snakes and lizards. Lizards she could handle, but snakes not so much. The sun was high above the mountains, so she thought that meant it was early afternoon. If only she'd learned more about the outdoors from the Indians. On the reservation, she remembered hearing stories of survival, and some of the natives had shown her which wild plants you could eat, but she didn't remember much of it since she'd only been eight years old at the time. She'd certainly never thought it might save her life someday.

Her legs were getting tired, and she needed to take a break. Just as she started to sit down, she spied a large hill ahead that could give her a view of what was down below. Maybe she'd see a ranger station or cabin. She had to at least check it out. Even though she was exhausted, she pushed forward.

When she reached the hillside, it turned out to be steeper than she'd thought at first. She put the bag strap over her shoulder and climbed, sometimes crawling to reach the top. At one point, she grabbed a rock to tug herself up, then yanked it away when she felt a sharp pain.

"Ouch! Crap." Crawling away was the ugliest brown spider she'd ever seen.

Two red marks that looked like they came from fangs caused her hand to throb. The spider had run off, but now she knew she had to watch out for more arachnids, which she'd never been fond of anyway.

She resumed climbing, being careful where she stuck her hand, and finally reached the top. Sitting on the ground, she took a deep, cleansing breath, then examined her hand. It was already red and swollen.

"Well, that's not good," she said while holding her hand.

She glanced down at the vast wilderness, but nothing came into view. Only trees, brush, and rocks. Her lips started to tremble, and she started to wonder how anybody would ever find her. No, she couldn't let herself think that way. Someone would rescue her, or she'd find her own way out.

"You stop that right now!" she said, tapping her quivering lips with her fingers. No, she wouldn't be a victim. Not now, not ever again.

Something drew her attention way down in the canyon, and she rubbed her eyes, making sure it wasn't her imagination. Yes, it was either a narrow river or wide creek. She'd heard someone say once that if you follow the direction of water, it's always going somewhere.

Now that she had a plan, she'd head down into the canyon and follow the flowing water. At least she'd be able to drink and wash up. Besides, someone had to be out there beyond the trees and bushes in the vast forest.

As she made her way back down the hillside, she made sure her bag was secure with the strap over her shoulder. Finally, she reached the path once again, then froze immediately when she heard footsteps.

Holy crap! Is it Peter?

She fell onto her stomach into the thick brush. Could Peter have tracked her here? There was no way he was capturing her again. She searched the ground for something to use as a weapon, and her hand touched a very large rock. Her palms began to sweat and her stomach fluttered as she held on to it. She would break his head open if she had to. She wasn't going to cower in fear. Slowly, she peeked just above the bush she was under.

Oh, God. Right in front of her, almost touching her nose, were the biggest brown eyes she'd ever seen, and they belonged to the most gorgeous baby deer in the world. She'd never been so thrilled to see a creature in her entire life. She sighed and laughed at the fawn with cute little spots. The mother had to be nearby, so Beth Ann scanned the area and saw Mom staring back at her. Very carefully, she backed away so they'd know she wasn't a threat.

After a few moments of enjoying the wildlife that didn't bite, Beth Ann continued on her way. The hours passed slowly and she found nothing in the way of shelter. Her legs were tired and hurting, and her hand was throbbing. She needed to stop and make camp for the night, and she was so hungry that her stomach was burning with sharp pains. Even a couple cookies would help, and she wanted to take inventory of what food she had.

Surveying the area, she spied a large tree surrounded by thick brush that seemed perfect and should offer her some protection. The carry bag was a blessing because it kept everything clean, safe and dry. She spread out her blanket at the base of the tree, then emptied everything out of the bag. Holy Treasure Alert, there were cookies and a pack of Tootsie Rolls along with three bags of potato chips and two small boxes of raisins.

"And look at this," she said, holding up a matchbook.

Then she couldn't believe her eyes as she pulled out a spare shirt, a bundle of rope and an unused toothbrush.

"Yay!" She cheered and tore off the bloody shirt, ripping it up and throwing it away. Even after washing it, there were still spots of Peter's blood on it.

"Gross." She wrinkled her nose.

Maybe the birds or an animal could use it for nesting. She slipped on the long-sleeved dress shirt and didn't care that it was extra large. It was fresh and had no scent of Peter.

All the snacks were looking almost as good as Kaylob's Chicken Marsala.

"Oh, Kaylob," she whispered. "I miss you so much. I promise I'm coming home."

Her heart ached, but she shut her eyes, trying to push back the tears. Wrapping her arms around herself, she could almost feel him cradling her. Her body needed food, but she needed him more.

Shielding her eyes from the afternoon sun, she looked around. There were tree branches and sticks that she could use along with the small rope. Peter the Pig had probably used it to tie her up when he'd kidnapped her, but now it could help secure a shelter instead of hurting her.

She gathered branches, leaves, and used the newspaper from Peter's car to build a tent, then she used the rope to secure everything in place. She needed to put all the food somewhere so the bears wouldn't smell it. An opening in the tree worked perfectly for that.

While she fluffed the jacket up to use as a pillow she felt something hard poking her. She hadn't thought about checking the pockets. She stuck her hand in one and was delighted to find some tissue, two candy bars that were a little squished and a Swiss army knife. Now with the matches she could easily start a fire to keep the big old bears away. At least she hoped it would. She thought she'd heard somewhere that wild animals didn't like fire.

She stared at the knife and smiled. "This might just come in handy."

She examined the jacket's other pockets and found some more goodies. Ten dollars and the receipt for the food he'd brought them for dinner, and she remembered that the food had still been warm when he got it to her. Of course, he could have turned on the heater in the car and blasted it like Kaylob used to do when he brought food home.

Then she looked at the receipt. It was from JB's Diner in Palm Springs, which she knew was on the main street down from Blake's office. She'd been there with him many times. Hope filled her heart because, if the food had still been warm, the restaurant couldn't be all that far away, that probably meant she was somewhere in Palm Springs.

She wrapped up in the wool blanket as she'd done the night before. At least it helped to keep the bugs away. With a deep sigh and dry throat, she thought about what the night might bring. She snuggled into her blanket cocoon under her woman-made shelter, nibbling on one of the candy bars and hoping and praying that nothing would find her and try to nibble on her.

The air temperature was dropping fast as the sun went down, and her teeth started to chatter. She decided to slip on the jacket and scoot as close to the base of the tree as she could, and it did offer some additional warmth.

"Kaylob, I hope you can feel me sending my love to you." Tears stung her eyes.

She started to drift off for the second night alone in the darkened forest. There was howling and rustling all around that woke her a few times as she slept. It was as though the forest was coming alive right when she was trying to rest. Sometime later, she jumped when the bushes started moving around her. She had forgotten to make a fire! Well, she was too scared and cold to do it now, so instead she said a silent prayer and reached in the bag placing her hand across the Bible.

Dear God, please keep me safe and let me return home to my husband. I ask you this with love and the belief that you will help guide me back to where I belong and not let me be dinner for a hungry animal.

Tomorrow she would make it to the river and start her journey home. Maybe she'd find someone camping or hiking who could help her. With that thought, she drifted off to sleep thinking about how happy she would be to see Kaylob.

Chapter Nineteen

Kaylob sat looking out his living room window at the early morning sky, holding Beth Ann's Tony award to his chest. His heart felt like he'd been sucker punched. Three more days had passed, and they were no closer to finding Beth Ann than they'd been in the beginning. Last night he'd thought he heard her talking to him, but when he woke up, there was no trace of her. His eyes burned and it was hard to breathe. All he wanted was his wife back home safe and sound.

He set the trophy down and gazed outside at the new winter blossoms.

"Beth Ann loves all those flowers," he whispered.

Frankie was in the shower, and Gram and Nickolas were still asleep. They'd arrived yesterday, and Kaylob had willingly given up his bed. He didn't want to sleep there until Beth Ann came home. Jean and Stanley had been staying at Blake's townhouse so they could help him go through files. They were checking every house that Peter had closed escrow on, and it seemed like it was taking forever. Some of the buyers were gone away on vacation, others seemed to be hard to get in touch with, then there were those who were not pleased at all to find out that their real estate agent was a kidnapper.

Blake had even been threatened with lawsuits, but Frankie said they couldn't do jack shit. It wasn't Blake's fault that a devoted father and a guy who looked perfectly normal was a nut case. Not to mention that he was a top-selling real estate agent.

Kaylob moved into the kitchen to fix a cup of coffee, but he jumped at the sound of someone pounding on the front door. Blake waved a folder at him when he opened it.

166

"I found something that looks promising!" He came in and handed the file to Kaylob. "This house is on a country road with no other houses around, very isolated." He rubbed his hand through his hair as he and Kaylob sat on the couch. "One of my agents said he went out there last month looking at some raw land for sale. He drove all the way down the road to see what the place was like and he saw some guys doing construction work."

Kaylob looked excited. "You think Steel could have her there?"

"It's a possibility," Blake said. "Donald Reid is the agent. He said he had clients with him and they didn't like the bumpy road leading out to the land. Reid said they had turned around to head back when he saw a black car in the driveway of the only house out there. He also remembered seeing a guy outside, but he had blond hair and Peter Steel's is brown." He arched a brow. "Could be a disguise. I know all about those, you know." He gave a small smile.

Kaylob tried to smile. "You mean, maybe he pulled a Blake Tanner?"

Blake nodded. "Maybe."

"Man, you look like hell." Kaylob notice Blake's haggard appearance. "Did you get any sleep last night?"

"Gee thanks, pal. No, I was up all night going through files. I have a feeling about this place and want to go check it out."

"How far away is it from here?" Kaylob asked.

"Maybe a little over an hour I think. And the road leading to the house is about twenty miles long. That's why I took Johnny's truck while he was in the shower. He was getting ready to go fishing, but the fish can wait. I had to show you this, and I thought Frankie might want to go with me."

"I'm going too." Kaylob looked at the phone and rubbed the base of his neck. "I need to get out of this house. I feel useless sitting here."

Blake shook his head. "You're not useless. Somebody had to stay here in case she called, and you know she'd want to talk to you first."

"If she hasn't called by now, she's not going to," Kaylob said, staring at the folder. "I don't think she's near a phone or can get to one."

Frankie walked into the room, drying his hair with a towel. "Hey, what's up?"

"I want to go with Blake to check out a lead," Kaylob said. "Can you stay by the phone in case Beth Ann calls? If she does, tell her I went to look for her and I love her."

Frankie nodded. "Sure thing, bud. What kind of lead is it?"

"We'll explain later," Blake said. "But this is the best lead we've had so far."

"Have you told the police?" Frankie asked.

Blake shook his head. "No, I was afraid they'd tell me to stay away, and I want to check it out myself. We'll call them after we check it out, but I guess it wouldn't hurt to call and give them this information after we leave. Where's a pen and paper?"

Kaylob went to the junk drawer and pulled out both. "Here you go."

Blake talked while he wrote. "This is the corporation that bought the property. I haven't been able to reach them on the phone, which seems a bit odd."

A few minutes later, they were getting in the truck. Kaylob climbed into the passenger seat and shut the door, then he took a deep breath. "I need to say something before we take off."

"Okay, what?" Blake took his hands off the key and looked at Kaylob.

"I want to thank you, first for helping search for Beth Ann, and also for how supportive you've been." Blake started to say something, but Kaylob held up his hand. "I know you're in love with her. Believe it or not, now I can imagine how hard it was for you to lose her. So thank you for doing this. You've worked your ass off."

A long minute passed, then Blake cleared his throat. "You're right, I've loved her since we were kids, but … I knew she was in love with you, even when we were together." His voice was thick with emotion. "I want her to be happy, and I know you're the only one who can do that." He looked up with a little smile. "So, my friend, let's go get her."

Kaylob nodded. "Let's do this."

Blake started the engine, and it roared to life. Kaylob continued glancing over at Blake and he must have felt it.

"What?"

"I need to say one more thing, but keep your eyes on the road," Kaylob said. "I don't wanna die before we find Beth Ann."

Blake nodded. "Okay, shoot."

"Look … I'm sorry I beat the shit out of you. It was wrong, and I was wrong about you."

Blake didn't say anything for a few seconds, then he looked at Kaylob and snickered. "Forget it. And I could've kicked your ass, but didn't want to embarrass you in front of everybody."

They both cracked up.

Blake shifted gears and a low grind jerked the truck. He shifted again and Kaylob almost got whiplash. "This stupid truck. I've never driven one before."

"Obviously," Kaylob said. "Pull over before you kill this old thing."

He didn't have to ask twice. Blake pulled over as soon as it was safe and they swapped places. Once they were on their way again, Kaylob chuckled.

"So you could have kicked my ass, huh?"

Blake shrugged. "Well, a man has to tell himself that."

"A man should know how to drive a truck." Kaylob shook his head. "Watch how I ease off the clutch and shift."

"A man shouldn't be driving this ugly beat-up truck."

They both chuckled again.

About forty-five minutes later, Blake pointed at an old dirt road. "Turn here. This is it."

Kaylob turned and the truck bounced as the tires crunched over the gravel. His heart was racing, and for some reason he knew they were in the right place. It was as though something electrical was pulling him down that road, and his foot pushed harder on the gas pedal. They drove in silence until a loud *vwomp* shook the whole truck.

"What the hell was that?" Blake was holding on to the dash with white knuckles.

"Shit, I think we blew a tire," Kaylob said as he pulled over.

"I'm not surprised at the way you were driving over those bumps at top speed," Blake said. "I hope he's got a spare."

They both got out and Kaylob walked around to the side and saw the flat tire. "I'll have it changed in no time." He had a feeling Blake had never changed a tire in his life. He got the jack from the toolbox and pulled the cover off the spare tire. "Uh-oh. This is not good."

"What's wrong?" Blake asked.

"The damn thing is flat as a pancake and has a giant hole in it." He stuck his finger in the hole and sighed. "I should have driven my own truck."

In a Southern drawl as thick as bean soup, Blake said, "Why in God's blue heaven didn't that man get another spare? I pay him enough damn money. I don't even know why he still drives this piece of shit." He looked around. "Now what do we do?"

"We walk," Kaylob said, I don't know what other choice we have. There's an ice chest in the back, let's see what's in it." He opened it and there were soda pops, a container of worms, and some wrapped sandwiches. "Let's take some of the drinks and sandwiches in case it gets late."

They both filled their pockets, then Blake said, "The police will come if we're not back soon. At least they know where we are."

"True," Kaylob agreed. "That's good because I don't know how many miles we've come down this road. If it's twenty miles like you said, we could have a long way to go. I didn't see any houses on the road before we turned down this one. It's better to keep going, than to try to find someone out in this isolated area." He slammed the ice chest shut and sighed. "Shit, I really blew it."

"Don't beat yourself up," Blake said. "This road is awful, and I don't know much about tread, but look at those tires." Blake pointed at the bald tires.

"Holy hell," Kaylob said. "You're right about that."

"Come on," said Blake. "Let's go find the redhead."

* * * *

As Beth Ann headed down the trail, she could hear branches cracking under her feet. She groaned at the way the pine needles stuck to her shoes because the darn sap acted like glue. The squirrels chattered and leaves rustled throughout the forest. The bag was slung across her shoulders, and the breeze chilled her a bit more than it had before. She was sure as heck glad to have a jacket and even more thankful that it no longer smelled like that creeper. Now it carried an earthy scent, like cedar and rotting wood, and she really enjoyed it.

Somehow the forest was comforting, something that really surprised her. It made her feel rejuvenated. The energy beckoned her deeper into the wilderness. It was if this place had a heartbeat, and Beth Ann could feel it and hear it. The screeches of what sounded like an angry animal startled her, but she just didn't feel afraid and had no clue why.

Maybe she had connected with the forest because it had saved her from Peter.

As soon as she got to the river, she planned on catching a fish and cooking it. That sounded really good about now. That bag of chips and one cookie for breakfast hadn't taken away the empty burn in her stomach.

After several hours of trudging through the forest, she still hadn't reached the river, but she needed to stop and eat again. Her legs were shaking, and she was a tad lightheaded. Ahead to the right was what she remembered the Indians calling a "nursing tree." She could sit there and eat a snack, and maybe heal the spider bite on her hand. This tree was especially powerful because of all the fauna growing from it. The Indians believe that when a tree falls, it sacrifices itself to heal others and give new life.

Once she sat down, she glanced around at her surroundings. The bugs weren't quite as bad here, probably because the breeze was keeping them away. She had to take a minute to enjoy the exquisiteness of the light that filtered through the trees. Like a spotlight, it showed off the lush green plants and leftover flowers that were beginning to fade.

"Food," she whispered after a few minutes, then she pulled out some more chips and one more cookie. Once she'd eaten it all, she stood and was just about to head down to the river when she spied a baby rabbit. She had a momentary thought that it could be used for food, but the bunny was so cute and fluffy that she couldn't even imagine killing it. She walked toward it, making crunching sounds, and watched it run away.

So far, she hadn't seen a bear or wild cat and hoped she wouldn't, but just in case she decided to carve a weapon when she got to the river. Even if she didn't need it for protection, she could use it to spear a fish. She had the knife and just needed to find a stick she could sharpen.

She started walking again and had a flash vision of Kaylob searching for her and thought she heard him calling out. She stopped and listened but didn't hear anything except the forest sounds.

When she came around the next curve in the trail, she could hear the whooshing sound of the water. There it was, less than fifty feet away with rocks everywhere. But what she had thought was a river from the distance looked more like a creek up close. This was where she needed to be, but disappointment washed over her at its size. Nevertheless, it was still big enough that it had to go somewhere, right?

She found another place right next to a tree hidden by the thick brush where she could set up shelter for the night. It was close to the water's edge, so it felt a bit cooler. That might not be such a good thing, but there were boulders she could use for heat when she started a fire. The Indians had shown her how to use them for warmth.

With a large piece of bark, she dug a hole in the ground then gathered firewood. Once she got the fire started, she collected the right type of rocks and placed them next to the flames. This would warm up the sleeping area and keep her toasty throughout the night. She was sure glad she had paid attention and remembered how well it worked.

Sitting by her fire and feeling rather proud of herself, she looked around and noticed all the beauty that surrounded her. It was lovely, the way the water curved gently through the forest and how nothing seemed able to stop the flow. Her mind drifted while she watched the flowing water. Just what would she find out there? Maybe a person, or a house, or a city. Better yet, maybe it would lead her home to Kaylob.

Okay, enough already. She needed to take inventory of her surroundings and gather her shelter. By the location of the sun, she thought it was around three o'clock or later. She had been hoping to make it here sooner, but there was still enough time to set up a safe place and maybe catch a fish.

First things first, she moved down to the edge of the creek and submerged her hands into the crystal-clear water. Holy Ice Cream, it was freezing. There was no way she could bathe in that. She'd freeze to death. Drinking it would be good, and maybe she could find a way to warm it up. She surveyed the area and something shiny caught her eye—an empty beer can that looked as though it had been left there eons ago. She could use the knife to cut off the top.

"Wow, I can boil some water now!"

The bite on her hand was still red but looked much better and didn't appear to be getting infected. She felt fine, so she wasn't worried. After gathering tree branches and building a shelter for the night, she sat by the fire and heated the can until the water came to a boil.

"Yay, it worked!" She was better at this than she would have ever imagined. "Maybe I found a new career as a survival guide." She had to laugh at that.

Once the water cooled off a little, she poured it over her hands and used a tissue to wash her face. Ah, it felt so good. Then she found a sturdy branch and sat down next to the fire to whittle it to a sharp point. When she was done, she held it up and admired her work.

"Wow! They can call me the jungle girl."

After she spent a few more minutes admiring her spear, she took a deep breath. The inner peace she felt was incredible and gave her a new sense of power. She'd been a helpless captive when Peter had her locked up, but she wasn't helpless anymore.

While night approached, she listened to the fire crackle outside her shelter and decided to try to spear a fish first thing in the morning. The flames should scare all the animals away. She'd planned to keep getting up throughout the night so she could keep it going, but after waking up twice and fanning it, she fell asleep.

Sometime later, a loud sound shattered her peaceful rest. A growl and rustle told her that danger was near, and the hair on the back of her neck stood on end. With trembling hands, she grabbed her spear and jumped out of the shelter, ready to fight.

What the heck, that's a skunk!

She watched it spraying what appeared to be a possum. Grrr! She jumped up and down, waving her spear at them, then watched as they ran away. However, the lovely skunk decided to leave her a gift and lifted its tail, dispensing a smell that made her gag.

Great. Just great.

She jumped back, not sure if he'd gotten her. Nothing was stinging, but the odor was horrific. She put some more wood on the fire to make the flames shoot higher, hoping that would keep any other critters away for the rest of the night.

Since she was awake and starving, she ate a few pieces of candy and another bag of chips. She was running out of snacks, and knew she needed real food to keep from feeling so weak. A little seed of fear sprouted. How much longer could she survive out here if there was no food? What if she couldn't catch a fish? Just thinking about that made her want to slap herself silly. Of course, she could catch a fish.

"Shut up Beth Ann," she scolded herself. "It can't be that hard to do."

The rest of the night was peaceful, and she stayed cozy with the rocks warming her. Her dreams once again were of Kaylob and Hawaii. She could see the crystal-clear water and glimmering sand. Her memories took her to the time they had pulled a blanket over them and made love on the beach while the sun sparkled across the water. Kaylob had called out her name many times that day.

During her beautiful dream, something once again was trying to wake her. *No, go away*, she thought. *I don't want to wake up.*

"*Arrooff, Arrooff!*" Sniff. Scratch.

"What the heck is that?" Beth Ann opened her eyes and felt her shelter moving around. "Is that a barking bear?" She had to giggle instead of being afraid.

She picked up her spear again, knowing full well that it would be no match for any kind of bear and would probably only piss it off.

"*Arrooff!*" Sniff. Sniff.

Of course that's a *dog?* Beth Ann stuck her head out and was greeted by a wet tongue across her face. She had to laugh at this golden dog who was so happy to see her. Maybe he was lost too. She rubbed his head and said, "Well, where did you come from?"

"Hello!" a man's voice called from a short distance away.

Beth Ann emerged from her shelter to see a tall, dark-haired man walking toward her with a fishing pole in his hand.

"Oh, my gosh," she almost cried. "I'm so glad to see you! I was kidnapped by a horrible man and ran away into this forest. My name is Beth Ann, and I've been trying to find my way out for three days and nights."

The man looked at her with concern. "Where are you from?"

"I'm from Novato, but I live with my husband in Riverside." She sank down onto a rock and hugged the dog, feeling her lip tremble. "I want to go home. Can you help me?"

The man walked over and set down his pole. "Yes, I can help you." He glanced around. "Where is your kidnapper now?"

"I stabbed him in the neck with a steak knife and ran away. I don't know where I am." Her voice cracked.

"A steak knife? Well, you're in the San Bernardino Mountains now. I live in a cabin about a day's walk from here, but I have no phone. I let my buddy borrow my truck, but he'll be back in two days." He sat across from her on another rock. "I have food and a real tent with me out here. We can get you home as soon as he comes back with my truck."

Beth Ann's initial relief faded a little. Was it safe to go with this man? He might be a killer or worse. But there was something about him and his dog that she trusted for some reason. He must have felt her hesitation, because he reached out a hand to her with a soft smile.

"My name is Charlie, and this is Rusty." He shook her hand then called the dog. "Come here, boy. I know you must be frightened, Miss, but I promise I'm not going to hurt you. You'll be safe with Rusty and me."

His voice sounded kind and ... wait, his name was Charlie? And the dog was Rusty? But he would be long gone. Could it be ...?

"OH MY GOD!" Beth Ann said. "Charlie, is it really you?" She felt tears trail down her cheeks.

He stared at her for a long moment "Elizabeth?"

"Yes, it's me!" She rushed toward him. "How lucky can one girl get? I've thought about you so many times!"

He stood up to embrace her with tears of his own. "Oh, my old friend and angel, I never thought I'd see you again." He held her tightly and kissed the top of her head. "I've wondered so often about you and your family. I'm so glad you're okay. Your family must be worried sick."

"My husband is sitting by the phone at home waiting for me to call." She tried to swallow the remaining tears. "I saw a news report before I escaped."

Charlie nodded. "We have to get you back home to your husband." He took her by the hand and sat down again. "How did you come to be kidnapped and why? Tell me what happened."

Beth Ann told him the whole story and finished with, "After I stabbed him, I just ran until I got into the forest."

"Do you think he was able to follow you?" Charlie asked. "I have a bow and arrow."

"I don't know, but it's been three days, and I haven't seen any trace of him."

The dog came and stood by her as though he understood. Her Rusty used to do that too.

"You called him Rusty. Is he related to my Rusty?"

Charlie nodded. "Yes, he's Rusty's son, so he's Rusty Junior. You're Rusty had a good long life and was a wonderful friend, I still miss him."

Beth Ann felt so much emotion that it was hard to put into words. "This is Rusty's son?" She laughed and cried all at once and hugged the dog until they both flopped onto the ground.

"He looks just like his dad." Rusty was the only dog she'd ever considered hers. That year they'd lived on the Indian Reservation, Rusty had followed her everywhere and became her best friend. Leaving him on the reservation had been awful.

Beth Ann stood, brushing the leaves and pine needles off her clothes. "I've survived out here by using some of the things you taught me." She pointed at her shelter and showed him the rocks, then she rubbed her arms against the morning chill. "I heated the rocks and kept warm last night. I know there are bears and stuff out here, but I felt safe for whatever reason."

"You did good, Elizabeth, and you're close enough to where you were born, that the wind knows your name. Here, take this." Charlie pulled off his jacket, but Beth Ann shook her head.

"Thank you, but I have a coat and yes, I remember you telling me about the wind." She smiled and started gathering her things.

Charlie was still big and handsome the way she remembered him. She wondered why he was all the way out here and why he wasn't on the reservation. He had been the tribal Chief when she was a kid. She'd have time to ask him about it on the way back to his cabin. The most important thing was that she was safe and going home. She said a silent prayer. *Thank you, God.*

Charlie took her bag and threw it over his shoulder. "Let's go get you some food and get your strength back. We'll head out for the cabin in the morning. I'll take you home to your husband as soon as my truck gets back." He smiled and held out his hand. "Now tell me about this man who won your heart. I want to know if my vision came true."

Beth Ann took his hand and gave it a squeeze. "I have so much to tell you, and I want to hear how it is that you're here and not on the reservation."

Charlie's expression told her, there was a story there, and she couldn't wait to hear it.

Chapter Twenty

"There's a house up ahead," Kaylob said, pointing. "Where the hell are the police? We've been walking for hours."

Blake shook his head. "So many of my leads turned out to be dead ends that they may not have taken this one seriously."

A second later, they heard the sound of a vehicle approaching and turned around to see Frankie's red Mustang heading their way. He stopped when it reached them and Frankie jumped out along with Johnny.

"Are you two okay?" Frankie said. "We passed the truck and saw that it had a flat."

Kaylob nodded. "We're okay, but that truck …" He glanced at Johnny.

"I know it needs new tires," Johnny said with a grin. "I only use it for fishing."

Blake shook his head and turned to Frankie. "What about the cops? Are they coming?"

"No, I couldn't get them to do jack shit." Frankie put a hand on Kaylob's shoulder. "Gram and Nickolas are waiting by the phone and won't leave for anything. I called Dana, and she sent Johnny to come with me." He rubbed his fingers through his hair. "We got lost three times. Man, were we happy to see that truck. At least we knew we were on the right road this time. Christ, there are a lot of long, unmarked, deserted roads around here."

Johnny nodded, then pointed toward the house. "Is that the place?"

"Let's go find out," Blake said. "I'm pretty sure it is."

They all climbed into Frankie's Mustang, and adrenaline started pumping through Kaylob, being so close to finding Beth Ann. All he wanted was to bring her home. No, that wasn't true. He also wanted to kill the bastard who took her.

The minute they got close to the house, Blake said, "That's Peter Steel's car. This is it!"

Kaylob jumped out and ran toward the house before the car even stopped.

"Wait a minute!" Blake yelled. "He could have a gun!"

Kaylob heard him, but couldn't stop. He wanted Beth Ann in his arms. He dashed up to the front porch and was about to kick the door when he saw it was ajar, so he pushed it open and ran in.

"Beth Ann! Where are you!" He heard the others behind him. "The door was already open."

As soon as they entered the living room, a godawful odor hit them all and made everyone gag.

Kaylob was all too familiar with that smell. The horrors he'd lived through in Vietnam suddenly merged with the horror he was facing now, and he almost went down to his knees.

"What the hell is that?" Frankie said as Johnny and Blake covered their faces.

"It's a dead body." Kaylob said, bending over and clutching his knees.

Johnny took out a gun. "Let me go in first. You guys stay here."

Blake grabbed Kaylob's arm. "Let him go look."

Kaylob nodded. If that was Beth Ann, he didn't want to see her like that. Tears stung his eyes and he swiped them away angrily. He couldn't let himself believe she was dead. She had to be alive.

They waited while Johnny went ahead, and after the longest minute of Kaylob's life, they heard Johnny yell. "Guys, get down here! It's not Beth Ann, but I'm pretty sure it's Peter Steel!"

They followed the lights down into the basement and when they entered the room at the bottom of the stairs, Kaylob froze dead in his tracks. The place looked exactly like their bedroom. Same furniture, curtains, everything. Except there was a dead man on the floor.

Frankie and Blake both coughed, but Kaylob walked over to him. Right away, he saw the steak knife sticking out of his neck.

"Holy shit." He glanced around. "This place looks just like our bedroom, only there's a dead guy on the floor."

"So this is Peter?" Frankie muttered.

"It's Peter all right." Blake looked sick. "But where's Beth Ann?"

They searched all the rooms in the basement and knew she had been there. Her clothes and shoes were in the closet, and Kaylob recognized her makeup and toiletries in the bathroom. What had this crazy bastard done to her?

Blake pulled a bag from the garbage. "Looks like they were eating dinner from a place I know well."

"Beth Ann must've escaped," Kaylob said. "She's alive, but where is she? And why didn't she call the police? Is there even a phone here?" Panic made him bend over to catch his breath.

"This place is surrounded by the San Bernardino Mountains," Blake said. "She could be anywhere." Worry washed across his face. "We need to get a search party organized. One with dogs."

"Let's make sure she's not hiding somewhere in the house first," Frankie said.

They all went back upstairs and ran through the rooms yelling for Beth Ann.

"Shit," Blake said when they met back in the living room. "There's no phone here. We have to go find one to call the police and get a search and rescue going."

"I'll wait here," Kaylob said. "She might come back if she's hiding somewhere close by."

Frankie threw Blake his keys. "You and Johnny go. I'll stay with Kaylob."

After they left, Kaylob and Frankie went back to the basement. Kaylob felt his stomach flip as he looked around. This had been her prison. But could she really have killed Peter? Kaylob had a hard time imagining that. Not his sweet Beth Ann …

Frankie grabbed a blanket and covered the body. "Man, this guy was nuts. But it looks like Beth Ann found a way to get away from him." Frankie looked down at the dead man and touched his chest in the sign of the cross, shocking Kaylob when he did it.

What was that all about? Kaylob didn't have a clue, but now wasn't the time to ask about it. He lifted the blanket once again to stare at the knife wound. Blood had oozed from his neck and left a small puddle on the floor, which was now virtually dry. The smell was horrid because the heater was up so high. Kaylob would guess he had been dead a good two days at least, maybe more.

He pulled the blanket back over the body, then walked into the bathroom and noticed an empty bottle of cough syrup in the garbage can. A fresh wave of panic rolled over him. Had Beth Ann been sick? What if she was really ill and out in the woods on the ground unable to move?

"I can't stand not knowing! I just want to find out where the hell she is!" he said to himself.

"What's wrong?" Frankie came bounding into the bathroom.

Kaylob picked up the garbage can. "Don't touch the empty bottle, but look."

"Is that cough syrup?" Frankie asked.

"Yeah. It's empty, but we can't touch it. The police will want us to keep our hands off everything." He set the can down again and felt the world tilt. "I just hope to hell she isn't sick out there all alone. I don't want to think about what might happen."

Frankie touched his shoulder. "Beth Ann is a lot tougher than you think. I saw that firsthand after you died." He looked embarrassed. "I mean, when we thought you died. But you're right, we shouldn't be touching anything. This is a crime scene, and they will want to question Beth Ann about the murder."

"Murder?" Kaylob frowned at him. "It's pretty clear what happened. This man kidnapped my wife and unless someone came to rescue her, she stabbed him to get away. She might not even know he's dead."

"Right, but they still have to investigate a homicide no matter what. We probably should go back upstairs."

"I want to look around just a bit." Kaylob walked into what appeared to be a small reading area. When he glanced around the room, he saw the Easter picture of Beth Ann and Gram, the gold cross was right next to it. "I'm taking these two items." He picked up the picture and the cross and knew she would want those.

Frankie sighed. "Okay, but hide them inside your jacket, until my car gets here and you can hide them under my seats. We shouldn't be tampering with evidence."

Kaylob nodded. "Alright."

Back in the living room, Kaylob plopped down on the sofa while Frankie looked around some more. Kaylob stared at the front door, hoping that Beth Ann would walk through it at any moment. She was alive and alone out there. Jesus, she didn't know anything about survival.

"Kaylob!" Frankie yelled. "Come here!"

He was up so fast he almost tripped over the coffee table. "Where the hell are you?"

"Down the hallway to the right. There's a secret room in here!"

Kaylob found the room and walked through the hidden door. "Holy hell," he said, looking around in disbelief.

There were pictures of them everywhere—on their honeymoon, up at Gram's house, at the pool and at work. Every part of their life in pictures. It was like a sick museum.

"This guy was a maniac," Kaylob said. "He's been following us for a long time, even on our honeymoon. What a sick bastard."

"Look at these." Frankie handed Kaylob some private pictures. You might want to hide these and don't say we took them."

Fury spread through Kaylob. "Shit, he was breaking into our house, too. This one is of our bed and Jesus, Beth Ann is sleeping."

Frankie nodded. "Listen, you better hide this stuff in your jacket with the other items or the cops will take it all as evidence. There's plenty of other things here for them to use."

Kaylob slipped them into his coat.

"I'm going to check outside," Kaylob said. "She might be hiding in one of the sheds I saw out there. Maybe in a bush or behind a tree. Although, I think she would have heard us yelling." He didn't have much faith that she was hiding right outside.

Finally, after searching all around the property and close by, they heard vehicles approaching and ran to meet them. Several police cars and an ambulance pulled up and Frankie and Kaylob were made to stay out of the house, while yellow tape was put everywhere. Kaylob felt like he was smack dab in the middle of a TV crime show. Everyone running around with Officer Deluca acting like *Kojak*.

Blake must have called everyone in the world. So long as they found

Beth Ann, Kaylob didn't give a damn. He planned to help lead the search party, after all, he'd been in the jungles of Vietnam and had experience with tracking. He couldn't stand the thought of his wife out in the wild, cold and scared to death. She had no idea how to take care of herself out there. They'd hardly ever been camping.

Deluca walked up to him and Frankie. "Kaylob, there's no speck of doubt that if your wife murdered that man in there, she did so in self-defense. By the way," he said, lowering his voice. "Did you see the secret room he had with all the pictures of you and Mrs. O'Brien?"

Kaylob nodded. "Yeah, Frankie found it." What he didn't tell him was that they had taken the ones that nobody else needed to see.

"You didn't take anything did you?"

"No." Kaylob lied and Frankie did too.

Deluca stared at both of them. "We found his journal with detailed plans, including this house and the bogus corporations. The guy has been following her since her Broadway shows."

"Christ all mighty," Kaylob said. "I had no idea she was being followed by this ass."

After Deluca walked away, Frankie shook his head and pointed at Peter's car. "Man, so that's the car that's been following her, right?"

Kaylob nodded. "Sure looks like it."

"Remember how much Beth Ann talked about that?" Frankie looked at the ground. "I wish I had paid more attention to her."

"You and me both," Kaylob said. "I thought it was the paparazzi, and so did she for the most part."

The guys from the coroner's office arrived, and it didn't take them long to remove the body on a gurney. Kaylob watched as they loaded it into the back of the vehicle in a body bag. That was the end of that asshole, and Kaylob didn't feel one ounce of sorrow.

After he watched them drive away, he said, "Come on, Blake. Where are you?" He paced back and forth, looking impatiently down the road ever so often. Finally, the sound of loud, approaching engines made everyone turn and look. Two truckloads of guys and barking dogs pulled up in front of the house, with Blake and Johnny behind them in Frankie's Mustang.

"Right on," Kaylob said to Frankie. "We can start searching for her now."

Blake got out and ran over to them. "The police said they were waiting until morning to start searching, but we're starting before it gets dark." Deluca walked up and Blake frowned at him. "I hired all these guys and they're dedicated. We'll find her, so we really don't need your search party."

"Hold on now." Deluca shook his head. "We should be able to get copters here tomorrow afternoon and I could send a couple of my guys with you."

"No, we have this," Blake said. "Look at all my guys."

"But the copters would be great," Kaylob said. "We want to start the search on foot tonight, and by the looks of it, we do have plenty of manpower."

"All right then," Deluca said.

"Thanks." Kaylob nodded. "I'm hoping we find her soon."

"If you do find her, it'll save the police department a ton of money. I'm sure the chief will agree. Good luck, guys." Deluca shook hands with all of them. "We'll be here all day tomorrow gathering evidence, so if you need us for anything, let us know. Send someone back if you don't find her."

"We will," Kaylob said. "Thanks again."

After Deluca walked away, Blake said, "We stopped by your place and got a sweater that had Beth Ann's scent on it. The dogs will track her from that. These boys have a great record."

That was the news Kaylob wanted to hear. "Okay, let's go find her."

"We're gonna work through the night if that's what it takes." Blake turned and addressed the group of men. "Can I see a raise of hands. Who can handle this all night?"

All the guys raised their hands, then headed toward the forest.

"Wait!" one of the guys yelled. "The dogs are picking up her scent on this road. Why don't we head on down while some of you bring a few vehicles and see where they lead us?"

Kaylob, Frankie, and Blake climbed into the Mustang and once the coast was clear Kaylob slipped the items from his jacket under Frankie's seat. Johnny and two other guys took off in a truck, trailing the dogs who were leading the way.

Kaylob prayed those hounds were right.

* * * *

When Beth Ann, Charlie and Rusty Jr. arrived at the campsite, relief swept through her. She was safe and sound with her dear friend. Finally, she knew without a doubt that Peter could never take her again. Her eyes were drawn to the pit in the ground with a grill on top. Food would be great about right now. Any kind.

Charlie pulled up a chair for her. "Sit down and let me get you something to eat," he said as though he'd read her mind.

He handed her a wool blanket, a lovely green apple, and a bottle of pop. "Here, wrap this around you against the chill in the air, it will be getting dark soon, and eat that apple until I get the food ready." He went over to a big ice chest and pulled out two fish, then he reached inside a pack and retrieved a can of pork and beans. He also lit a lantern, even though the sun had not set yet. Never had she been so glad to see some beans, even though she would still pick out the pork.

Charlie also pulled out a skillet from that same carry pack along with some oil. After he got a fire going, he put the fish in the skillet and placed it on the grill. While it sizzled, he opened the can of beans with a funny-looking can opener.

"Now let me get Rusty fed, so he won't try to steal our food." He laughed and used a rag to wipe off his can opener. While he opened the dog food, Rusty Jr. barked at him twice, demanding to eat right now. "Here you go, boy. I'm not gonna let you starve."

He wagged his tail and stood at alert. Beth Ann found herself giggling. Looking around, she couldn't help but wonder how Charlie had gotten all this stuff here with no vehicle. There was a tent, food, sleeping bag, two small chairs, and utensils to eat and cook with. Plus that nice fishing pole he'd had when they found each other.

"Charlie, how do carry all this stuff?" Beth Ann asked.

"I have a system. See this tote bag?" He picked it up and showed her. "Everything is hooked onto it, and I carry it on my back. You'd be surprised how everything fits." He handed her the tote to look at. "And these chairs come apart. Everything is compact."

Beth Ann examined it with awe. There were hooks and even a compartment that the dishes fit inside. But she still didn't see how the

185

chairs and tent would fit.

Her confusion must have shown because Charlie smiled. "You'll see tomorrow. Everything fits right on my back."

The aroma of the apple was wonderful. When she bit into it, her eyes rolled back in her head from pure delight.

"Yum," she said. "You have no idea how good this tastes. Thank you, Charlie."

She gobbled down the entire apple before she even took one drink of her cola. When she glanced up at him, his smile reached his eyes, reminding her of the days on the reservation. Charlie had always made her feel special and had tried every way he could to persuade her dad to stay put and not drag them around anymore. Anyone could see that living out of that old car had been hard on them. But back in those days her dad had only cared about getting famous, which was why her mom had finally left.

At first, Beth Ann had been sad, but after a while she understood. And the truth was clear now. That divorce had led to her meeting Kaylob. Everything seemed to happen for a reason, and her belief was that when one door closes, you just have to find the key to the next one and see if that's the door you want to go through.

Those thoughts made her wonder if Charlie had ever found another love since his wife had died so young. Beth Ann remembered that she had been beautiful and so full of life. In fact, she had died while playing with the children. According to what the elders said, she fell to the ground because her head was bleeding and was gone instantly. Now that Beth Ann was an adult, she understood that it must have been an aneurysm.

She wanted to ask Charlie if he'd ever met anyone and fallen in love again, but she didn't know if she should. They hadn't talked about that on the way to the camp, but she had told him everything about Kaylob and her life in Novato. She had also shared the details about Blake. Charlie had listened and even stopped her a few times to ask questions, wanting to hear more. He had always been interested in what she had to say.

Now that she and Charlie had found each other, she had no intention of letting him vanish again. Gram would call this God's Plan, and Beth

Ann would most certainly have to agree. Maybe this was the silver lining of her being kidnapped.

Just saying that word made her head start to spin and her palms sweaty. Just like before, she thought she heard Kaylob calling her and stood straight up, looking around, but she didn't see or hear anything. Maybe he was searching for her, even if it was only in his mind. They'd already been through this situation once before. And the thought of him feeling anything close to what she had experienced tore her heart to pieces.

Charlie came over and took her arm. "Elizabeth, are you okay?"

She opened her mouth to answer, but nothing came out. She gripped the bottle so tight that Charlie pulled it from her hand. If he hadn't, it might have broken and cut her. Everything that had happened hit her all at once. She could see the knife in Peter's neck, and the blood made her feel as though she was going to faint.

No, she had to be stronger! But every muscle in her body tightened, and she knew her legs were not going to hold her up much longer.

Charlie helped her back into the chair. "Tell me what's wrong, child."

Beth Ann finally choked out the words. "I think I must have murdered Peter or he would have come after me!"

Charlie's dark eyes clung to hers for a long moment. "No, it was self-defense. He kidnapped you and had plans to hurt you. He might have survived and still be looking for you, but if he is, he won't get far." He wrapped his arms around her shoulders.

Beth Ann held on to his strong arm and let out a heavy sigh. "You're right. I think it's just all sinking in."

Rusty Jr. barked suddenly, and when they turned to look at him, they saw smoke coming from the pan.

Charlie ran over to the fire. "I almost burned the fish," he said. "But it's good. Now you just sit there and try not to worry about anything." He glanced over his shoulder. "Rusty, good job saving dinner, boy. Go on over there and keep Elizabeth company."

The dog came and put his head in her lap. As soon as she touched him, the stress started to fade and relief filled her. She leaned down to kiss his head and got a very large, wet kiss in return. *That would make anyone feel better, she thought* as she wiped off the slobber.

With her hand on Rusty Jr's head, she sighed and glanced out at the creek. She was just days away from being home. She lay back her head and closed her eyes. The brisk winter breeze blew all around, and just for now, for this moment, all her worries floated away. When she opened her eyes again, she saw a little bird staring at her, and for some reason, hope and promises floated over her. She had a strong feeling that life would be stable from this point on, as if God was promising that she'd never have to be away from Kaylob again. Whatever it was, it made her heart fill with gratitude.

"The smell of that food is making me feel like I'm in heaven," she said, getting up to come stand by Charlie. "That looks amazing. Thank you for doing this and rescuing me."

"I didn't rescue you, Elizabeth. You did that all on your own. I'm just cooking and helping you get home." Charlie shook his head as he picked up the skillet from the grill. "Now, this is done. Want to hand me those two plates out of the tote?"

While she got the plates and silverware, she thought about what Charlie had said. He was right, she *had* rescued herself. She had escaped and survived in the woods for three nights all by herself. Just maybe she was her own *heroine*.

That's when the truth hit her and she made a decision right then. From this point forward, she would listen to her own instincts. Three times now, she had pushed those feelings aside or let others tell her what to do. Once when she'd known that Kaylob was alive even though everyone thought he was dead, then when those guys down in the garage had given her the creeps, and now all the things that happened because of Peter. If she was being honest, Peter had always given her the willies, even from that first meeting with Blake. The way he'd held her hand too long that she'd had to wiggle it loose, then that time at school when he'd kissed her hand again, and the way he'd looked at her gave her a funny feeling, but she shook it off and thought she was being silly.

"You're deep in thought," Charlie said as he handed her a plate then sat down with his. "I remember seeing that look on your face. Let's eat and you can tell me what's on your mind. By the way, I deboned the fish, so it should be pretty clean."

Beth Ann nodded and sat down with her own plate of food. Never had anything smelled so good. She took a very large bite and swallowed. Maybe it was because the food was already making her feel stronger, but she decided to tell Charlie the rest of everything.

Chapter Twenty-One

Five hours after the search began, the dogs led the search team down a trail into the forest. They hadn't found anything yet, but the dogs kept barking and running. Some of the men had slowed down from pure exhaustion, and Kaylob had to admit that his legs were feeling the burn. He wasn't stopping though. He'd keep on going even if they couldn't.

"Hey, Kaylob, how you doing?" Blake appeared tired and winded.

"Hanging in there. Never thought I'd have to tromp through the jungle again."

"Hey, are you okay with this?" Blake stopped him with a hand on his arm. "I mean, are you dealing with everything okay?"

"So far all I can think about is finding Beth Ann. I was hoping we would find her by now." Kaylob bent over and rested his hands on his knees, but straightened up fast when the dogs suddenly got frantic.

"We found something!" a guy named Gary shouted. He shined the lights around a bush.

"Boss, you might want to come and check this out!" Johnny called.

Kaylob, Blake and Frankie took off running.

"What is it?" Kaylob asked, trying to see what they were all looking at. It was almost as if they didn't want him to see.

He pushed several guys out of the way. "What the hell did you find?"

Johnny handed it to him. "Do you recognize this?"

It was a woman's shirt shredded to bits, as if some type of animals had torn it off. It was also stained with what appeared to be faded blood.

"No, I've never seen that top before." Kaylob shook his head and glanced at the dogs going crazy again.

"The dogs are picking up her scent." Gary signaled for the dogs to stop barking, but one of them was tugging him to continue down the trail.

Kaylob stared at what was left of the blouse with a rolling wave of fear going through him. When he finally glanced up, Frankie had worry wrinkled across his face, and Blake's eyes looked as scared as Kaylob felt.

"Hey, come on, guys," Johnny said. "That don't mean nothing. She's a redhead, and they're tough as hell. Besides, those dogs want to keep going. That means she's still out there somewhere."

"She's okay." Kaylob nodded. "I can feel her."

"Let's keep going then." Blake agreed.

An hour later, the men were yelling again. "We found something else! It's a plastic baggie with cookie crumbs in it. And it looks like she slept in this area." They shined their lights against the tree and picked up some sticks.

Kaylob jogged over to take a closer look. It did look like a fort or some kind of shelter that had been made. That couldn't have been Beth Ann. She didn't know the first thing about stuff like that.

"My wife knows nothing about the wilderness," he said, shaking his head. "We hardly ever went camping. This must be from someone else."

Gary shook his head. "No, my dogs are getting her scent all around here. She was here and they're trying to pull me down the trail." He gently pulled on one of the leashes. "I know she made it out of here alive. I can promise you that."

"If that shirt back there was hers, maybe she just fell and got hurt. We need to keep going," Kaylob said as he turned to Frankie and Blake. "Or maybe that shirt had Steel's blood on it."

"That's true," Blake said. "After all, she did stab him in the neck."

Frankie nodded. "I bet that's it."

"Are you guys okay with going further, or do you need to rest?" Gary addressed the other men.

"We need to rest," one of the guys yelled out. "It's almost morning and we haven't stopped."

"Yeah, she more than likely got chased by a bear or something," one of the other guys said.

"Ignore that." Gary shook his head and looked at Kaylob. "There are no bear tracks out here. Plus, she was walking, not running."

Another guy said, "I need to stop and rest or I'm gonna turn around."

"Okay." Blake held up his hands. "Take a two hour break. If you need more time than that, I'll pay you for the hours you've worked and find someone else to help out."

"I need to feed my dogs and let them rest," Gary said. "Two hours is good." He turned and looked around at all the guys. "Right, men?"

Everyone nodded and started finding places to take a load off.

Except Kaylob. He stared down the road, then turned to Frankie. "I'm going on ahead. You guys can rest and meet up with me later."

"Like hell," Frankie said. "I'm going with you."

"You two go ahead. I'll stay with the team and keep them going." Blake handed Kaylob a flare gun. "If you find her, shoot this to let us know where you are. Or if you get in trouble and need us."

"All right, Blake. I might get scared by a bear or something." Kaylob shook like he was afraid.

"Sorry, pal." Blake gave him a sheepish grin. "I sometimes forget that in 'Nam you had a lot more to worry about than bears."

"I'm not terribly fond of bears." Frankie glanced around with wide eyes. "Are they out this time of year?"

Kaylob and Blake laughed. Kaylob had never thought about Frankie being such a city boy and not knowing anything about the wilderness. Now that Kaylob thought about it, he couldn't remember ever hearing about Frankie being in any kind of woods, let alone a forest.

"Frankie, I'll go," Johnny volunteered. "You can stay here with the other guys."

"No way," he said, looking a little embarrassed. "I want to go. I just think maybe we should take a gun or something."

"Gotcha covered." Johnny held up his gun and put his arm around Frankie with a wink. "Don't worry, big guy. I'll protect you."

"Very funny." Frankie pulled away.

Blake insisted that they take some food, blankets and rope with them. "In case you decide to rest for a bit, these blankets will keep you warm. And here …" He handed Johnny some small sticks. "In case you need a fire."

Kaylob was surprised that Blake seemed to know that much about camping, and tilted his head towards Blake.

"I did a lot of camping with a girlfriend and her family in high school," Blake said.

"Oh, yeah." Kaylob nodded. "I think I remember hearing about that."

"Her dad was a forest ranger and taught me stuff about the woods. Bet you didn't know that."

"You had a girlfriend in high school, Boss?" Johnny asked with a grin.

"Yes, for one whole summer. Imagine that." Blake waved them off. "Go on and get out of here. We'll catch up with you later."

The three guys headed down the path, each with flashlights and wool blankets wrapped up with rope. Kaylob didn't give a shit about sleeping. He intended to stay on the trail until they found her. At least they knew she'd been alive when she left this spot.

But he still had one lingering question. How did Beth Ann know how to build a fort? He tried to imagine her doing it and just couldn't. She was a small town girl, and although he knew she'd lived on the road as a child, she'd never said anything to him about camping. Maybe she'd read a book about it. She was a fast learner.

That made him think about the book she'd read before they'd made love for the first time. She had blown his mind with all she did. Hell, she was still blowing his mind, and right now. he just prayed that those dogs were right and this was Beth Ann they were following and not some hiker who was camping out.

* * * *

When Beth Ann and Charlie finally arrived at his cabin, Rusty Jr. bounced around barking, then ran into the back yard as though he were chasing something.

Charlie laughed. "He's gonna find some creature to chase, and when he catches it, he'll try to make friends."

Beth Ann had to giggle. "He's a cute guy no doubt."

Once she got a good look at the place, it reminded her of a miniature log cabin. It had steps leading up to the porch with wood piled high on the left side. Two old rocking chairs sat centered within the middle of the window and a flowerpot that held wilted plants.

"Welcome to my humble abode," Charlie said with a smile. "It's rough but clean. I've got running water, a good-sized kitchen, two bedrooms and one very large bathroom with a soaking tub." He pushed the door open with his foot and carried the stuff on his back some place outside the kitchen. "Come on in and get comfortable."

The place looked like paradise to Beth Ann, with a large oversized couch, wooden floors and a few throw rugs. In the center, against the wall, was a wood-burning stove with a pile of cedar on the side that she could smell all the way across the room. Charlie must keep the place toasty warm.

"This is adorable," she said. "Did you build this place?"

"Yes, with my own two hands." He walked into the room and pointed to the couch for her to sit down. "I'm gonna build us a fire and put on some stew I have frozen. Got enough to feed an army." He stopped and turned to look at her. "Oh, would you like to take a bath or change? I have some female clothes in the spare room if you'd like to go take a look."

"Female clothes?" Beth Ann grinned.

"Remember my sister Benita? She comes and stays with me once a year and leaves some of her clothes behind. She says it's the ones she won't wear in the city and that they're her ugly clothes." He smiled and shook his head. "She wouldn't be caught dead wearing them anywhere but here."

"Well, I like ugly clothes." Beth Ann thought of her house-cleaning shirt that Kaylob loved. "And a bath sounds wonderful. Anything clean to wear would be great."

"It's down the hall to the right. You can sleep in there tonight. She's got a warm blanket on the bed, and this stove keeps everything cozy, almost too cozy. You can use anything you need on her shelves and in the bathroom."

"Thank you, Charlie. That sounds wonderful." Beth Ann took off and could almost feel the water running over her skin from just thinking about it. When she entered the bedroom, she caught the scent of more cedar and some other woodsy aroma. It was so comforting, and for the first time since she'd left Peter's house, she felt safe to soak in a tub.

The clothes in the closet were a little big, but they were fresh and clean. The green plaid shirt and black pants worked just fine. She even found a brand new pair of underwear and a bra that were two sizes too big, but who cared.

In the bathroom, she found vanilla lotion and a hairbrush. It was more than she could have wished for. Charlie even had a new toothbrush and minty toothpaste. She would feel human again.

The tub was charming and oversized, with shampoo and conditioner sitting on the side. After she turned on the water, she got undressed and waited for the tub to fill. Stepping inside made her almost melt on the spot. Gosh, it felt good. The warm water soothed her tired and exhausted muscles, allowing her to completely relax.

Out in the other room, she could hear Charlie humming a song she didn't recognize. Somewhere between the warm water running over her and his voice, she drifted off and didn't wake up until she heard Charlie calling her from outside the door.

"Elizabeth? The food is ready when you are. It's been over an hour. You didn't fall asleep in that tub, did you?"

"I almost did," she fibbed. "Thank you, Charlie. I'll be out in a few minutes." After she dried off and put on the clean clothes, she finally felt normal again, with clean hair and a clean body she was rid of Peter's blood.

When she sat down to eat, she practically inhaled the large bowl of stew and buttered bread. "This is so good," she said between bites.

"Glad you like it." He wiped his mouth and studied her. "Elizabeth, did you ever do anything with your singing?"

"You might say that," she said with a grin. "I won a Tony, and I teach at a very well-known school of performing arts. I traveled around for over six months doing tours." She watched his eyes sparkle with joy. "I saw a lot of places and mostly enjoyed it. That was during the time that Kaylob was missing. I guess I forgot to tell you that on the way here."

"No kidding." Charlie's eyes got big. "You left out some mighty important events. I'm so proud of you. I always knew you were talented. So will you be doing another show soon?"

"Not right away. I was so tired after being on the road for so long that I just wanted to stay home for a year or two. If the right show comes along later, I might consider it, so long as I don't have to be away for six months. I did get another offer, but at the last minute I backed out." She rose and took their plates over to the sink. "I'm going to sing at Kaylob's restaurant though. He's so wonderful, Charlie. He built me a stage and everything."

"He sounds like a great guy," Charlie said. "I can't wait to meet him."

Beth Ann insisted on washing all the dishes and cleaning up.

"Would you like some dessert?" Charlie asked when she was finished.

"No, not right now. I'm so full." She rubbed her stomach.

"Thank you for cleaning up." He walked over to the refrigerator and pulled out a pie. "Are you sure you don't want some blackberry pie? It's made from scratch and tastes really good." He held it up and showed her.

"Who made it?" Beth Ann asked.

"I did. I love to cook. Remember, you always told me you'd never marry a man that didn't know how to cook, and since your husband's a chef, I guess you meant it." He sliced a piece of pie and put it on a plate. "You sure you don't want a small one?"

"Oh, okay." Beth Ann licked her lips. "How can I refuse?"

After they ate their pie and talked some more, Beth Ann yawned. "I'm getting sleepy." She glanced at him and saw that he had droopy eyes too.

"Yeah, we'd better turn in for the night. I think Benita has some flannel gowns in her drawers, but anything you find in that room you can use to sleep in. Help yourself."

Beth Ann walked over and gave him a big hug. "Thank you, Charlie. I'm so glad you're in my life again."

He kissed her head, and his eyes looked a bit glassy. "I'm a happy man, too. You sleep well and know that tonight you're safe. My doors are solid, and they all lock this way." He walked over and pulled down a steel arm that went across the door and slid inside a holder. "See? Bear proof. They tried to come in a few times when I first built this place, so I had to make it secure."

"Good idea." Beth Ann grinned. "Good night, Charlie."

The minute she stepped inside the bedroom and shut the door, emotions rocked her and she started to cry. She didn't want to be a big baby, but it was so hard to wait to get home to Kaylob. For some reason she was feeling him right now and knew he was worried. She just missed him so much that her heart ached.

In the drawer, she found a flannel nightgown and a pair of thick socks. Charlie's sister had left a lot of stuff, and Beth Ann would be sure to wash everything and buy her some new cotton underwear.

She brushed her teeth and crawled into bed, then she took a pillow and hugged it. Despite the pain in her heart from missing Kaylob, tonight she would say a prayer for just how grateful she was to be safe with Charlie. She was in a warm bed with clean clothes and a shelter where nothing could bite her, spray her, or scare her.

"Thank you, God," she whispered. "And please watch over Kaylob until I get back to him."

Chapter Twenty-Two

Kaylob was pissed at himself for having to take a break, but when he almost passed out, Frankie made him stop and eat a candy bar and some pretzels. Not a healthy diet, but it would give him some energy. As Kaylob took his last bite, he stopped chewing and stared at his best friend on the ground rolling in the dirt.

"Frankie, what the hell are you doing? Have you lost your mind?"

"No, I read once that bears can smell humans. I figure if I get my human scent off, they'll leave me alone. You guys should do this too." He rolled over again.

Kaylob and Johnny looked at each other and did their best not to laugh.

"Frankie," Kaylob said. "Get up off the ground before you roll over a snake or get poison oak."

Frankie was off the ground in a flash. "Snakes? What kind of snakes?"

That did it. Kaylob and Johnny busted out laughing. Maybe it was being exhausted and hungry, or maybe it was just a release. Whatever the reason, they both howled at Frankie looking around for snakes with wide eyes.

"What the hell are you two laughing at?" he said with a scowl.

Kaylob was still cracking up and could only point, because now he could see that Frankie was covered with dirt and what appeared to be some type of animal dung.

"You didn't have to do that," Johnny said, trying to catch his breath. "I told you I'd protect you."

Kaylob had to look away. Seeing his friend covered in poo was not a pretty sight. "Okay, enough of this," Kaylob said. "Let's get back to searching." As soon as he stood up, he heard the dogs. "Hey, the guys must be close."

They all turned to see Gary with the two dogs who headed right to Frankie and started sniffing. Gary backed up, wrinkling his nose.

"What the hell is that smell?" He looked Frankie up and down. "Man, you got crap all over you. What happened? Did a bear try to mate with you or something?"

Frankie looked down. "Oh, shit."

"Exactly," Johnny said, and they all laughed.

Blake walked up then, but he stepped back as soon as he got close and held his nose. "What in the world happened to you, Frankie?"

"Never mind." Frankie picked up some leaves and tried to wipe off his clothes, but it didn't seem to help.

"I'm glad you're all here," Kaylob said. "Let's get going."

Blake nodded. "We rested for a little over an hour and decided we wanted to try and catch you guys."

"We had to stop too," Kaylob said. "My stupid legs gave out on me."

"Mine too," Frankie said.

Blake sniffed the air and glanced at Frankie. "What the hell, man? Did you fall in shit somewhere? You smell like an outhouse."

"All of you can kiss my ass," Frankie said and walked off.

Kaylob snickered and leaned closer to Blake. "He thought rolling on the ground would keep the bears away."

Blake shook his head. "He's a funny guy."

After they'd been walking another hour, they found a shelter built against a tree near a creek, and this time there was a hole in the ground with burnt firewood and rocks inside the fort.

"Wow," Gary said. "This chick knows how to take care of herself."

Kaylob felt sick. Gary was right. Whoever had done this, did know how to take care of themselves. That meant it couldn't be Beth Ann.

The dogs had a hard time picking up Beth Ann's scent again. Finally, after hours of taking the dogs up and down the creek, they picked it up again. Kaylob prayed that they'd find her before another day passed.

* * * *

After another long but beautiful day at Charlie's cabin, twilight was setting in. Beth Ann spent most of the day playing with Rusty Jr. in the front yard and tried to keep her mind off how much she wanted to go home. She also decided to start calling him by his right name. It wasn't fair to keep calling him junior even though Charlie had named him after his dad. He was the only Rusty they had now.

Beth Ann loved her time with Charlie and Rusty, but she hoped Charlie got his truck back soon. They had talked about her life and friends, but he hadn't talked much about himself at all. She still wanted to ask him what he was doing out here, but hadn't known how to broach the subject.

"Elizabeth, I made a pot of coffee and I'm cutting some pie," Charlie called from the doorway. "Want some?"

"That sounds wonderful." Beth Ann got up and brushed Rusty's hair off her baggy jeans. "I need to wash up first. I've been running and playing with Rusty."

When she came back to the kitchen a few minutes later, Charlie was sitting at the table with two pieces of scrumptious looking pie and two cups of coffee.

"Thank you." Beth Ann pulled up a chair and sat down. "This looks yummy."

"You're welcome." He lifted the cup to his lips and took a sip. "I'm sorry about my truck. I wish he would hurry and bring it home."

"Me too, but I'm happy to be spending time with you." She took a bite of pie and decided now was as good a time as any, to ask him about his life. "I don't mean to be nosy, but why are you here and not on the reservation? And did you ever get remarried?"

He wiped his mouth with a napkin. "I moved out here because I love these mountains, and also because this piece of land was cheap." He dropped a piece of pie for Rusty. "I never married again because I've never met anyone I loved that way."

"So you've had some girlfriends then?"

"I've dated, but nothing serious."

"Ah, okay. I get it," she said. "Frankie always dated a lot of women, although right now he's with a girl named Debra."

200

Charlie took a bite of pie. "Frankie? That's your good friend, right?"

She nodded. "Yes, I love him like a brother."

After a minute or so, Charlie said, "I just really didn't want to live on the reservation anymore. We had a lot of new people move in, and it was getting out of hand. A lot of drinking and all-night parties."

"Oh, I'm sorry to hear that," Beth Ann said. "I loved it when we were there."

Rusty suddenly jumped up and ran to the door, scratching at it frantically.

"What is it, boy?" Charlie asked.

The sun had gone down, so there was no telling what was out there. Beth Ann stood and felt her stomach turn. Charlie went into the living room and picked up a shotgun leaning against the hutch. He loaded it, grabbed a flashlight and stepped over to the front door.

"Rusty heard something, and I did too. If that kidnapper is anywhere near us, he's about to be shot."

Beth Ann's head started to spin. If Peter had followed them, he must have done a great job of hiding, and why would he risk coming here?

"Charlie, be careful! If it's him, he's crazy. And I don't know if he has a gun or not."

He unlocked the door and shook his head. "Get in the hallway and look in that drawer." He pointed at the hutch. "If anything happens to me, you shoot him."

She pulled open the drawer and retrieved a small handgun.

"It's already loaded," he said.

As soon as he opened the door, Rusty knocked him out of the way and dashed outside. Whatever was out there, Rusty didn't like it.

"Who's out there?" Charlie yelled into the darkness. "I'm gonna fire one shot in the air, then I'm shooting to kill, and I have good aim!" He blasted off a shot, then they heard barking—and it was more than one dog.

"Holy night," Beth Ann said, going to the door to look out. "Charlie, those dogs sound vicious. They might kill Rusty. Let's get him back inside."

"Rusty, come here!" Charlie yelled, then he put his fingers in his mouth and whistled.

"Don't shoot!" a man's voice called out. "My dogs are trailing someone who was kidnapped. They won't hurt your dog."

Beth Ann's heart leapt in her chest. Kidnapped? Their dogs were trailing someone? Could it be her? She stepped out onto the front porch.

"I was kidnapped, but I escaped!" she yelled back, still not able to see who was out there in the dark behind the moving flashlight beams.

"Beth Ann!"

As soon as she heard her husband's voice, Beth Ann's eyes flooded with tears and she set the gun down. Her feet were moving as if they had a mind of their own.

"Kaylob!" she cried out.

She wasn't sure where she should run, but knew he was out there somewhere, and that was all that mattered. With her heart pounding, she kept running and heard male voices hooting and hollering, then she saw Kaylob running toward her with his arms outspread to catch her. She flew into his arms, and he lifted her as if she weighed nothing. Then, with every bit of strength she had, she wrapped her legs around him and buried her face in his neck as they both sobbed.

"Oh, my God, baby! I've been so worried, and I didn't know if you were alive or dead!" He kissed her with tears streaming down his face. "I love you so much!"

"I love you too, Kaylob!" She held his face in her hands. "I was so scared, but all I could think about was getting back home to you."

They kissed again, then Kaylob finally put her down. Beth Ann looked around at the group of men with him and saw Frankie grinning at her and Blake looking down at the ground. Johnny was there too. She had so many questions, but she would have plenty of time to ask them later.

"Frankie, get over here and give me a hug!" When he got closer, she held up her hand and backed away. "Holy cow, what happened to you?"

"Nice to see you too." He scowled, but hugged her anyway.

Johnny laughed and wrapped his arms around her. "Hey, Ms. B. It's good to see you."

All the other guys came over to shake her hand. Except Blake. He hung back from everybody, looking uncomfortable.

Kaylob turned to Charlie. "I'm her husband. You must be the guy who rescued her. Thank you so much." He shook his hand.

"Pleased to meet you," Charlie said. "But I didn't rescue her. She did that all by herself. We just found each other in the forest. Well, my dog found her sleeping in one of her woman-made shelters. This young lady was surviving just fine all by herself. But I've known her since she was eight, so I'm not surprised."

"What?' Kaylob looked around at Beth Ann.

Beth Ann grinned. "True story. Charlie and I go way back."

Charlie motioned toward his cabin. "Come on in and make yourselves at home. I'll fill you in while I make coffee for everybody. I've also got plenty of stew and fresh bread. I should have my truck back in the morning and can get everybody home."

Gary held his dogs on the leash that were still trying to get to Beth Ann. "I'll take that stew and some water, but I want to head back and let the cops know that we found her. Is there a shorter way to get to somewhere to a phone?" Gary asked.

Charlie nodded. "About five or six hours up the river there's a ranger station and they have a phone there. But you want to be careful and stay by the river."

Another guy said. "I'll go with you."

Blake still hadn't said anything, but when Beth Ann looked at him, he stared at her with emotion all over his face. Kaylob must have seen it too, because he walked over to Blake and put a hand on his shoulder.

"Okay, Blake. You're the reason we found her, so I'll let you talk to her alone. Just don't keep her too long." He smiled and held out his hand. "Thanks, buddy. I'll never forget it."

Blake shook his hand and nodded. "Glad to do it, pal."

They walked over to Beth Ann and she could feel her mouth hanging open. Kaylob kissed her on the cheek again. "I'll see you inside in a few minutes." He turned to Charlie and said as they walked toward the cabin, "So tell me how it is that you know my wife."

Beth Ann looked into Blake's eyes with a lump in her throat. "I can't believe what I'm seeing between you and Kaylob."

He picked up her hand. "We both love you and we're determined to find you. At first, they thought I'd taken you, but I finally convinced them that I was searching for you too. Plus Dana finally remembered to give me the cuff link that wasn't mine. I bought those for Peter as a sales reward. As soon as I saw them, I knew who had you, but he gave some lame excuse, which the police believed. It was actually Lenard, who recognized his picture from when you and Kaylob were out of town that brought it all together." Blake pulled her closer. "He didn't hurt you, did he?"

"No, he didn't hurt me, and thank you for helping Kaylob find me." She wrapped her arms around him, and when she looked at his face again, she wiped away the tear trailing down his cheek.

"Kaylob's a good man. I always knew that, I just didn't want to admit it before. But somehow through all this, we became friends." He looked toward the cabin. "Good friends."

"Then my kidnapping served more than one purpose," she said, looking up at him with a trembling smile. "I found out that I'm stronger than I ever knew, and you and Kaylob became friends, not to mention finding Charlie."

"I'm so happy that you're alive and well, darlin." Blake touched her cheek. "Now let's get you inside to your husband before he comes back to get you. We may be friends now, and I want to keep it that way." They both laughed. "Seriously, he's been a real sad sap since you've been gone, so I know he doesn't want to be away from you for long. Besides, I'd really like some of that coffee and food your friend Charlie mentioned."

Beth Ann felt like she was dreaming. Once again, she realized that going through something horrible can lead anyone to something beautiful.

When she and Blake went through the front door, she was met with a round of applause. Kaylob strolled over and kissed her forehead.

"Charlie was telling us some of what you did to survive, and I can't believe you knew how to do all those things, Beth Ann. We saw the makeshift shelters and the carving you did to make a weapon, but to tell the truth, I thought we were tracking the wrong person." He took a deep breath. "You are one amazing lady, Mrs. O'Brien."

Beth Ann glanced around the room. Charlie was pulling down bowls and cups from the cabinet in the kitchen, Johnny was sitting on the arm of the couch, and Frankie …

"Good God, Frankie." She scrunched up her nose. "What in the world happened to you?"

She saw Kaylob trying not to laugh, but he failed badly, then the entire room was cracking up. All except Frankie.

"Can I use your shower to wash up?" he asked Charlie.

Charlie nodded with a smile. "Let me get you a clean shirt and pants. I can stick your clothes in the washer." He winked at Beth Ann and led Frankie down the hall with the other guys still laughing. Beth Ann was sure they'd let her in on the joke, but right now she felt bad for Frankie.

"What did he fall in?" she asked Kaylob.

"Nothing. He was rolling around on the ground to take away his human scent and rolled in something." He had a hard time spitting it out without laughing. "I found out that Frankie doesn't like the wilderness or bears."

"Poor Frankie," she said, trying not to laugh too. "He's never going to live this one down."

Kaylob nodded and Blake laughed again.

Most of the guys slept out back in a little guest cottage that Charlie had. It was rustic but had bunk beds. The men were so tired they didn't care.

Charlie went to bed finally, but Beth Ann stayed up with Kaylob, Frankie, Johnny and Blake. It just didn't feel right for her to go sleep with Kaylob in the bedroom. Nothing was said, but she could see in Kaylob's eyes that he agreed. They all wanted to hear more about how she'd escaped, so she told them as much as she could bring herself to tell. Of course, she'd tell Kaylob everything when they were alone.

Later, when Beth Ann found out that she had killed Peter, she cried. She had never meant to kill him. Frankie assured her that it was self-defense and she wouldn't be charged, but she still felt so bad for little Cathy. She had taken away her daddy, and Beth Ann would have a hard time forgiving herself for that.

The guy named Don showed up with the truck the next morning, and things started to roll. Beth Ann insisted that Charlie come home with her to see her mom, and the reunion was overwhelming. Tears of joy filled their townhouse. Before Charlie left, he promised he would spend time with the family, and Jean said she was going to hold him to it.

When they were done with all the police interviews, reports and meeting, Beth Ann finally had some time to relax. She and Kaylob had barely left each other's side since she'd been home, and as much as she loved her family, she couldn't wait until they had some time alone together so she could show him how much she had missed him. Sure, they'd had those stolen moments when they almost forgot they had company, but they only made her long for him in a way she couldn't describe.

They were sitting around in the living room, talking to Gram and Nickolas, Beth Ann's head on Kaylob's shoulder, when Kaylob said, "Oh, I almost forgot something I have for you, baby." He got up, went to the closet and pulled out a small box. "I knew you'd want these, I'm glad you have the Bible, but I was sure you'd be happy about this too." He handed her the picture of her and Gram and the cross.

"Oh, Kaylob, I wasn't sure I'd ever see these again." She kissed the picture, then sat beside Gram on the love seat to show her. "Look, Gram."

"Oh my, I remember that moment like yesterday," Gram said with tears in her eyes.

They spent the afternoon journeying down memory lane and savoring the fact that Beth Ann had survived. She swore to herself that she would never take for granted the love she had with her friends and family.

Chapter Twenty-Three

It took a while, but everything went back to normal. Beth Ann and Kaylob could breathe a sigh of relief because nobody was following her. They were happy and adjusting to a quiet, normal life. Things were finally stable, although Beth Ann was still jumpy.

The biggest effect of Beth Ann's ordeal was that she continued to worry about Cathy a lot and wondered how she was dealing with the loss of her father. Beth Ann's therapist said that Cathy would understand someday, and Beth Ann prayed every night that it was true.

Beth Ann decided not to go back to the school, at least for a while, but she had been singing at the restaurant and helping Kaylob. It was good for her, plus it also allowed them to stay together most days. They didn't want to be apart, for good reason. Over the years, they had been separated too many times.

One Friday afternoon when Beth Ann walked in the door alone to a ringing phone, it sent a chill up her spine, and she said hello with the tiniest bit of fear until she heard Blake's drawl.

"Hi, darlin. How are things?"

"Hi, Blake. Things are good—really good. I've been singing three days a week and just puttering around the restaurant."

"I'm glad to hear that. I just wanted to call and check on you. I'll stop by some time and hear you sing. I'll give Kaylob a call later."

"Blake ..." Beth Ann paused. "Are you okay?"

Nothing but silence for a few seconds, then he said, "I'm good, Beth Ann. I miss you, but I'm good."

"I miss you too. And I think I need to tell you something." She cleared her throat. "Your secretary, I think her name is Melissa. Well, she's in love with you."

He laughed. "She's just a kid, and I know her daddy really well. She's infatuated, not in love."

"I think you're wrong. I saw how she looked at you. Why don't you bring her to the restaurant some time?"

"Listen, little darlin, I won't have my ex-fiancé playing matchmaker for me. Is that clear? Now, you tell that husband of yours hello, if I don't get in touch with him today, then I'll stop by and have lunch or dinner soon."

"All right," she said with a sigh.

"Beth Ann?"

"Yes?"

"Stop sulking and dragging your lip on the ground." He laughed again. "Goodbye."

Almost as soon as she hung up, a knock on the front door made her jump. For safety reasons she always peeked out the hole, and in truth she was still way too jumpy. But before she could even look, Frankie's voice rang out.

"It's me, Beth Ann."

She opened the door with a big smile. "Frankie, what a nice surprise." Then she noticed he looked like hell. "What's wrong?"

"Oh, nothing really."

He came in and followed her to the living room where they sat on the sofa. "Debra's moving out today, and I needed someone to hang out with. She really didn't want me there."

"Oh no, Frankie." She turned to give him a hug. "I'm so sorry. What happened?"

"We both knew it wasn't going anywhere. I didn't love her the way she needed." He honestly looked sad. "She's a great gal. I wish I could have fallen in love."

"Then it's for the best." Beth Ann felt bad for him, but she had to be honest. "She's very sweet and deserves to be loved completely."

"You're right, and I want her to have that." Frankie nodded. "We parted friends."

Beth Ann took his hand. "Even though you weren't in love, I can see that you still cared, and it must be hard to say goodbye."

"I know," he said. "I'm gonna have to wait at least a week before I can go out again."

"What? Oh, you!" She grabbed one of the throw pillows and smacked him upside his very large head.

"Why'd you go and do that?" he said, holding his head. "You messed up my hair, and I want to take you for coffee and some cheesecake at that new place that just opened down the street."

"Frankie Dean Russo, you're impossible."

"Yes, I am." He winked. "You know, a week is a long time for me."

Later that evening, after Frankie and his so-called broken heart had gone back home, Beth Ann was in bed, reading, while she waited for Kaylob to get off work. He was closing that night, so he'd be later than usual. As she got deeper into the story, she didn't even hear the front door open.

"Hey, baby."

She looked up and climbed out of bed to welcome home her handsome husband. "I didn't even hear you."

He lifted her into his arms, and she wrapped her legs around him. "You smell so sweet," he said, burying his nose in her hair. "I want to eat you up."

Beth Ann giggled. "You're always hungry, Mr. O'Brien."

He set her back on the floor. "Right now I'm famished. But there's something I've been meaning to talk to you about."

"Uh-oh. You look serious." She plopped on the bed and crossed her legs under her. "Am I in trouble?"

"No, not this time. I was thinking about this more than once and wanted to ask you before I forget again."

"Okay, what is it?"

He sat beside her on the bed and took one of her hands. "Why is it that you never told me about Charlie and your time on the reservation?"

She thought for a moment. "The subject was very painful for me, and I had honestly tried to push the memories away. I know now that it was a mistake, because seeing Charlie made me remember some special times." She looked down at their hands and sighed. "I told you how we lived most the time in our car, but there were some things I was embarrassed about."

He lifted her chin with his finger. "If you don't want to talk about it, that's okay, sweetheart."

She took a deep breath, then let it out. "No, I want to tell you now. We lived on the reservation for almost a full year. Charlie was our friend and my teacher. He spent a lot of time with my family, and I adored him. When my dad announced that we were heading out on the road again, Charlie tried everything to get my dad to stay, even finding him a local place to entertain. But it didn't matter." Her voice broke and Kaylob tried to wrap his arms around her, but she held up a hand to stop him. "Wait, I want to do this without falling apart."

"Okay," he said. "I understand."

"Not only did we have to leave our small but comfortable home, we left behind Charlie and my beloved dog Rusty. He was the daddy to Charlie's dog—that's why he called him Rusty Jr. He was the only animal I ever felt was mine, and I loved him so much." A lump in her throat made her pause. "When we got the station wagon all packed and ready to leave, I watched my mom cry, and that was hard enough. But when we all got in the car and were saying our last goodbyes, Rusty jumped inside and howled. It was like he knew we were leaving."

"I'm so sorry, Beth Ann. That's awful." He kissed her forehead.

"Oh, Kaylob, there are moments I can still hear his cries." Remembering that day brought tears to her eyes.

Kaylob took her in his arms, and this time she let him. He held her in silence until all the tears dried.

"No wonder you never talked about it. I feel bad for bringing it up."

"It's okay. I know I was just a kid, but the memories still hurt. We left behind people we loved, and about two years later my mom came home and announced she was leaving my dad."

"Jesus, Beth Ann. I've been such a giant ass."

She looked up at him in confusion. "Why would you say that?"

"Because I was always leaving you. You spent most of your childhood saying goodbye to people and things you loved, then you had to do the same thing with me, too." He took her face in his hands. "I'll never leave you again. I promise."

She smiled and threw her arms around his neck. "I believe you."

When she released him, she could tell by the look on his face that he was thinking hard about something else, and she didn't have to wait long to find out what it was.

"Beth Ann, I know you can never replace Rusty, but what if you had a chance to get a puppy from his bloodline. Would you want to bring home a baby dog?"

"Yes!" she said, hugging him again. "I'd love that. But how do we know that will ever happen? Charlie didn't say anything about it, did he?"

"No, but we don't know it won't happen." He leaned down for a kiss. "I'll talk to Charlie."

* * * *

By March, spring had sprung and life was blooming. Beth Ann and Kaylob's restaurant had grown more than they had ever dreamed. Her performances were making the newspaper, and she was getting interviews with TV stations and magazines. One of the most exciting things for her was that Charlie was trying to breed Rusty. He was a bit old, but Charlie said it could still happen.

Beth Ann suspected that Kaylob had talked him into it. If she'd been a gambling woman, she would've bet that was why he'd gone fishing with Charlie, not once but three times. She supposed that was called bribery, but she couldn't help being excited.

They'd also been searching for a new home outside of Riverside. Their townhouse just held too many upsetting memories. With the attacks and kidnapping, the shadows of the past lurked around every corner. Besides, they'd need something with a real yard since they were getting a dog. They had two more houses to look at on Saturday, and one sounded very promising. It was between Palm Springs and Riverside—not too far for them to commute to the restaurant, and they both loved that area.

That Friday evening, standing on the stage, getting ready to sing, Beth Ann's heart swelled as she looked out at the audience. So many friends, new and old. When she glanced at the door she spotted Blake with Dana and Johnny, they all waved to her and she gave them a big smile. She had grown to love all of them. They were in her dearest friends category.

"Elizabeth!" one of her fans called out from the audience. It was

Tina, a new friend who was in her mid-forties and was a really neat lady.

"Hi, Tina."

"Will you sing *I Left My Heart in San Francisco?*"

Beth Ann smiled and spoke into the microphone. "Yes, just for you. By the way, you look exceptionally pretty tonight in yellow."

Tina blushed, which turned her light skin to crimson and highlighted her blonde hair.

Once the band signaled to her, Beth Ann took the microphone out of the stand and caught her husband staring in her direction. He gave her one of his charming smiles that sent butterflies scattering around in her stomach. Funny how he always seemed larger than life when she stepped onto the stage.

She blew a kiss to Kaylob as she did every night just before she sang the first note. She absolutely loved having him there when she sang. Each time the emotion was more powerful than the first. Way more than she'd experienced doing Broadway.

Right after she began singing, Charlie walked in and stopped when he heard her voice. A broad smile washed across his face. For the first time since she was eight, Charlie was there. What more could a girl ask for?

After her last song, *Imagine,* by John Lennon, everyone stood and gave her a standing ovation.

"Thank you." She smiled and waved toward the band. "Please give a big round of applause to Billie and the Band. They are the best."

Everyone clapped, whistled, and cheered. Beth Ann felt elated when she left the stage.

While she was saying goodnight to everyone in the lounge, she noticed Tina staring at her and Charlie. An idea hit. Tina had lost her husband three years ago from a heart attack, so they were both single.

"Charlie, I want to introduce you to someone."

"Sure." Charlie smiled and held her hand as they walked over to where Tina was sitting by the stage.

"Tina, I'd like to introduce you to my friend, Charlie," Beth Ann said when they reached her table. "We go way back. Charlie, this is Tina."

"Pleased to meet you," he said as they shook hands.

Beth Ann didn't miss the glint of interest in Tina's eyes. "I don't mean to be rude or presumptuous, but I thought maybe you two might have some things in common. You both lost spouses and ... well, I just thought you should meet." She was saved from more awkwardness by the sound of her husband's voice. "Excuse me, I'll be back in a bit."

She scampered off, hoping they would like each other and find some more things in common. When she reached Kaylob, he pulled her into the office and locked the door. Had he seen her matching making? Maybe he didn't approve of that, but he had a big smile on his face.

"What?" she said. "You look serious but sorta happy."

He moved to his desk and picked up a white envelope that he held out to her. "It's from Aunt Lillian in Ireland. Read it, Beth Ann."

She pulled out the folded letter.

Dear Kaylob and Beth Ann,

Please accept these tickets as a gift and come to Ireland. I've longed to meet Kaylob, and now I'd love to meet you both. I've heard such wonderful things about the two of you. I scheduled the flight for April 15th and hope that works for you.

Please consider doing this. I feel like I've waited forever to meet you, and I love you with all my heart. Plus, you also have a cousin and other relatives who want to finally meet you.

Love always, Aunt Lillian

"Wow." Beth Ann glanced up and saw his eyes fill with sentiment.

"Can we go, honey?" Beth Ann asked.

"Of course we can. I've got a great management team here, and it will take at least thirty days to close escrow even if we find a place tomorrow." He put his hands on her shoulders and grinned. "And our agent said if we find a house, they can get a later closing date if we need it. After all, we are paying cash."

"Well, great then," she said. "I'm good with everything. I've always wished you could meet your relatives, and I want to meet them too."

She knew this would be a good thing for them. They'd both been looking forward to going to Ireland. His Aunt Lillian sounded like a sweet lady, and Beth Ann especially noted how she said she'd been waiting forever to meet him.

"Kaylob, I know she's telling the truth about always wanting to see you. I overheard a phone conversation between your mom and Aunt Lillian while you were in the hospital. I couldn't hear her side, but I heard your mom saying she hated that Lillian never had the chance to see you. From what I gathered, I believe your dad might not like her."

"Now why doesn't that surprise me?" He shook his head. "My dad is a hard nut to crack. But still, I wonder why she didn't come around while he was on one of his trips."

"Maybe your mom didn't want to cause trouble. She's always seemed to do what your dad wanted."

"True. But it's all good. We get to meet her now." He picked her up and swung her around. "And we finally get to go to Ireland!"

When they went back to the lounge, Beth Ann was thrilled to see that Charlie and Tina were still talking and laughing.

"Well, look at that," she told Kaylob, pointing at them with a little wiggle. "You can just call me the matchmaker."

Kaylob grabbed her by the hand and pulled her into the kitchen. This time she knew she *was* in trouble from his stern look.

"Beth Ann, don't even go there. Blake told me you already tried to do that with him too." He swatted her butt then leaned over to whisper. "Maybe I should really spank you."

She giggled and moved closer to find a surprise. "Oh my ..."

He picked her up and carried her into the produce room in the back. After shutting the door, he lifted her onto the table and pushed up her dress. "Oh my is right."

"Kaylob, wait." She pulled down her dress.

"No, I can't." He laughed and pulled it back up.

"I went off the pill, and you don't have one of those things."

He used his touch to show her what he knew she wanted. "Oh, baby, can't we just make love without worrying tonight?"

"Kaylob, I don't want to get ... oh, okay. It'll be fine." She quivered as she pulled off her panties and wrapped her legs around his waist. "Show me what you want, Mr. O'Brien." She ran her fingers over him in a way that made him shiver.

His pants hit the floor and he moaned. "You got it, Mrs. O'Brien."

He ended up showing her not just once, but three times.

Chapter Twenty-Four

Beth Ann and Kaylob arrived two days early on April thirteenth to surprise Lillian. They were both so excited about meeting his family and being in Ireland. The Dublin airport was just as busy as the one in Ontario, but nobody seemed to be in the same kind of rush as they were back home. Beth Ann noticed two men standing around, pointing to something in a magazine and cracking up. There was a certain exhilarating madness that can only be found in airports.

Outside the airport, they waved for a taxi from the long line, and one of the closest drivers pulled over in front of them and got out.

"Where can I be taking the two of you today?" His beautiful Irish accent washed over them. They gave him the address and his eyes widened. "Will they be expecting you?"

Beth Ann thought that was an odd question, but Kaylob just nodded. "Yes, my Aunt Lillian lives there."

"Aye, I know all about Lillian Rafferty, but I wasn't aware she'd be having any siblings," the man said. "Well, let's get your luggage loaded and get ya to your destination."

Beth Ann loved his accent, but it wasn't what she had expected from the movies she'd seen.

"We'll be heading outside of Dingle." He put their luggage in the trunk. "That will be taking us about four hours, depending on what we find on the road."

"Four hours?" Kaylob said with his brows scrunched. "That's a long trip."

"That it is, lad. Once we get you out of the city, the countryside is a beauty, but we do have to go slow because sometimes the sheep will be taking over the road. The Manor is quiet and private, and the views of

216

the Atlantic Ocean and mountainside will be taking your breath away."

"Oh, it sounds lovely and I can't wait," Beth Ann said and smiled. "I love animals and don't mind having to share the road with them."

"Sometimes the sheep will want to see what's in the car," he said.

Kaylob grinned. "Sounds good, so long as they don't eat us."

"Speaking of eating, we can stop somewhere if you need to grab a bite. By the way, my name is Clancy, and you can be calling me that if you'd like."

"Is that an Irish name?" Beth Ann asked. "It's very nice."

"That it is indeed." He nodded. "I only charge a set fee, not by the mile or hour." He handed them a card with the rate, and they were glad to see it was in American dollars and not the pound.

"Thank you, Clancy," Kaylob said. "We're ready to go when you are."

After thirty minutes of driving, they started to spot the amazing hillsides Clancy had predicted. Beth Ann couldn't recall ever seeing anything that shade of green before.

"So, did your ma and da live here in Dublin or in Dingle?" Clancy asked Kaylob.

"No, they've never been to Ireland, and this is our first trip." Kaylob squeezed Beth Ann's hand and smiled.

Clancy nodded. "Well, I'm sure you'll be loving it."

"I'm sure we will too," Beth Ann said. "I wonder how long Lillian has lived here. Do you know, Clancy?"

"Ah, she's been living here as far back as I can remember. I was just a wee lad when I got to know the Rafferty family. Of course, that would be her husband's family, but I would be seeing those two together when they were young."

"I take it they were childhood sweethearts." Beth Ann touched her heart and glanced at Kaylob.

"You'd be taking that right." Clancy laughed.

Funny, Beth Ann wondered why Lillian didn't seem to have much of an accent, at least the time she called for Kaylob. Not like the cab driver.

"Wow," she said. "Kaylob, look at those stone huts."

Clancy pointed at one of them. "That one is actually called the

Beehive. We could stop if you two want to be taking some pictures."

They pulled over and also did it a few more times to snap some shots, use the restrooms, and grab a snack. The view only got more and more spectacular as they drove by all the country homes, some of them looking hundreds of years old. The emerald waters and the green countryside combined to make everything appear to be a beautiful painting.

"You'll be experiencing sea smells wafting through the air—pungent but refreshing." Clancy rolled down his window "And never will you be experiencing a view like this." He gestured proudly.

Kaylob and Beth Ann inhaled the salty air, and as Clancy had said, it was refreshing and new. As tired as Beth Ann was, she wouldn't dare close her eyes and miss anything. The drive ended up taking almost five hours, and they totally enjoyed every minute of it.

"Here we are at the Manor," Clancy said as they turned down a long paved driveway. The outside of the massive structure was all mismatched stones and made it look like a castle from long ago. As far as they could see, were unparalleled ocean views, with lush grounds that surrounded the home as if it were sitting on emerald velvet. Beth Ann rolled down the window to take it all in.

"I can't believe the beauty." She glanced at Kaylob who seemed to be speechless. "Or the size of it."

As they stepped out of the taxi, the sounds of the waves gave Beth Ann goose bumps. Clancy helped them unload their luggage and carry it to the large double doors. While Beth Ann paid him along with a large tip, Kaylob just stood there staring at the door.

"Kaylob," she finally said. "Ring the doorbell."

He stuck his finger to the ringer and pushed twice. After a few seconds, a skeleton of a man with an old-style butler jacket came to the door. His white gloves nearly matched his skin color. Beth Ann wondered if they had been let off at the wrong house.

Kaylob must have been wondering the same thing, but he leaned over to her ear and whispered, "This is unreal."

"May I help you?" the butler asked.

Kaylob must have swallowed his tongue, because he didn't seem to be able to talk again.

"Yes, we're the O'Briens," Beth Ann said. "And we're here to see Aunt Lillian."

"You were expected on the fifteenth," he said without a smile. "You're early."

"We wanted to surprise her." Beth Ann said. If her husband didn't say something pretty soon, she was going to kick him.

The man looked at them a few seconds more, then he opened the door wider and waved them in. "Welcome to Queens Court Manor," he announced in a formal tone. "I'll let your aunt know that you have arrived. I'll take you to the library where you may wait for her."

"Thank you," Kaylob managed to say.

They both stood in the foyer, if that's what it was. All Beth Ann knew was that it was bigger than their townhouse.

"We will take your luggage upstairs," the butler said. "We are putting you on the second floor in the Villa Mar suite." He finally smiled slightly and gestured toward a large staircase, the biggest that Beth Ann had ever seen. "You should find it very comfortable, as it has the best views of the ocean from its private terrace. It also has a sitting area with music of your choice, and a fireplace for the chilly evenings. Shall I get you some tea and biscuits in the library?"

"Thank you, yes," Kaylob said. "That would be wonderful."

Beth Ann almost laughed as she noted that it was amazing what the prospect of food did for him.

"So is that why you haven't spoken in the last five minutes?" she whispered. "You froze up from hunger?"

He scowled at her. "Funny, Mrs. O'Brien."

The butler led them down the hall past two young housekeepers. One was a girl with curly blonde hair dusting the furniture, and the other was a strawberry blonde up on a ladder, dusting high ridges. They both looked at Kaylob then back at each other before trying in vain to suppress spontaneous giggles. Kaylob acknowledged them with a smile and a wink, and the blushes on their faces were priceless.

Beth Ann elbowed him. "You're going to cause that girl to fall off her ladder."

He brought her hand to his lips and kissed her palm. "They remind me of how you used to blush." He chuckled. "Actually, sometimes you still do."

"I do not," she said.

After following the butler for what seemed like an hour, he finally stopped and opened a door. "Here we are. I'll be back shortly with some tea and biscuits. There is a powder room off to the left. You'll see a sign on the door."

Stepping through the library's doorway, Beth Ann froze in awe. Holy bookworm, right in front of her stood cherry wood bookcases that stretched from floor to ceiling, with at least a bazillion books.

"Oh, my gosh, Kaylob!" She turned in a circle. "I can't believe this."

"Yep, it's pretty amazing," he said.

Along with all the wonderful books, a gorgeous stone fireplace filled the entire north wall. Two lavish couches faced it, inviting anyone to come in and curl up with a book.

"I want to live in this room," Beth Ann said as she looked around with wide eyes.

"No way. I'd be neglected." Kaylob pulled her into his arms and nibbled on her neck.

"I'd never neglect you, Mr. O'Brien. Do you smell that?" She giggled. "This room has the scent of adventure."

"Hmm ... I'm not sure what adventure smells like." He sniffed the air and laughed. "Oh, wait. I do smell adventure. My favorite kind." He moved his hand across her bottom and pulled her close. "We've never made love in a library."

"Stop that!" She smacked his hand teasingly. "Someone could walk in."

"See, I've already been replaced."

"Don't be silly." She reached around and patted his bottom. "Nobody or nothing could ever replace these buns."

Five minutes later, the butler returned with a tray of tea and cookies. Beth Ann was pleasantly surprised since he'd called them biscuits.

"I have informed Mrs. Rafferty of your arrival," he said. "Currently, she's in the upstairs parlor finishing a business meeting, but she will be down shortly. If you need anything else, please don't hesitate to ask." He pointed to a small cherry table in the corner. "Every room has a phone.

Just dial the number one and it will ring me."

Beth Ann didn't care about the cookies or tea. All she could do was walk around touching all the books. On the other hand, she could hear her hungry husband already chomping down.

"Man, these are good," he said with his mouth full. "You didn't want any, did you?"

She sighed and walked over to take six out of the ten cookies away from him, shaking her head. "Give me those. You don't need that many." She placed them back on the tray.

"Beth Ann, you're awfully bossy."

"I'm not bossy. I'm keeping you from giving yourself diabetes or heart disease."

He gave her a sly smile. "Oh, my little redheaded dancer, you do plenty of other things that keep that from happening."

"Kaylob, hush." She grabbed one of the cookies up from the tray and strolled over to the books. "Someone might hear you."

His laugh echoed through the room.

She pulled out a couple of books just to peek, half expecting to find spirits lurking behind them. One was titled *The Philoctetes of Sophocles* and the other was *The Works of Jonathan Swift,* which appeared to be an original written back in 1751. Beth Ann was captivated and amazed at its flawless condition.

Kaylob put his hand on her back and kissed her neck. "Would you like some tea?"

"Sure, honey, I'd love a cup," she said, not taking her eyes off the books. "I do believe I'm in heaven surrounded by all these books, because nobody could ever read all these in one lifetime."

Kaylob went to fix her cup of tea, and she knew he would make it just the way she liked it. He always remembered little things like that about her. How had she gotten so lucky? He was the best husband in the whole wide world.

"Oh my gosh," she said when she picked up another book.

"What is it, baby?" Kaylob asked.

"This is a book of Irish history written in 1840. It's all about the Great Famine that ravaged the island. How awful."

"Yes, it was awful, but it's our history," a silky-soft voice said from the doorway. "Hello, Kaylob. Hello, Beth Ann. I'm so happy you decided to come early. What a nice surprise." She glided across the room to Kaylob with tears clearly shining in her eyes.

Beth Ann was flabbergasted at Lillian's beauty, and also by how much she and Kaylob looked alike. She was tall with blonde hair down to her shoulders that showed only a hint of gray. Her almost royal blue eyes matched Kaylob's, and she had the most beautiful skin. But the thing that shocked Beth Ann the most was the dimple in her chin.

It was just like Kaylob's.

When he moved to greet Lillian, Beth Ann could tell he saw all the same similarities from the shocked expression on his face. And when Lillian put her arms around him, Beth Ann knew the truth from the way her shoulders shook and the way she enveloped him in her arms.

This was not Kaylob's aunt.

Beth Ann had no proof, but from the way Kaylob was looking at Lillian, she was sure there was a *storm* coming. After everything they had been through, finding out a *secret* like that was not the *April* in Ireland they had envisioned.

To find out what happens next and if those dreams come true.

Follow the Seasons of Love and War Saga.

About the Author

Brenda Ashworth Barry's first book was a memoir titled, Healing the Voices Within, which was never published but sponsored on a local TV station and flew off the shelves at her Healing Center in Redding California.

Her most recent work is a six-part saga of star-crossed lovers separated by the war in Vietnam, entitled Seasons of Love and War. Brenda worked for over five years to bring the six part Saga alive.

Brenda lives in Roseburg, Oregon, by the Umpqua River, and has raised four children three birth children and one adopted born in her heart. Her husband, who was in the military for 21 years, gave her help and encouragement while writing her novel. When she's not writing she can normally be found walking the trails with her husband and their little dachshund, or in their RV enjoying nature.

Twitter: @sunsetsky52
Website: http://www.brendaashworthbarry.com
Facebook: www.facebook.com/pages/Seasons-of-Love-and-War-Author-Page/411210412247684
Blog: brendabarry.blogspot.com
Blog: brendabarryashworth.wordpress.com